'Can I help something I or my men can do?

He leant forward. His hand brushed her shoulder. 'Tell me, and if it is within my power it shall be done.'

She gazed at the point where his tunic kissed the column of his throat. More than anything she wanted to turn to him and lay her head against his chest, to feel his arms about her, holding her. She only had to take one step closer and she'd be there, her body next to his, her hands entwined with his.

The image shocked her, made her hesitate. Her thoughts were not those of a priestess in training but of a woman. She should despise him as her enemy...

Author Note

Ancient Rome has been a neglected era in historical romance. But it is a period I have long thought well worth exploring as the potential is huge—stories of passion and adventure combined with oracles, soothsayers and some of the most memorable figures in world history.

From celebrity adoration, populist politicians and consumer crazes to complicated and complex personal lives, the Roman world has many echoes of today's society. It was the first civilisation to struggle with the problem of what happens when a Republic becomes the world's only superpower. Culturally diverse and socially mobile, it was a place where sons of slaves became senators, and senators, slaves. And yet there are many differences—spectator sports were literally a matter of life and death, animal sacrifice was prevalent in religion, and no one could conceive of a society without slaves.

I hope you will enjoy reading my tales of sandals, swords and sex as much as I enjoy writing them. I would love to hear from you, as reader feedback is a gift. I can be contacted either through my blog, http://www.michellestyles.blogspot.com, through my website, http://www.michellestyles.co.uk, or write to me care of Mills & Boon®.

A NOBLE CAPTIVE

Michelle Styles

MILLS & BOON®

First published in Great Britain 2006
Paperback edition 2007
Harlequin Mills & Boon Limited,
Eton House, 18-24 Paradise Road, Richmond, Surrey TW9 1SR

© Michelle Styles 2006

ISBN-13: 978 0 263 85155 7
ISBN-10:   0 263 85155 9

Set in Times Roman 10½ on 13 pt.
04-0107-81581

Printed and bound in Spain
by Litografia Rosés S.A., Barcelona

Although born and raised near San Francisco, California, **Michelle Styles** currently lives a few miles south of Hadrian's Wall, with her husband, three children, two dogs, cats, assorted ducks, hens and beehives. An avid reader, she has always been interested in history, and a historical romance is her idea of the perfect way to relax. Her love of Rome stems from the year of Latin she took in sixth grade. She is particularly interested in how ordinary people lived during ancient times, and in the course of her research she has learnt how to cook Roman food as well as how to use a drop spindle. When she is not writing, reading or doing research, Michelle tends her rather overgrown garden or does needlework, in particular counted cross-stitch. Michelle maintains a website, www.michellestyles.co.uk, and a blog, www.michellestyles.blogspot.com, and would be delighted to hear from you.

A recent novel by the same author:

THE GLADIATOR'S HONOUR

To my god-daughter, Silvana Greene,
and my daughter Katharine

Chapter One

⚜

*75 BC—An island in the Mediterranean,
a few miles north of Crete*

'The sibyl of Kybele wants to see you.'

The harsh voice of a pirate cut across Tullio's troubled dreams and jerked him awake.

Marcus Livius Tullio, junior tribune Legion II Fourth Cohort, winced as he stood up in the overcrowded hold where he was confined with what remained of his men. Every part of his body from his neck to his knees ached. The leg wound he had received in the pirate attack throbbed.

How many days since pirates had overrun the trireme transporting him and his men back to Rome? Four? Five? In that short time, seven of his men had died in this stinking rat-infested place.

Some might say they were the lucky ones.

In the dim light of the hold, Tullio could make out the dispirited faces of the twenty who remained alive. Already they moved like prisoners, shuffling towards the entrance with heads bowed.

'Helmets on, boys.' Tullio forced his voice to sound as firm and calm as it would on the parade ground outside Ostia. 'Let's show this priestess of theirs that we are Roman legionaries, not slaves or pirates who skulk in corners and attack in the dead of night.'

At his words, the men stood straighter.

Tullio jammed his helmet on and flicked his red cloak back from his shoulders. He ran a hand over the stubble on his chin. He needed a bath and shave, something to make him feel human again. But he refused to allow the scum who had captured him or their so-called priestess to see any weakness.

Their retribution day would come.

Bright sunlight blinded him as he stepped from the hold on to the gangplank, then on to the shore with its collection of whitewashed Greek-style buildings clustered around the harbour and the rock-strewn mountain rising behind.

He inhaled, savouring the way his lungs filled with fresh air. The faint scent of jasmine and other spring wild flowers tickled his nose, reminding him there was more to life than salt air and the stench of unwashed bodies.

A young legionary knelt down and kissed the earth. Tullio motioned to the one remaining centurion. Quintus moved swiftly and raised the lad up, shaking his head as he did so. Tullio cast a practised eye over his men—ragged, bearing injuries, but alive. Twenty men out of the original two cohorts on the ship. Jupiter willing, he intended all of them remaining would return to Rome.

The guard shoved them forward towards a small group standing on the quay. Tullio ignored the pirate captain who had captured them, concentrating instead on the slender figure dressed in flowing white robes who was surveying the scene from a golden chariot pulled by a pair of lions. The sibyl.

Although a gold mask obscured the majority of her face, sea-green eyes were clearly visible. She should be ancient, but held herself erect like a young woman. He glanced at her hands. Save for the shortened little finger on her right hand, they appeared to be as unmarked as those of his late wife.

What sort of woman hid behind that mask? Interested in her people's welfare? A leader? Or merely an apologist for the pirates?

Tullio grimaced as he shifted his weight from his bad leg. This woman gave religious sanction to piracy, acts of barbaric terrorism against Rome.

'The prisoners, my lady,' the pirate captain said.

'Guests, honoured guests, Captain Androceles,' the low melodious voice from behind the mask said. Younger than Tullio had anticipated but it held a definite note of command.

'Just so, my lady.' The pirate captain gave an ironic bow towards Tullio and his men. 'My men risked their lives to rescue these poor wayfarers. We expect payment for our services.'

Rescue? This was the first time Tullio had heard such a word used for an unprovoked night attack. He choked back his anger.

'I had assumed you would unload the amphorae of oil first,' the sibyl said, her hands tightening on the lions' reins. 'As you have always done, keeping your guests on board until the tribute is paid.'

Tullio concentrated on staring straight ahead. How dare

she talk as if he and his men were objects! Chattels worth less than wine or olive oil. They were soldiers, Roman soldiers.

'What is a fair rate of passage for unwillingly rescued guests?' Tullio bit out through clenched teeth, tired of the charade.

The sibyl started and Tullio gave a grim smile of satisfaction. Human after all?

He narrowed his eyes and stared harder at the woman standing with her shoulders back, sword in one hand, reins clasped in the other. A living statue. Her eyes had changed to a deeper green, but that was all. He looked again at the priest-ess in the golden chariot, her shoulders held stiffly as if she was unaccustomed to the weight of the mask she wore. He searched his memory for what he knew of sibyls and their cult that worshipped Kybele, the Mother Goddess.

A scrap of a ritual from his childhood. Nothing more.

'You must know, Sibyl,' Tullio persisted, hating her even more than the pirates. At least the pirates were honest about their terror and did not take refuge behind masks.

'The captain will tell you,' she said in a low voice. 'The *negotiatii* set their prices, not the sibyl. They bore the burden of your rescue.'

The pirate captain broke the silence, naming a sum about the annual wage of a legionary. He paused, fingering his gold brooch. His voice became oilier. 'But for you, I had thought perhaps three hundred. You are used to…shall we say…the finer things?'

Tullio heard a small smothered gasp from the sibyl. He offered a prayer of thanksgiving the amount requested was less than that he had agreed with his agent before he left Ostia for his posting in Cyrene, North Africa.

'You ask too little for me, Captain. I would have thought I was worth at least five hundred gold pieces,' Tullio drawled, using his most affected patrician accent, and brushed a speck of dirt from his cloak.

The pirate's eyes shone with greed and his pink tongue flicked over his lips. Mission accomplished. Tullio had suddenly become a valuable property, one who would have to be handled with care and not left to rot in a hold.

The sibyl's knuckles shone white against her sword. What was it about this business that she did not like? The haggling over money? Or that he and his men were on shore? Tullio doubted that it was the traffic in humans. Kidnap, ransom or selling on those who could not pay as slaves—it was all in a day's work for a pirate.

'Five hundred gold pieces it is, then,' she said, 'but the other soldiers are to be charged at the usual rate. We're not greedy merchantmen seeking profit out of misery, but rescuers seeking to save lives.'

Tullio drew his lips together, biting back sarcastic words asking for her definition of 'saved'.

The pirate's smile increased. 'Kybele will receive her usual proportion in thanksgiving for her protection.'

'See that the grain is fresh this time. Your son's last offering was mouldy.' The sibyl gave a flick of her wrist and the chariot started forward.

The pirates started to prod the Romans towards the trireme with painted eyes on the prow, a device pirates believed made it easier to spot their prey. The black hole of the pupil stood out from the yellow decking, ready to swallow them. He and his men were to be returned to rot in that ship, to wait for the day when the tribute arrived. This brief scent of fresh air, the feel of solid ground beneath their feet, had been part of some cruel game.

How many of his men would give up the will to live and cross the River Styx?

Three men had breathed their last early this morning as the trireme docked. Rufus's life hung by a slender thread as it was.

His men gave him desperate looks. Twenty unarmed and injured men against the whole island. Suicide. He needed to remember the ritual that would invoke Kybele's protection. Now. The words hung tantalisingly just beyond the edge of his tongue. He willed them to come, but nothing. He could not take the risk of getting them wrong. With a heavy heart, he motioned that his men should go.

'Have a care. When we are free,' Mustius Quintus said in a low voice as a guard prodded him with a spear, causing the large man to stagger, 'we will hunt down each one of you pirates and crucify you as a warning to those who would harm Roman soldiers.'

'Brave words, but foolish, Quintus. Who gave you leave to say such things?' Tullio muttered. He offered a prayer to Mercury that the remark would go unchallenged.

Quintus shrugged and looked unrepentant. The line of legionaries continued shuffling towards the ship. Rufus half stumbled as a pirate stuck his foot out. A seagull screamed overhead.

No response from the pirate captain. Tullio exhaled a breath. Mercury was with him. This time.

'Halt!' the sibyl cried. 'Who threatens this island?'

'Stand firm, comrades,' Tullio said in a low voice. 'We are Romans, not slaves. We face this together.'

Helena's robes quivered with indignation as she fought to

keep the gold mask of Kybele from slipping down her face. She glared at the group of men standing before her, their helmets and breastplates shining in the afternoon sun, their leader's firm chin tilted towards the sky and a defiant look flashing in his dark eyes.

How dare the Romans issue threats against her people! What else could go wrong?

Because of the Roman, she had haggled over the tribute money like a fishwife. Aunt Flavia would never have done that. She would have remained aloof—the perfect sibyl, living symbol of Kybele, protectoress of this island. Not Helena, the sibyl's assistant who had trouble keeping the mask straight and the lions under control.

Helena pressed her lips together. If she wasn't careful, everything would be revealed.

This masquerade had failed to go as she had planned back in her aunt's apartments. She blamed the tall Roman tribune for unsettling her. There was something about his eyes and the way he held his shoulders. Captain Androceles's wilful misunderstanding of her request to see the cargo had not helped. She had wanted to inspect the grain, wine and olive oil, to make sure he did not cheat them. Roman soldiers were kept in the hold. It was understood. It was tradition.

What did Androceles hope to gain?

The cold prickle of sweat ran down the back of her neck. She had to react to the Roman's threat, but how?

'Your ears are sharper than mine, Sibyl. I missed the Roman's threat.' Captain Androceles's words pierced through the pounding in her head. 'Shall I have him killed?'

One of the seafarers lifted his sword as another grabbed the soldier who had uttered the threat.

Her breath stopped in her throat. Another mistake. Blood would flow. Kybele would never sanction murder.

The masquerade would be over. The true state of the sibyl's health would be discovered. This was an unqualified disaster.

What would her aunt do? Allow the Romans to march back to their hold?

Helena tried to think, but her mind was a blank. She offered up a prayer. *Come to my aid, now at the hour of my need, Kybele.*

Time stood still. She had to say something. But she had no guidance from Kybele. Sunlight glinted off the sword that hung poised over the man's neck, blinding her for a heartbeat.

'No!' the tribune roared. 'Stay your hand.'

'Let the Roman speak.' Helena risked a breath. 'The sibyl is not without mercy.'

'If you will punish someone, punish me.' The tribune stared directly at her, shoulders back, head held high. 'He is under my command. He spoke without thinking. He means your island no harm. Our only quarrel is with those who would abuse us.'

The seafarer hesitated, looking from the tribune to his captain and back again.

'Very well, Tribune, if you are so eager to go to Hades…' Captain Androceles tapped his vine cane against his thigh. 'One Roman is very like another.'

The tribune calmly removed his helmet, his red cloak and coat of mail until he was clad in only his short tunic. His shoulders were wider than she thought possible, and his legs sculpted muscles save for an angry red wound. His black curly hair ruffled in the breeze.

Helena gulped.

She had to stop this bloodshed before it began—but how?

'I am ready for whatever the Fates decree,' the tribune said. No fear or tremor in his voice, and his eyes blazed defiantly. 'But I warn you, Sibyl, no one will pay for a dead body.'

'Perhaps I am prepared to take a chance on that,' Captain Androceles sneered.

The seafarer lifted his sword higher.

'No, wait,' Helena called out. Everyone turned to look at her. She felt her face grow hot and was grateful for the mask. 'The tribune speaks wisely. If you kill him, you will not be able to claim his ransom. Five hundred pieces of gold is too great a sum to throw away on an idle boast. Rome holds no sway over this island. Since when have they been able to attack here?'

'You have a subtle mind, Sibyl,' Captain Androceles said with a bow as he signalled to the seafarer, who lowered his sword. 'In my anger at the insult to you and this holy place, I had forgotten about the money.'

'I trust you won't again.'

Helena clutched the edge of the chariot as her knees threatened to give way. No blood would be shed today. The rugged tribune would live. The sibyl's position would remain untouched. She had recovered from the mistake. Helena closed her eyes and offered a small prayer of thanksgiving.

'Kybele welcomes the tribute you and your fellow adventurers bring, but she will not sanction bloodshed.'

She risked a glance at the tribune. He should be down on his knees. She had saved his life. She gave him a nod, indicating he could begin thanking her. But he stood there, feet wide apart, glaring at her.

'The centurion told the truth. Rome will hunt out pirates and all who support them.' His black eyes bore into hers as if he could see the woman behind the mask and was aware of who she was. 'Rome has no quarrel with this island. Allow us to go free without tribute.'

'Rome has not been able to trouble us so far,' Helena said, but her hands trembled. 'Mind making promises you cannot keep.'

'I never make promises lightly…even to pirates or their priestesses,' he said defiantly with his shoulders back. He slammed one fist into the other.

'This Roman will be punished, my lady, tribute or no,' Captain Androceles said. 'I refuse to allow any man to talk to you like that.'

The guard raised the sword again.

Helena stood frozen in her chariot.

This whole thing was a mistake from start to finish. She longed to fling the mask away and step from the chariot, to go back to being herself, not her aunt's stand-in. But it was too late for that. She had to continue. She had to play the part she was born to play. She needed a miracle—fast.

'I ask for Kybele's protection. My men are seriously injured after the unprovoked attack,' the tribune broke in, forcefully. His low-timbred voice cut across her words. 'They need medical attention, some place sheltered to sleep. They do not need to go back on that stinking hulk. Enough have died already. I ask for your help in this matter, Sibyl. I ask for Kybele who is the Mother Goddess of All's aid.'

'Kybele cares about all storm-tossed strangers, Tribune,' Helena recited automatically, falling back on her learned responses and ignoring his dark intent eyes. 'She does so now.'

He paused and seemed to search his memory, a crease appearing between his eyebrows.

'My name is Marcus Livius Tullio,' the tribune said, his voice growing in confidence with every word. 'And my men would be pleased to have Kybele's protection. We beg and require Kybele's protection and assistance in this matter.'

Helena bit her lip. Marcus Livius Tullio had used the exact ritual words. How did this Roman tribune, this Tullio, know the correct ritual? She had no choice now. Was this her miracle? 'Kybele always gives protection to those who request it.'

'My lady?' Captain Androceles said with surprise in his voice.

Helena swallowed hard. She had to keep a clear head. She might yet emerge triumphant.

'The tribune has invoked the protection of Kybele and I have given it.' Helena forced her voice to sound strong. 'There will be no killing here today. Captain, you may continue to load them back on to the ship.'

Androceles stroked his chin and nodded. He signalled and the tribune's chain mail coat was thrown at his feet. Helena released a breath. He had accepted her explanation. He would now march the Romans on to the ship to await the tribune. She would leave and the masquerade would be over. She would go back to being Aunt Flavia's assistant and hopefully next time a pirate ship appeared on the horizon, Aunt Flavia would be healthy again. She flicked the reins.

'Pardon, my lady,' Androceles said, bowing low. 'The temple is the proper place for the Romans to reside.'

'Why?' Helena pulled back on the lions. Not another complication. 'I understood…that is, guests are always kept aboard ship. They can receive medical attention there.'

'When we attempted to…rescue these guests, we lost a

number of men. In view of their threats, I wish them off my ship while we wait in your harbour for the tribute to arrive. I have no wish to lose any more men to these Roman scum. These animals. You have given them protection, therefore they should be housed in your temple.'

A cold shiver passed through Helena as she gazed out at the Roman legionaries, standing at attention despite their injuries. The tribune's eyes defiant. Not scum. Not her allies either, but they were more than animals. The beginnings of a headache gathered at her forehead. If the Romans were housed at the temple, the risk of Aunt Flavia's condition being discovered was that much greater.

'It is something to be taken into consideration—' she began.

'The Romans will stay with you until the tribute is received, my Lady.' Captain Androceles rubbed his hands together. 'Otherwise how can they be sure of your protection?'

'Very well, Captain, I will house them at the temple. But if we look after your guests, Captain, I expect compensation. This was not part of the original agreement.' Helena forced her voice to sound firm. She tilted her head and stared at the captain.

'As would I…if any die in your care.' Androceles rearranged his cloak and gave a practised smile that failed to reach his bloodshot eyes.

'Kybele makes no such promises. One never bargains with the goddess.' Helena gave a quick glance at Tullio's wound and thought about the different herbs in the garden. After such misplaced bravery in defence of his men, surely the man would live. 'We can speak of this later should it come to pass.'

'I will trust in the goddess's mercy then.' Tullio's voice did something to her insides.

Helena ignored the curls clinging to her forehead. Nerves, nothing more. When she returned to the temple, all would be as it always was. She would fall back on routine.

'When you are ready, Captain, the temple will receive the guests.' She nodded to her bodyguard and flicked the reins a third time. The lions started slowly forward, moving the chariot at a steady gait as they had been trained to do since they were cubs. Her arms trembled.

'I thank you for looking after my men, my lady. We Romans do not easily forget an act of friendship.' Tullio stepped forward and caught her free hand.

He brushed it with his lips. A tremor went up through Helena's arm, and warmth flooded her body. She jerked her hand away.

'Not friendship, Tribune. There can never be friendship between our people.'

Chapter Two

~∽∾∿~

Tullio welcomed the coolness of the temple. Every step up the steep rock-strewn hill from the harbour, past the palace and the peasants' huts interspersed with a few olive trees and fields of vines, had sent ropes of fire along his shoulders, but he refused to show the pirates how much they ached. One blow more and he would have crumpled to the sun-baked earth.

His men walked with firmer steps than when they had first shuffled off the ship. Not quite legionaries, but no longer prisoners. A small boon.

The scent of cinnamon and other incense assaulted his nose as he and his men were escorted into a large antechamber adorned with statues and smaller altars. Tullio frowned, and tried to ignore the slight stab of disappointment.

Instead of the sibyl with her snow-white robes and masked face, a solitary young woman waited to greet them with a tablet in her hands. His eyes roamed up from her rose-coloured gown pleated in the Greek manner, to where a jet black curl of hair peeked from under her cap of red and white ribbons. Her lips were a bit large and her nose a tad small for the woman to be truly a beauty, Tullio decided, but poets probably wrote odes to her anyway.

'Welcome to the Temple of Kybele,' the woman said, her voice sounding anything but welcoming as she tapped a wooden tablet against her hand. 'I am Helena, the sibyl's assistant. You are to be housed here, waiting for your passage money to arrive. I pray it will be soon.'

She reminded him of the marble statues in Vesta's temple in Rome. All beauty, but no heart. An efficient administrator. He doubted if she had one-tenth the passion the sibyl had displayed on the quayside.

'We all look forward to its arrival,' Tullio answered smoothly. 'The sibyl's kindness is beyond measure, but my men are in need of medicine and food.'

'The temple has a long and proud tradition of tending storm-tossed strangers in their time of need.'

Looking after strangers by conniving with the pirates?

With a great effort, Tullio bit back the sarcasm. He shifted his weight and the pain from his wound shot through him.

'Are we to be treated as prisoners or as men?' he asked.

Helena's eyes flashed. He noticed with a start that her eyes were the same colour as the sibyl's. Could she be? He looked towards her right hand, but it was hidden beneath her robes. Within a heartbeat, he dismissed the thought. She had no reason to mask her identity here.

'The rules of the temple are straightforward. The rules of hospitality must be honoured. You may use the grounds and the public buildings during day, but at night, you and your men must be in your rooms for your own protection.' She led the way back to the courtyard and gestured towards a complex of austere buildings.

'As Roman citizens, my men and I shall have no problem following the dictates of civilised men,' he said with a smile and a shrug. 'We have already declined the captain's offer to swim back to Rome. It is better to keep our armour dry.'

Helena's shoulders visibly relaxed. Her lips curved up briefly. 'Your logic is faultless, Tribune.'

'You should take care, my lady, these are dangerous men,' the pirate grunted. 'Captain Androceles suggests —'

'Pilgrims from all lands have graced this temple.' The chipped marble voice was back.

'These are soldiers, Roman soldiers, not pilgrims.' The pirate's voice became strident. He slammed his fists together. 'If you had been on the waterfront, you would not dismiss them so lightly. I was there. They threatened the very existence of this island. Only the personal intervention of my esteemed captain prevented a physical attack on the sibyl.'

Tullio ignored the protest of his muscles and forced his body to the rigid attention of the parade ground and indicated to his men to follow his example. Instantly all obeyed him. This time there would be no breaking ranks.

He focussed his attention on Helena. He had to assume that the sibyl had told her everything. Like Pandora after her box was emptied, all he had left was hope.

'The sibyl made no mention of this when she returned.' Helena tapped the tablet against her mouth. She must say nothing to indicate who was at the quayside. After all that, she could not give into her temper. She had to stay calm. 'No mention at all.'

The sailor with a gold ring in one ear leant forward. His

finger twisted a strand of his greasy beard. Helena struggled not to recoil in disgust.

'These men are dangerous, my lady. You will need extra help,' he said. 'See how they seek to defy you. If they could, they would be beating their swords against their shields to signal the start of battle.'

'The sibyl would have informed me if she felt in danger,' she repeated, disliking the man more with each word he uttered. The good Captain Androceles had set a crude trap, one that she had no intention of blundering into. These Roman soldiers were not going to be a pretext for stationing his armed men within the temple. 'We are not without protection.'

'I tell the truth, lady,' the seafarer whined. 'And as you were not there, will you trust the word of a Roman or the word of your ally?'

'I trust the sibyl's judgement. Kybele guides her.' Helena's fingers, tightening around the tablet, snapped it in two. The faint crack brought her back to her senses. Any more provocation, she'd start blurting out the whole story.

'But the captain is only thinking of your welfare.' Gold Earring continued his protest and the rest of the seafarers echoed his sentiments.

'The lions roam the grounds at night,' Helena said as if he had not spoken. 'We have our guards during the day. Above all, Kybele protects and defends this temple. I doubt the Romans will be foolish enough to abuse our hospitality and risk the wrath of Kybele. Where would they go? All the triremes and boats are guarded. The harbour provides the only way on or off the island.'

Her gaze met Tullio's steady one.

How dangerous was he? She remembered his fingers on her hand, the way the tingles dashed up her arm. Her whole body seemed to be aware of him in a way she had not felt before. She offered a prayer up to Kybele that her face showed none of her disquiet.

'The captain's concern is solely for the temple,' the pirate said, his hand going to where his sword belt normally hung.

'The temple thanks you for your concern.' She crossed her arms and squared her jaw. Perhaps she should be grateful to the Romans for showing her Androceles's naked ambition. 'But I shall trust the sibyl's judgement. You have delivered the guests. You may return to your captain.'

'Captain Androceles has ordered that we remain as guards, in case the Romans try anything.' The seafarer planted his feet firmly and rocked back and forth. The other seafarers bristled. 'I must respectfully request that our swords are returned. We desire to provide the proper protection for the sibyl.'

Helena's arms started to tremble. Androceles's stratagem was obvious to any who had spent time with a *latrunculi* board. If his men became guards at the temple, he would try to dictate the sibyl's pronouncements, destroy her aunt's carefully built neutrality between rival factions of sailors. All because Helena had made an error.

'You may thank the good captain from me, but when we need assistance, the sibyl will ask for it.' Helena increased the volume of her voice so that it echoed throughout the antechamber. She knew her guards in the vestibule would hear and start their final preparations. Captain Zeno had been tricked six months ago, but would Gold Earring be so gullible? Did she dare take the risk of revealing the true extent of the temple's weakness? 'The temple is a place of peaceful contemplation. No arms are permitted to sully that. The sibyl refuses to allow the temple to be desecrated.'

'I am very grateful to the sibyl for providing us with lodging as we wait for the tribute.' Tullio stepped forward, his metalled sandals ringing out on the mosaic floor.

Helena ignored him. Romans were less a danger than the pirate. He had to leave.

'Your job has finished. The guests have been delivered safely. Go.' Helena used the same intonations her aunt used when she was declaring what the goddess wanted. Forceful, but with no hint of the desperation she was beginning to feel.

Gold Earring took a step towards the gateway, then hesitated. 'Captain Androceles ordered—'

'This is not the captain's ship.' She moved towards the main altar. In her mind, she recalled the number of times Aunt Flavia impressed on her the need to glide and not run. This man must have no hint of what was to come. If it taught the Roman with his knowing smile a lesson as well, so much the better. 'Perhaps you will believe after a small demonstration, but I warn you, Kybele protects her own.'

She gave a small clap of her hands and then pulled the curtain cord and allowed the mirrors to show. Instantly temple guards swarmed into the vestibule and stood in line behind Helena, each brandishing a long curved sword. She bit her lip. Hopefully the concealed mirrors and dim light would make Gold Earring think there was twice the number of guards.

'You called, my lady,' the lead guard boomed.

'The seafarer expressed a concern about our ability to look after the temple properly.'

'We have never had any trouble before, Helena.'

Tullio took pleasure in watching the pirates shift uncomfortably as Helena stood, head held high in front of her troop of guards.

Helena was unexpected. She managed to confront the pirate without flinching. He doubted many women of his acquaintance in Rome would have the courage to do such a thing. Most, like his elder sister and his ex-wife, would have run screaming before they dared speak back to a man like that.

From where he was standing, he could see the trick she had played with the bronze mirrors. It had been the vogue when he had been a boy and his mother had gone from temple to temple searching in vain for a cure for his younger sister's illness.

The question was whether or not the pirate would know about the trick or would he simply see the images without questioning and leave?

'I had no idea the temple had that many guards,' the pirate said before he brought his sandals together and gave an elaborate bow. 'Captain Androceles thinks only of your welfare.'

'Should the temple be in mortal danger, someone who is of pure heart would blow Neptune's horn and aid would appear.' She indicated a large bronze trumpet etched with shells and inlaid with precious stones. 'No doubt the good captain has forgotten the legend.'

'No doubt.' Droplets of sweat shone on the pirate's face.

Tullio allowed a breath to escape from his lips. The pirates would go. His men would be given a bit of dignity back and he could begin to discover why the sibyl had agreed to have him and his men housed here. Given the mirror trick, he doubted the sibyl left anything to chance.

Helena clapped her hands again. The curtains shut, concealing the mirrors once again. All the guards except the two directly behind the woman left.

'The temple has sufficient protection.' She waved her hand. 'I trust Captain Androceles will refrain from making that mistake in the future.'

'We have no quarrel with the sibyl. Her closeness to Kybele is well known.' The pirate put his hands together and bowed low.

'See that it stays that way. Kybele would not look kindly on her sanctuary being violated—by anyone.' Her eyes blazed green. A force to be reckoned with, truly, but her mouth held a pinched look as if she was not accustomed to defying pirates.

The pirates backed out of the temple, the swagger of earlier gone. The interview seemed not to have gone as planned. Maybe there was a breach between pirates and temple. Something he could use. Maybe the gods had favoured him after all.

Tullio's head and neck pounded from the earlier beating as he tried to concentrate on the implications. He had to get this right. The Republic could not afford a mistake.

The vestibule became quiet except for the breathing of his men. He regarded the slender woman standing in front of him. The time had come to start pleading Rome's cause.

'Thank you.' Tullio bowed low. 'The temple's hospitality is unparalleled. Rome will be grateful.'

'You are here as guests, soldier, and welcome on the sibyl's wishes, not mine.' Her pearl-drop earrings swayed as she lifted her chin higher. 'Leave your armour here. To be returned when you depart.'

Tullio heard the low murmur of his men. He refused to

repeat the folly of the pirate and anger the woman. But armour held almost sacred significance to his men. Even the pirates had not attempted to take it.

'We have no weapons. Our armour reminds us of who we are.'

'Armour offends the goddess. You will do as I request.'

Tullio took off his helmet and placed it at her sandal-shod feet. He motioned to the men. The last one to take off his armour, throwing it down with a loud clang, was Quintus. Tullio glared at him. Although Quintus was an experienced centurion and invaluable in the defence of the trireme, this was the second time he had defied orders in the space of an hour.

'I believe your guardianship will be more considerate than that of the good captain,' he said, hoping to draw Helena's attention away from the belligerent centurion.

'Captain Androceles and his house are well known to this temple.'

Tullio curled his fingers about his belt, tried to read the woman's expression and the unspoken meaning in her words. Was she saying that she didn't trust the pirate captain? He tried to smile, but it turned into a grimace as his wounds protested.

'On my sacred word as a Roman citizen, I promise you that my men and I will behave like guests as long as we are in this place, waiting for the tribute.'

'Spoken like a true Roman—a promise with conditions.' Helena crossed her arms. Her expression became more remote, her voice chilled. 'The price Rome exacts is often great.'

Tullio cursed the pounding in his head. He had behaved like the worst diplomat. Quintus had more finesse.

'Rome always treats its friends well,' he said.

'I have seen how Rome treats its friends. We are extending the same courtesy we would extend to any stranger who requests Kybele's protection. You used the ritual words, I believe.'

A jolt ran through Tullio. Her intonation echoed the sibyl's too closely. However, if they were one and the same, he failed to understand why she chose to hide her identity. Surely her word would have carried more weight with the pirates if she appeared as the sibyl?

'Your humble servant.' He paused for dramatic effect, caught her hand and raised it to his lips briefly before letting go. As his lips brushed her palm, he felt a faint trembling. 'Sibyl.'

Helena stared at Tullio, icy fear gripping her insides. It took all her powers of concentration not to snatch her hand out of his warm grip, but to move away with a fluid and easy motion.

How much had the Roman tribune guessed?

Her mind raced back over the conversation. Nothing she said had given any clue to her charade of this morning. He had to be guessing. She had to stop seeing shadows where there were none. It was one of her worst faults, according to Aunt Flavia, always trying to react rather than letting the goddess take charge.

'I am the sibyl's assistant, her niece. The sibyl is busy…busy with other matters,' she said quickly before she lost her nerve. But the excuse sounded feeble.

'My mistake.' His words were too smooth. 'You sound and look very much like her.'

'Look? How would you know? The sibyl only ever appears dressed in her robes and mask.'

'Your eyes are the same.'

Helena's heart sank. Such a simple thing. Hopefully no one else had noticed. Aunt Flavia's eyes were deep emerald green, not her much paler shade. She gazed over his head at the frieze of Kybele's life and attempted to draw strength from that. 'We are very alike. People have commented on that before.'

'Many apologies.' A small dimple appeared in his right cheek. 'Beautiful eyes must run in your family.'

A tiny flutter in her stomach caused Helena to swallow hard. She tried to damp down the tiny bubble of happiness by calling his words flattery, but they did please her.

'The sibyl does not take kindly to such mistakes,' she said, making her voice sound stern. She kept her eyes carefully trained on the frieze. 'Please refrain from making them in the future.'

'Will I be able to meet her and express my gratitude properly?' His voice was smooth like polished wood or the touch of silk.

Helena blinked and regained control of her wayward thoughts.

'If it can be arranged…' Helena allowed her voice to trail away. 'But for now she has given me authority to house you and is busy with other things.'

'It appears we are to be here for some time. I sincerely hope the sibyl might find time in her busy schedule at some point. I believe we have much to discuss.'

He knows.

Helena cleared her throat, unsure of what exactly to say, when Tullio took a half-step forward and swayed in front of her.

Her hands came up to catch him, to break his fall. His shoulder knocked into a statue of Kybele and caused it to rock. Helena held her breath. If the statue fell, it would be an omen of Kybele's disapproval. The statue stayed upright on its plinth.

Tullio's strong fingers gripped her forearms for an instant before he stood up straight. His masculine scent enveloped her and she felt the fluttering begin again in her stomach. Two of his men rushed to grab him. He waved them away.

'Forgive me, it has been a long day and we have not been fed at all.'

Helena tilted her head and eyed the tribune. Was this a ploy to make her feel sorry for him? Then she caught sight of the jagged wound running down his leg.

She clapped her hands and motioned to one of the guards.

'Show the Romans to the pilgrimage rooms and provide them with any medicine they require.' She turned to go before she made a bigger fool of herself. 'There is lentil and barley soup with cheese bread. We eat simply at the temple, but you should have sufficient.'

'Helena, wait,' Tullio called.

'Is there some further problem?' she asked and tried to ignore her heartbeat pounding in her ears.

His dark eyes crinkled at the corners, and, despite the marks from the beating, Helena could see that he was a handsome man, possibly the most handsome she had seen. Not in a pretty sort of way, but rugged. A man who could fight battles. But whose?

'Shall we meet again?' he asked in a low voice as his eyes seemed to deepen.

Helena hesitated, confused.

He was her enemy. Rome had always been the temple's and the seafarers common enemy. It was Rome who had

driven them to this remote island and forced them to live off
the seas. She had to remember that. She had no business
thinking he was handsome. Her hand trembled as she tucked
a stray lock of hair back into place.

'I doubt that very much. The temple guards are well versed
in solving pilgrims' problems.'

Chapter Three

Helena shut the door to her aunt's apartments with a decisive click, closing it against the world and the Roman tribune with the piercing gaze.

He unnerved her. She'd admit that. First at the quayside and then just now, when he had nearly guessed... That was all it was: a guess, a ploy, a Roman trick. He wanted her off balance.

Worse, her treacherous body reacted to him. A Roman. The last sort of man she wanted to be attracted to.

She'd ignore it and it would disappear. Her passions would not rule her as they had ruled her mother. She knew what she wanted in this world and why she would never have a life like an ordinary woman. She had her duties and responsibilities. Her path was clearly laid out before her.

She breathed deeply, enjoying the mixture of incense, pine and cinnamon scents that filled the room. When she was a child, she had been frightened of the ornately decorated apartments, with their strange friezes and heavy smell of incense, and more frightened of the imperious woman who inhabited them. Now, she found them a pleasant refuge from the day to day concerns of the temple. It was here she could relax and learn.

She peeped through the doorway.

Aunt Flavia looked small and pale against the white linen pillows. So different from the woman who had dominated Helena's life with her no-nonsense ways and determination to promote the interests of Kybele. Her aunt always exuded energy. Now she was an empty husk whose every breath was laboured.

'Did she wake?' Helena asked Galla, the maid she shared with her aunt. She had hoped that somehow, when she returned, the sibyl would be better. That Helena's assumption of her role would have jolted Aunt Flavia back to the land of the living.

Galla shook her head. Helena hurried over and touched the sibyl's cool hand—no response. She resisted the temptation to hold the tiny bronze mirror in front of her aunt's lips.

Aunt Flavia had to get better.

With each passing day, the danger that her affliction would be discovered grew. Without her aunt, there would be no orderly passing of the sibyl's mask. Uncle Lichas and the other seafaring houses would demand a say in who became the next sibyl, would require greater control over the temple. Aunt Flavia, through a combination of her own personality and the accuracy of her predictions, had managed to keep the temple away from the seafarers' clutches. The islanders led a better life. Helena tried to count how many lives her aunt had saved—at least twenty, including Niobe, the temple's goose-girl who could not talk.

The scene on the quayside, and just now with the Romans,

would surely have never happened if her aunt had been in control. Helena knew that. She stilled as she noticed the bronze hands that the sibyl used in the highest of ceremonies. She had thought about wearing them to the quayside, but it would have made the lions difficult to control. A mistake? Had anyone noticed? She had to believe she had escaped…this time.

Lately, Kybele ignored all her prayers. The goddess certainly had not sent any help—no dreams, no premonitions, nothing. And all the while, the problems kept multiplying.

Helena ran a hand along a carved box, her fingers tracing the strange carvings and ancient runes. She had expected some guidance from Kybele, who always guided her aunt's actions.

'Did Aunt Flavia say anything? Make any noise at all?'

'The sibyl remains as you found her,' Galla replied. 'When she stirs, I will send word immediately.'

Helena shut her eyes, willing her aunt to improve. They had a few more days at most before her uncle returned from his own fishing expedition, loaded with spoils and expectant of the sibyl's blessing. If the Roman tribune had noticed the similarities between hers and the sibyl's eyes, how long would it take Uncle Lichas? Even if she wore the bronze hands? He could surely tell the difference between his niece and his sister. And then what would happen? Would he demand an immediate passing of the mask…to his niece to keep the balance of power within the family?

She knew instinctively that she could never command the same sort of respect as her aunt. The Lady Zenobia, her uncle's Cilician wife, took every opportunity to make waspish comments about how like her disgraced mother Helena was, pointing out each and every mistake. Part of the reason Aunt

Flavia had not let her make her final vows was down to Zenobia's interference.

'How did the performance at the quayside go?' Galla asked, laying a friendly hand on Helena's shoulder. 'Did anyone guess?'

Helena slowly traced one of the runes with her forefinger—piety. There was no need to worry Galla about the possibility of her hands being noticed.

'Luckily, the trireme belonged to Captain Androceles,' she said. 'He only uses this port occasionally and I don't think he noticed. We agreed the normal terms. You've made *itrion*? They're my favourite sweet.'

'I've heard that somewhere before.' Galla gave a laugh.

Helena walked over and popped one of the biscuits made of sesame seed and honey into her mouth, savouring the taste.

'I made them for you. You need something after your performance, but don't try to change the subject with your flattery.' The salt-and-pepper-haired woman shook her forefinger at Helena. 'There is something wrong. I can see it in your face. There have been movements in the temple. The guards have been hurrying everywhere. You might be able to fool the others, but I have known you since the hour you were born. This was a mistake, you know it was. You should have informed the palace of your aunt's illness.'

Helena pressed the tips of her fingers together, then tapped her forefingers against her mouth before replying. Galla had been against the charade from the beginning, arguing that they should announce the sibyl was ill, indisposed. What had happened was the sort of disaster she had predicted. 'We have visitors…guests, courtesy of Androceles. Roman soldiers.'

'Romans? Here?' Galla gave a wild look at the bed. 'What will the sibyl say? After what they did to your family! Why did you allow them to disembark? Your aunt would never have allowed that. They are inhuman, the Romans.'

'I had no choice, Galla.' Helena stared at the floor mosaics rather than meet her maid's eye. She didn't dare admit the stab of attraction she felt for the Roman. He was human, she knew that. His concern for his men showed. It took a brave man to offer to take another's punishment. She wondered how many of the islanders, let alone a seafarer, would do such a thing. Then she dismissed the idea as unworthy. 'After the last time when Androceles's son cheated us with mouldy corn, I thought it best for him to reveal his cargo. He unloaded the Romans first.'

'The sibyl would have stopped him. Or she would have forced him to reload the Romans.' Galla shook her head. 'If you had listened to me—'

'If I had listened to you, all the seafarers from the Pillars of Hercules to the shores of the Black Sea would have known the sibyl was ill and would have set sail to conquer this island.'

'And what will happen when the Romans learn of her illness? Rome is a good deal closer than those two places you named.'

Helena's headache began to pound in earnest. She knew what Galla said was true, but there had to be a way. She refused to surrender everything her aunt had worked for over these past twenty years. Aunt Flavia would recover, as she always did. It was simply taking longer this time, that was all.

'Your aunt—'

'The tribune asked for help. He used the proper words, the correct ritual. He invoked Kybele.' Helena leant forward and grabbed Galla's forearms. 'In the name of Kybele, I could hardly refuse. Aunt Flavia has never refused anyone using the ritual.'

'You didn't lock them in the warehouse and throw away the key?' Galla's shawl quivered and her eyes grew as round as the wheels on the chariot. 'We shall be murdered in our beds!'

'Our *guests* have arrived. Anyone who invokes Kybele's protection with proper ritual words is a guest.' Helena drew on her training to remain calm. She needed Galla's help. 'Some of them were injured and need medical attention, if they are to remain this side of Hades.'

'They won't be getting any from me.' Galla crossed her arms and glared at Helena, looking for all the world like a ruffled hen. 'You should have told those soldiers to swim for it and to take their chances with Neptune. That's what I would have said.'

Suddenly, Helena had a picture of Galla confronting the tall tribune. It would be an unequal match. Helena's lips curved upwards, but she pressed them into a stern line. 'Are you refusing to help me, Galla?'

'This is another one of your crazy schemes, Helena. We need to inform the palace. The Lady Zenobia will know what to do. They can throw the Romans in the palace's prison and we will be rid of them.'

'If I did that, Aunt Zenobia would demand to see Aunt Flavia. Can you imagine what would happen when she found out?'

Galla's face sobered. Her hands plucked at her gown's folds. 'I know what Zenobia is capable of,' she whispered. 'I used to be her slave until the sibyl rescued me. But please, I beg you, don't ask me to wait on the Romans. I have heard the stories of how they behave. They are worse than the seafarers.'

'You must help, Galla.' Helena placed an arm about Galla's waist and rested her head briefly on the older woman's shoulder as she used to do when she was a child. 'How many of the guards are loyal to me? There is no one else I can trust or turn to. Will you do this for me?'

The maid walked over to the bed and straightened the cover. 'This is one mess you will have to clean up yourself, Helena.'

Tullio stretched and ignored the aches and pains in his body. What more could be done for his men? The severely injured lay on pallets with their cloaks rolled as pillows. All had feasted on a simple bowl of barley and lentil stew.

The next problem he faced was how to arrange another meeting with Helena. The way she had kept her head despite the pirate's best efforts. Beauty and brains together were a rare combination. There was much more to her than met the eye. Despite her denials, he couldn't rid himself of the feeling she was the sibyl from the harbour. But it made no logical sense.

'You wanted to speak with me, Livius Tullio?'

Tullio regarded the burly centurion. How best to approach the reprimand? Back on the trireme when the pirates had boarded, Quintus's bellows had saved his and half his men's lives. The number of brasses he wore on his belt and the vine cane he carried attested to his courage and devotion to Rome.

'My life is not so cheap, Quintus, I would have you throw it away on mere words.'

'It was them pirates, sir and that priestess of theirs.' The centurion hung his grey-flecked head. 'Standing there as if they owned the whole world. Them's our amphorae, our grain. My tongue got the better of me. Hercules's club, I never expected them to hear.'

'You are a soldier, not an orator, Quintus. I shall need you by my side when the fighting does begin, but any repeat…' Tullio allowed his voice to trail off.

'If you'd like, I'll fall on my sword. I don't know any other tribune who'd have put his life on the line for me. Think about what a mess young Julius Caesar would have made of it. The gods were with me this time.'

Tullio lifted his eyes heavenwards. He had enough troubles without being reminded of the mercurial tribune. Although Caesar possessed a great deal of charm, Tullio privately doubted that he would progress far if he did not learn to control his arrogance. Caesar might claim descent from Venus, but when was the last time any of his family were elected consul?

'We have enough troubles, Centurion, without adding your death to them. Against the odds, your outburst worked. These quarters are more comfortable than the trireme.'

'And the woman who greeted us is much better looking than the pirate captain!' one of the legionaries cried.

'That wouldn't be hard!' Another shouted to howls of laughter.

'Remember we are here as guests, not as legionaries.' Tullio held up a hand and the laughter stopped. 'I have no wish to alienate the sibyl or her assistant.'

'What do you mean, sir? They're allies of the pirates. Followers of Kybele, and you know what those women do to men.'

A sharp rap on the door prevented Tullio from replying.

The door swung open to reveal not one of the loin-clothed guards, but Helena. She had discarded her cap of red and white ribbons for a rose bandeau. He had no doubt some artist would have enjoyed using her profile for one of those red and black vases that the Greeks specialised in. In her hands, she carried a bowl and a large bag hung from her wrist.

Why had she appeared?

'Helena, what an unexpected pleasure,' he said, giving a deep bow, but keeping his eyes on her face, searching for any hint. 'Is there something we can do for you? The food you sent filled a hungry man's belly. I don't think lentil and barley soup ever tasted so good.'

'I promised you medicine,' she said. Her chin tilted upwards and he received the full force of her green eyes. 'You and your men are guests in the temple.'

'Was there no one else to bring it? I thought you were busy with your temple duties.'

'The other healers had rituals to attend to.' Helena shifted on her feet. 'We have no desire to lose any of you. If you would please tell me your injuries? Exactly what did this storm do to your men? I was surprised. The sea around here has been exceptionally calm of late.'

Her look implied that she considered Romans to be very poor sailors.

Tullio rapidly listed all the injuries his men had suffered, sparing Helena no detail. He watched her face carefully to see if she felt some sort of compassion for his men. He wanted her to acknowledge what the pirates had done, to see their barbarity. 'They attacked at night, Captain Androceles and his men.'

Her face changed. A crease appeared between her

eyebrows. Her eyes blazed green fire. Inwardly Tullio cursed. He had allowed his anger to get the better of him.

'I am here to speak of your men's injuries, not what caused them. Captain Androceles assures me that he rescued you. You invoked the goddess to aid your men.' Helena's head raised another notch. No matron in the Forum could have had an icier chill to her voice.

'I apologise, my lady.' Tullio had to keep control or risk losing any sort of support. Now was not the time. 'My concern for my men is such that I wanted you to understand how the injuries occurred.'

'Let me worry about the healing and you can worry about how it happened.' She turned her head and Tullio found himself staring into her eyes, which were deep unfathomable pools of green. 'We don't throw away lives here.'

Without saying another word, he led the way to the pallet of his most injured man, his optio, Rufus. Rufus with his laughing eyes and quick wit, everyone's friend as well as being a useful solider. He had saved Tullio's life several times with his fast thinking, using his shield to deflect the pirate whose knife had stabbed Tullio in the leg. Now he lay muttering and thrashing about on the pallet with eyes that were far too bright.

'He has a fever.' She knelt down by the pallet and poured some liquid into Rufus's mouth. The optio gurgled slightly and lay still. Quintus started forward, but Tullio held him back. He wanted to see what this woman was going to do. 'He should sleep for a while and give the goddess a chance to work her miracles. My guards will move him to the hospital.'

There was a murmur of protest behind Tullio and he knew

Quintus's reminder about the strange practices of female followers of Kybele had struck home. He did not need the men
rioting from fear. They had to save their strength.

'Will I be able to see him? Will someone be able to be with
him?'

The murmurs behind him quieted.

'You are free to move around the compound during the day
as long as you don't interfere with the work of the temple. If
you desire it, one person may stay with your wounded
comrade.'

'Thank you.' The intense pain in Tullio's shoulders and
neck eased at her words.

'It is not in the interests of the temple to let any of your
men die, Tribune.'

'The name is Tullio. Marcus Livius Tullio.' He waited to
see what her response would be. She raised an eyebrow. 'If
we are to be guests here.'

He detected a slight easing around her mouth.

'Very well, *Tullio*, we attempt to keep people on this side
of the River Styx. Kybele is a healer on this island, not a de-
stroyer—whatever her critics might say. She makes no judgement on whether or not you belong to this island, or are a
Roman. The goddess only sees the living person.'

A small victory, but an important one. He felt sure of that.
She had used his name. Was it to distinguish between him and
Rome? It did not matter. He had to take what was offered.

'Will you be taking any of my men to the sibyl?'

'I will present a list of your requirements to the sibyl and
she will consult the goddess who will decide the best way
to proceed.'

'How long will that take?'

'Several days. The goddess operates on her own time, Tullio.'

Tullio drew in his breath then took another before he trusted himself to speak. He wanted to know all his men would survive. He intended to leave no man behind when they departed from this island. 'But you say that he will live.'

'The goddess moves in mysterious ways, Tullio. He is in good hands.' She placed the herbs and bowl down. 'If you make a paste with these and apply them to your wounds, you will discover that the wounds heal more quickly. It is what I use when any of the villagers injure themselves.'

Tullio could see the questions in his men's eyes. No one moved towards the herbs. They were frightened, scared to trust. The last thing he needed was Quintus muttering more curses. 'We will trust in the goddess then.'

'You are welcome. Please ask if you need more herbs.' She spun on her heel and half-stumbled on the uneven flooring in the room.

He put his hand under her elbow to steady her and felt the warmth of her body rise up his arm. Her face was but a few inches from his own. He could count the lashes that fringed her green eyes. He fought the urge to pull her more fully into his arms.

She moved away from him and he let her go.

'In due course, you may visit your comrade in the hospital. I will send a guard when he is awake again. There is a small yard two doors down. Pilgrims use it for exercising and contemplation. Your meals will be delivered to this room. We are a humble establishment...Tullio. Now I bid you farewell.'

With that, she turned and walked out of the room, leaving only the faintest scent of jasmine in her wake.

* * *

The hospital wing was cool and dark by the time Helena reached it. She had intended to check on the Roman earlier, but every time her sandals turned towards the hospital, someone else approached with a difficulty. Not only did she have the usual problems of making sure the temple was running smoothly, but the sibyl's audience with the villagers was much larger than she anticipated. The first petitioner had been the local goatherder, Pius. When Helena, wearing the gold mask and this time the bronze hands, inclined her head, he had approached, twisting the end of his cloak in his hand.

Would Kybele really know where Pius's goat was? Or if the sailor on the third trireme from the left fancied Pius's sister? And, if so, would he pay the proper dowry? Helena provided what help she could. The goat was easy—she had seen it chomping away in the sweet grass on the other side of the temple. The other, she gave what she hoped was a reasonable answer. It appeared to satisfy Pius. He smiled, bowed and left. Helena released a breath.

Normally, the villagers attended to their own lives and only went to the temple during the high days. But the curiosity about the Romans had brought the villagers to the temple in a way she had not seen since just after the great storm had destroyed half the village and the women worried about the men on the sea. Helena gained a bit of confidence as the audience wore on. Common sense, that was all. At the end of the session, she thought she saw the porter from her uncle's palace, but her attention was distracted.

Thinking back on it now as she walked through the deserted corridors, she was certain it had been the porter—the jagged pink scar on his right cheek and all.

Her feet tumbled into each other when she saw the man sitting by the Roman's bed, his head rested on his hands. The golden light from the single oil lamp made his hair appear as black as the stones that edged Kybele's pool in the innermost grotto.

Helena stopped.

Her heart began to pound slightly faster. She arranged the folds of her cloak more tightly about her body. She should have taken time to change out of the sibyl's gown, but she had not expected to find him here. She had assumed his words were mere bravado, intended to make certain that his man was looked after, rather than the intention of actually carrying out the vigil himself.

She had only thought to stop for a brief time to check that the injured man's breathing was easy and that the opium held him in its painless sleep before retiring for the night.

At the movement, Tullio lifted his head. Large dark rings encircled his eyes as if sheer strength of will was keeping him awake. Helena tore her gaze away. She refused to think what he had been through. But the sneaking thought that none of the heads of the trading houses, from her uncle to Androceles, had ever been to see any of their sick men crept in and refused to leave.

She pulled the cloak tighter and tore her gaze from the line of his shoulders. She had to think about the tribute she would receive for him and his companions.

'The sibyl's audience lasted longer than expected,' she said to fill the silence. She had to say something. It would be impossible to walk by without saying a word after the time she had spent looking at him. 'I wanted to be here sooner.'

He lifted an eyebrow, but his eyes held a certain measure

of kindness. It surprised her—she had always considered Romans to be without human feelings. 'Is the sibyl giving audiences? I wish I had known. I greatly desire the chance to speak with her.'

'Her audiences are finished. She needs time to recover.' Helena's mind raced. She had to find a more solid excuse, but her mind refused to co-operate. 'It will have to be tomorrow at the earliest. I'm not sure of her schedule.'

He stood up gingerly, reminding Helena of the injuries he had suffered. Most men would have looked to their own needs first, rather than sitting by the side of a fallen comrade. A grudging admiration filled her. The man bore all the hallmarks of a great leader, but that made him all the more dangerous.

He was the true enemy.

'There is a salve in the medicines I left that will ease the pain,' she said to draw attention away from his desired meeting with the sibyl.

'Aches and pains are nothing for a soldier.' He rotated his right arm and a flash of discomfort crossed over his features. 'My man was more important. I had to make sure he received proper treatment.'

'Are you questioning his care?' Helena released a breath and felt her lungs fill with more air. She walked over and felt the soldier's forehead with her right hand. Cool to the touch.

'Not at all.' Tullio passed a hand through his black locks, making them stand straight up. 'He became calmer after one of your guards gave him something to drink.'

'He has had opium mixed with wine. He will sleep until the morning. We are used to such things here. All the seafarers from across the Mediterranean bring their sick here to be cured. He should recover.' She nodded towards the door. 'You ought to go and rest. One of the guards will call you if his condition changes.'

'One brought me here when I asked. Your words explain why the hospital is so large.' Tullio gestured to the airy but nearly empty hospital room. Most of the pallets lay neatly stacked in the corner and had obviously not been used for some time. His smile reached his eyes and caused them to twinkle in the lamp light. 'I had wondered. There are whispers about the rites of Kybele in Rome.'

'Is that how you knew the ritual words?' Helena leant forward and waited for his answer.

'I took a gamble with my memory. Something I heard as a child.'

His long fingers stroked the line of his jaw while his eyes assessed her. A trembling filled her stomach. Was he looking at her in the same way a man looks at a woman? The Lady Zenobia had told her enough times that no man would do such a thing to a creature like her, especially since Helena had seen more than twenty summers.

'Your mother was an adherent of Kybele?' Helena asked, not bothering to hide her surprise. Only she could have such a Roman land here.

'My mother sought help wherever she could.'

'You did well to remember such a thing. Without the exact words, the sibyl would not have been obliged to help.'

'I know,' he said quietly and his dark eyes caught hers. Helena looked down at her hands.

'I can remember very little about my mother,' she said to cover her confusion. 'A smile here, a laugh there and always her white robe.'

'Your mother was involved with the temple?'

'Before my aunt, she was the sibyl. Her healing powers were renowned throughout the eastern Mediterranean.' Helena kept her voice neutral. She had no wish to relive her mother's disgrace or the fact that she was living proof of that disgrace.

'Are sibyls always related by blood?'

Helena knew she should cut the conversation short, that there were too many pitfalls. But it had been so many years since she had talked to anyone about such things. There was something in his voice that lured her on and made her want to linger. But for how long?

'Sibyls are traditionally related to the king of this island.'

Tullio inclined his head. He moved away from the pallet where the man lay sleeping soundly. He was so close that she could nearly touch his tunic. All she had to do was to reach out her hand. Helena shivered. Was this how it happened with her mother?

'And your father is king?'

'My uncle, Lichas, is the current king. He assumed the throne after my grandfather…died.' Helena's hand plucked at her cloak, aware she had strayed too near old wounds for her liking. She regarded the man on the pallet again as he gave a loud snore. 'We should go. Leave this man in peace.'

He made no move from beside the bed.

'I made a promise to Rufus's woman that I would bring him back safe. He is from my father's estate. I will stay by his side if I can.'

She opted for the bland words she had recited a thousand times since childhood. 'It is in the goddess's hands.'

'Thank you for taking care of all of us.'

'Your friend will wake in the morning. You should try to get some sleep.'

you.' His eyes deepened in the torchlight.

inside of her cheek and refused to think about
must look like asleep and how intimate this hospital
had become with just the two of them, alone. Had she
ever been alone with a man before like this?

Her eyes lifted. Once again their gazes locked. His hand caught hers and very deliberately brought it to his lips. All the while his steady gaze seemed to devour her soul. A tingling jolt ran up her arm and she moved a step closer. His other hand reached out and touched her shoulder.

A butterfly touch, nothing more. Helena felt the breath stop in her mouth. She wanted him to kiss her. She wanted to know what his lips tasted like. She ached to find out. She took a step closer and his tunic brushed her gown. The dark bristles of his stubble contrasted with the golden olive of his skin.

What would the bristles feel like against the pads of her fingers? Sharp or smooth? Her hand came up, hovered in mid-air.

'My lady, the sibyl desires a word.' One of the guards broke the spell.

Helena jumped back, allowing her hand to fall to her side. What had she been about to do? She had never behaved like that with any man before. She refused to look at Tullio. He was supposed to be her enemy, however attractive he might be. She had to remember that.

She hurriedly straightened her cloak, and ignored the man standing next to her. She had to concentrate on the guard's words. Something had happened, some change in Aunt Flavia's condition. 'Now?'

'That is what Galla said when she found me.'

'What were her exact words?'

'Find Helena and tell her the sibyl wishes to see her.'

Helena forced breath through her mouth. For a wild instant, she had hoped Aunt Flavia had spoken, that her prayers had been answered. But Galla's coded message meant there were signs of improvement, a flicker of life. 'Yes, I will go now. Please make sure the Roman stays here tonight. The lions are out and I have no desire to lose such an important tribute.'

Tullio watched Helena hurry away, her dark red cloak billowing slightly, revealing the hint of her slender figure and her sandals tapping on the smooth stone floor. The message had meant something. He was sure of that.

She intrigued him. A puzzle he felt he had to solve. There was much more to her than met the eye. There was a pull there he had not felt before. If the guard had not interrupted them, he would have kissed her red lips or at least tried.

He turned and saw the temple guard regarding him. His broad arms were folded across his chest. These were not the arms of someone unaccustomed to work. The knotted muscles stood out clearly. This was a bodyguard, an enforcer. Who did the sibyl need protection from?

Tullio tilted his head, going back over the conversation he had just had. There was something there, some clue. 'Do all the priestess have a short little finger on their right hand?'

'It is not a requirement.' The guard's voice sounded cautious.

'I noticed Helena's and wondered.' Tullio considered how best to continue without alerting anyone from the island to his suspicions. Who exactly had been the priestess on the quayside and why was she there? His instincts told him that it was Helena, but she had denied it. 'I like to know about different customs and rituals. What purpose does it serve?'

'Helena lost that finger in the accident that killed her mother, the late sibyl.'

Tullio had remembered how the sibyl had held the lions steady at the quayside. The woman holding the reins had had a shortened little finger. 'So the present sibyl has no shortened fingers?'

'The sibyl is renowned for the beauty of her hands,' the guard answered without hesitation. 'They are without blemish.'

Chapter Four

Time. She had no time.

Helena stared at the barely touched pile of the pyramid cakes laid out for her breakfast. She knew the honey-and-wheat-flake cakes were required eating after the morning ritual, but when did the sibyl get the time? She gulped down one or two morsels with a mouthful of cold mint tea and resumed her pacing of the apartment.

Today was going to be no better than yesterday.

There was no safe haven. Although Aunt Flavia had opened her eyes yesterday evening and patted Helena's hand with her fragile fingers, her voice had not worked. Helena gave a brief explanation about their guests—nothing to cause alarm. Her aunt had nodded and mouthed the words 'good' and closed her eyes.

Last night, it had been enough, but this morning?

She crumbled a cake between her fingers. She was not going to think about last night, about the way sleep refused to come and how she kept remembering the feel of Tullio's hands against her back.

Time was dripping drop by precious drop from the water-clock.

She had to concentrate on the words she'd use when she confronted him this morning. Galla had done her a favour by taking the medicine this morning, and she'd returned red-faced and stammering. And Helena refused to have Galla intimidated like that.

It was all too easy to imagine what had happened to her.

The tribune wouldn't dare trying something here in her aunt's apartments. Here, she could reassert her authority without being distracted by the breadth of his shoulders or the line of his mouth. Here, she'd remember who she was and her place in life.

She gave one last glance around. Everything about this room, from the carved wood furniture to the wall hangings, spoke of the sibyl's power and prestige. It would give the correct impression—efficiency and control, not the quiet intimacy of the hospital wing at night.

The door to her aunt's apartments gaped open, revealing the slight figure on the bed. A sudden lump formed in Helena's throat.

'You must get well, Aunt Flavia,' Helena whispered. 'The Lady Zenobia was at the morning ritual, and you know she never comes to anything but the most grand events. She's plotting something and I don't know what to do.'

Helena held her breath, waiting for a sign. The mention of Zenobia was sure to get a reaction. Aunt Flavia's fraught relationship with Zenobia was legendary.

'Please get well. The temple needs you.' Helena paused. She had to try once more, and hope for a miracle. 'I need you. I am not sure I can do this, that I am ready for the responsibility.'

She waited for as long as she dared, but heard only her aunt's soft breathing intermingled with the incessant dripping of the water-clock. Helena shut the door. There would be no miracle before the Roman arrived. She was the temple's last defender.

The ornate box that held the sibyl's mask and hands lay open and the light from the flickering oil lamps gave it an eerie otherworldly look. Helena rose to her feet and closed the lid with a decisive click. Her hand lingered on the carved frieze, her forefinger tracing Kybele's face.

Did Kybele truly talk to Aunt Flavia?

The goddess certainly did not talk to her. The only thing she felt when wearing the mask was its cold heaviness.

The sound of tramping feet in the corridor brought her back to the present.

The Roman had arrived.

Hurriedly she stood up and smoothed her gown, Nothing to show distress. Calm, cool, collected. She was in charge, last evening a distant memory.

'My lady? The tribune waits outside.' A temple guard entered the room.

'Very good.' Helena again ran her hands down her gown and attempted to quell the butterflies that fluttered in her stomach. She tried to picture how the interview would go, what she would say and how she would say it. She would make her authority felt.

'The tribune desires to speak with the sibyl if at all possible after he has had this interview with you,' the guard informed her.

'The sibyl is busy and wishes to remain in seclusion for the rest of the day.' Helena gave her standard response. She had given it so often lately that she began to feel like Aunt

Zenobia's mynah bird, echoing the last phrase time and time again.

'I already told him she receives petitions in the evening. It is tradition.'

Helena resisted the temptation to curse. Her diversionary tactic of last night had not worked. She had to think of something else, some concrete reason why Tullio should not have a private interview with Aunt Flavia. The guard regarded her with a quizzical expression.

'What the Roman asks is impossible.' She ran her hands a third time down her gown. 'I will inform him of that. When the sibyl deems the time is right, she will grant him an audience, but she must be allowed to attend to her goddess-appointed tasks.'

'That is a pity,' a low-timbred voice said, reminding Helena of a cool waterfall tumbling over rocks to a deep pool and sending a glorious thrill down her spine. 'I did so wish to thank her for yesterday morning at the quayside and for the medicines. Food and a bath can make you believe the gods are smiling. It has done wonders for my men.'

'I'm pleased our humble facilities meet with your approval.'

She glanced down at her sandals and gave her mind a shake. She wasn't going to think about such things. She was about to prove to herself that she was capable of ignoring this attraction. She could do it if she tried. Helena's breath stuck in her throat. He was even more handsome today than yesterday. Her eyes travelled from his sandalled feet up his bare legs and short tunic to his broad shoulders, and finally to his face, which was framed in short dark curls. There was a look of fierce determination in his eyes, despite the smile on his lips.

Romans were supposed to be monsters, but this one made her senses tingle. His quizzical expression intensified. Helena drew a deep breath and launched into her prepared speech. She explained about the island's history of hospitality towards strangers.

'We discussed the need for your soldiers to act as guests,' she said, feeling her stomach start to tighten as she came to the difficult portion.

'Guests.' Tullio broke in. He was careful to say the word without rancour or irony. 'I hope we behave as such.'

He moved further into the room. It was not a formal audience chamber, but a room that looked as if it were used for the day-to-day running of the temple. Scrolls and tablets lay piled on the floor and in the centre of the room on a pedestal was an ornately carved wooden box. The golden mask? After last night's conversation with the guard, he would be prepared to wager several estates that Helena was the woman underneath yesterday's mask.

His eyes searched Helena for a sign of weakness. Nothing out of place. No stray locks of hair tucked behind her ear. Every fold of her gown hung perfectly. Her makeup had been applied with a precise hand. Her gold earrings matched the slender gold chain about her neck. The perfect administrator. The warm woman he had held briefly in his arms had vanished.

'Hospitality is the defining mark of a civilised society,' he said.

'Do not take our hospitality for granted, Tribune.' Her eyes flashed green fire. 'You are here and you are alive.'

'For that I am grateful, Priestess. It is my sincere wish some day Rome may properly express its gratitude.'

Tullio watched to see how she'd react to his deliberate

choice of words. Woman or statue? One of the first lessons
he had learnt from his drill instructor was: your opponent's
true state of mind will be revealed in little movements.

Her fingers plucked at the folds of her simple white gown
and her tongue flicked over her lips. A faint frown showed
between her eyebrows, allowing Tullio a glimpse of the
woman. The strain in his shoulders eased.

'Call me Helena, please.' She made a small gesture with
her hand. 'The only priestess is the sibyl. I am, as I explained
yesterday, merely her assistant. Pray remember that.'

'Helena, then.' Tullio rolled her name on his tongue,
allowed his eyes to roam over her curves, but kept his mind
alert. 'Is there some reason in particular you have called me
here? Or did you wish to pass the time of day with me?
Continue last night's interrupted conversation?'

The colour rose higher in her cheeks, until they matched
the delicate pink in her lips.

He lifted an eyebrow and invited her to continue the flirtation. It had to be the reason she had summoned him. A bold
move. He felt his body respond to her nearness, and wondered
if he risked taking her into his arms. A little physical persua-
sion perhaps. His smile grew wider. He took a step closer.

Her gaze moved to the desk and she picked up a stylus,
toyed with it. Then she placed it down and turned back
towards him. The administrator was back, and the woman in
full retreat. Silently, Tullio cursed his action. He had moved
too quickly. The quarry had flown.

'I have called you here because my maid encountered disre-
spectful remarks when she delivered the medicine this morning.'
Each word spoken with care and precision. 'If you Romans wish
to be treated as guests, you must obey the rules of hospitality.'

'I spent the night by Rufus's side and had only just returned to my men when I was summoned.' He held out his hands, palms upwards, but felt the muscles in his jaw clench.

Who had transgressed? Quintus?

The centurion had seemed pleased with himself to the point of humming a tune. Tullio had not had the time to pursue it before the guard had arrived. But after what happened yesterday, Quintus would not risk further upsetting their hosts. Even he would not be so bold and reckless as to disobey a superior officer. His medal for bravery would not protect him.

'I have no knowledge of this. When and where did it take place?'

'Are you denying it happened?' Her earrings started to swing, brushing the top of her gown. The ease between them vanishing as surely as a smoke curl from a brazier. 'How typically Roman.'

'Tell me which soldier and he shall be punished. I have no wish to discipline the wrong man.' Perhaps there was a misunderstanding. Perhaps the maid was not used to the rough banter of soldiers. But he refused to condemn Quintus without knowing the full story. He had to be certain. 'Wrongful punishment will only inflame the situation.'

'Inappropriate comments were made to my maid. That is all you need to know.' Her eyes were green ice. 'She was visibly distressed when she returned.'

Tullio drummed his fingers against his thigh. Helena was not going to meet him halfway.

'Some light-hearted banter may have been exchanged. Nothing serious and certainly nothing designed to offend. Much as we spoke last night.' Tullio forced his voice to sound light, but every muscle was alert. When he returned to their quarters, he'd give all the soldiers a dressing down. They had to behave properly. The gods had given him this chance to save their lives. None of his men should jeopardise it. 'These are soldiers, not silver-tongued diplomats.'

He waited and watched. Helena pressed her lips together until they were a firm white line. Her eyes became like hard green marble.

He resisted the temptation to run his hand through his hair as he silently cursed whichever solider had tried to flirt with the maid.

'It is not up to me to pinpoint the troublemaker, merely to inform you that I refuse to have the servants of this temple molested in that manner.'

'I apologise unreservedly if anything my men or I have done or said caused distress.' He made a bow.

'I need more than simple words. Words are easily spoken.' Her eyes looked directly at him, challenging him. 'Unlike you Romans, we expect courteous behaviour here. I assume your men are capable of it. You will do something about this and give me your promise that it will not recur. It must not!'

Tullio managed to choke angry words back. The arrogance of the woman. How dare she preach to him about how he should discipline his men! He had apologised. That should be enough.

'And I refuse to punish innocent men on a vague feeling. I have explained it is most likely a misunderstanding. I will speak to my men, but these things can happen.'

'We are at an impasse, I see.' Helena walked over to a table, picked up a sheaf of tablets and rapped them sharply against the wood. The line between her eyebrows deepened. 'There is little point in continuing this conversation. My word that one of my maids was upset should have been enough for you.'

There was no mistaking the threat in her underlying words. Tullio regretted he had not chosen more diplomatic words, but, by Jupiter's thunderbolt, his men were important and he refused to punish them on a whim.

'I mean you no harm,' he said quietly, making sure his voice held nothing of the parade ground. 'I will speak to my men, but I need to know what bothered the woman, so I can tell them specifically. These are soldiers, not courtiers. If their language is rough, I can only apologise. We are grateful to be out of that hulk. The sibyl—'

Helena lifted her eyes and met his gaze. A flash of fear shot through the green. What had caused it?

'Tribune, you must understand that your position and that of your men is somewhat unique. I will not have temple routine disrupted…'

'Only pirates have something to fear from me.'

He took a step closer to her, watching for any sign that she understood, that he had reached the woman again. Her hand went to her hair and loosening a single curl at the back of her neck, twisted it around her finger. Her lips softened. His hand sought the reassurance of his sword belt and encountered thin air. The time had come, he judged. 'Allow me to do something in return for the sibyl.'

'You used the ritual words. The sibyl needs no thanks,' Helena said, staring straight ahead and not at him. She had to ignore the way his black hair curled at the temples. 'It is not my place to question the rules.'

He took a step closer. If she took a deep breath, her breasts would brush his chest. His masculine scent tickled Helena's nose, holding her. She wanted *him* to hold her. She wanted him to look at her with his dark eyes. The way he done when he first came into the room. Her tongue flicked over dry lips.

It had been a mistake to dismiss the guard, she thought. She had to remember the Roman was a soldier and she knew what Roman soldiers did and how they behaved. The pull she felt was her overactive imagination. How many times had Aunt Flavia criticised it?

This man was her enemy. He had the potential to destroy everything she held dear. She refused to be attracted to him.

'I wish to speak with her, to thank her for the supplies she has sent the men.' Tullio spoke as if he were trying to soothe a frightened horse. His hands hovered as if he sensed her fear and wanted to protect her. 'Let me speak to her. Tell me the words I need to use to unlock her door.'

Helena found it difficult to breathe. Her heart thumped in her ears. She wondered what it would be like to be engulfed in those arms. A woman could feel safe in those arms, she was certain of that. The atmosphere seemed charged with something and she longed to lay her head against his solid chest. Helena put a hand to her throat and grasped her gold necklace as if it were a lifeline. The movement broke the spell.

'I'll let her know of your gratitude. She will be pleased to be thanked.' She made her voice as brisk as possible as she stepped towards the table, away from his arms, away from him. Her body's reaction to his nearness shocked her. For the first time in her life, it was as if she was on shifting sands, unable to find a proper response.

'You do that. I wanted to let her know that we Romans

never forget our friends.' His voice held warmth, more warmth than she had heard in a long time.

Helena wrapped her arms about her waist and tried to ignore the slight trembling in her limbs. Normally, she had no hesitation, everything had a ritual, a proper place. There was a certain order. She knew again where she stood.

'The sibyl would behave in such a manner towards any…any storm-tossed stranger who used the correct ritual.' The edge of the table dug into her thighs. 'The goddess guides her every move.'

He made a small dismissing gesture and then moved closer. If she put out a hand, her fingers would brush his tunic. Her fingers curled.

'I do not search for reasons. I look at results. My men will live because of what she has done.' Again, his voice sent thrills down her spine. 'She holds my and my men's life-debt.'

She could only stare at him and his deep fringed eyes. There was a certain untamed power about him. She had never been able to understand why women might find men overwhelmingly attractive, enough to gossip in the corners and giggle, but, faced with this man, she felt the stirrings of something inside her. It both excited and frightened her.

'I will let her know.'

'I would like to explain it personally to the sibyl.' His eyes were focussed on her lips, making them feel full and heavy. 'You can arrange that for me, can't you?'

The words were like ice water. Helena turned and broke his gaze. She had allowed this conversation to progress too far. The spell he held over her shattered. Helena drew a shuddering breath. All the warnings she had over the years about Romans came flooding back. What was his game? Seduction? Too late, she remembered her aunt's warnings. Men were not to be trusted.

Did he hope to turn the temple away from its people?

'The sibyl is no friend of Rome. She has no use for Roman life-debts,' she stated flatly.

He had to understand this. If anyone from her uncle and Captain Androceles even suspected a hint of co-operation with Rome, retribution would be swift and harsh.

'She cares only for her people. She would never betray her people.' Helena watched Tullio as her words echoed around the room. Something seemed to die in his eyes. Cold hardness replaced the warmth.

'I see. I mistook the situation.'

'My lady, your aunt, the Lady Zenobia, and her entourage approach,' a temple guard said, bursting into the room.

Helena pressed her fingertips together. A new wave of pain crashed around her head. The Lady Zenobia. She had to prevent Aunt Zenobia from seeing Aunt Flavia. It was that simple and that fraught with danger.

Why now? Had Zenobia reached a similar conclusion to Tullio? Her aunts never spent any time in the same room together. Aunt Flavia blamed Aunt Zenobia and her extended Cilician family for many of the excesses of the seafarers.

Oh, Kybele, what had she done?

Chapter Five

The Lady Zenobia, dressed in a heavily embroidered purple gown, stood in the centre of the sibyl's reception room. Everything about her posture proclaimed she was consort to the head of one of the most important seafaring houses in the islands. Next to her stood Captain Androceles, resplendent in his green tunic and darker green cloak. With his sharply pointed nose, his resemblance to a bird of prey was striking.

A great pit opened where Helena's stomach used to be, and her limbs started to tremble. She had expected the captain to sail with his trireme, but he hadn't. There had to be a reason why he had let the trireme sail without him. Normally, he was content to leave behind one of his men, while he took charge of negotiation with the Romans for the disposal of his goods. It was this attention to detail that had earned in part his nickname of the Eagle.

What had his eyes picked up this time? And he had enlisted his distant cousin in his plans. The combination could spell disaster for the temple unless Helena kept Aunt Flavia's illness hidden.

Helena straightened her robes and made the necessary obligations in front of Kybele's statue before turning to her aunt. She concentrated on her breathing, steady and sure, the same as she practised before the libation water ritual. Everything she did had to appear unhurried when, in reality, she wanted to flee from the room and lock the door behind her.

'How good of you to call, Aunt Zenobia.' Helena made an expansive gesture with her hands. 'The sibyl did mention that you were in the congregation for this morning's ritual. What can the temple do for the queen of this island?'

Helena paused to see if her aunt would use any of the ritual words, but Zenobia stood fingering her deep purple gown and the expression in her eyes turned to one of deep distaste. Helena looked behind her. Tullio stood, arms crossed, face stern—an unrequired bodyguard. Helena pressed her tongue against her teeth. The Roman presumed much. When she needed help, she'd ask for it.

'This is not a social call, niece. I, that is, *we* desire a word with Flavia, with the sibyl. My dear maternal cousin and I wish her to read the portents.' Zenobia glanced at Androceles who nodded.

Helena's heart plummeted. What was Zenobia doing, deferring to Captain Androceles? She never deferred to anyone. It was one of Aunt Flavia's standing criticisms. The Lady Zenobia would not even bow to Kybele herself.

'Is there some matter in particular you wish the sibyl to consider or is it a more general request?' Helena forced her face to remain impassive. She must wait until her aunt spoke. She must not offer anything, jump to any conclusions.

It might only be about temple business.

Had one of the temple's goats escaped and eaten her precious orchids? Had she not had her feet washed first during the ritual? What possibly could warrant this visit, rather than sending a tablet as Zenobia normally did when she had a prayer request?

'As we are caring for the good captain's guests, the temple hums with activity. There are many demands on the sibyl's time. Making sure the strangers are looked after according to tradition is very important to us.'

'I have a matter I wish to discuss with Flavia.' Aunt Zenobia's face wore an expression as if she tasted a very sour grape. 'You will fetch her for me. Tell her I am here and desire an immediate audience.'

'The sibyl must attend on us at once.' Androceles took a step forward. He placed a hand on her aunt's shoulder. Helena bit back a gasp. No one used that tone with Aunt Zenobia or touched her person with such familiarity. It would be demeaning to her status. 'Zenobia, you have forgotten what we discussed earlier. You were to use the exact wording we agreed on. We are concerned about the sibyl. Her behaviour yesterday was extraordinary.'

'Androceles is right.' Zenobia fluttered her eyelashes and gave a simpering smile to Androceles. 'Her behaviour at the quayside was…unusual.'

Helena's hand instinctively sought the Kybele amulet that hung from her belt. Its familiar curves and indentations provided a measure of calm. Giving way to panic would undermine everything. Shouting at Zenobia that Androceles was using her would serve no real purpose. Some sort of accord had been reached between the two rival seafaring houses. She had to find a way of distracting them and reassuring them that everything was normal. Only her mind was as blank as an unused wax tablet. 'The sibyl…'

'The sibyl is resting at present. I believe I have first claim on an audience with her.' Tullio's rich tones came from behind her, drowning out her words.

The pair turned towards him with an identical astonished expression on their faces. As distractions went, his intervention was a good one, Helena had to admit with grudging admiration.

'Why?' Zenobia asked. 'Why should you wish to see the sibyl?'

'The sibyl did a great service to my men last night. Several received medical attention and I wish to thank her for her assistance.'

'Who is this man that he dares speak to me like this? Does he not know who I am?' Zenobia's elaborate mass of curls shook. Her face turned red underneath the white lead paste she wore.

'Marcus Livius Tullio. The sibyl graciously consented to our lodging with her until the tribute arrives from Rome.' Tullio made a flourishing bow towards the captain. 'Captain Androceles is responsible for our presence in this place. I do not believe it was the sibyl's intention.'

Captain Androceles returned the bow. Helena was reminded of two gladiators giving each other elaborate courtesies before the games began.

Helena forced air into her lungs and kept her hands still. She wanted to cry out, but did not dare.

What if they came to blows in this chamber?

It would give Captain Androceles the excuse he needed to station men here. At the very least, he would demand a personal audience with Aunt Flavia. There had to be a way of preventing that from happening.

'Are you denying that you wished to be rescued?' Captain Androceles's lip curled. 'By the beard of Alexander, your trireme would not have lasted much longer upon the sea.'

'Typical Roman seamanship, no doubt.' Zenobia's face was crimson with poorly concealed rage. She moved away from Androceles. Her eyes shot daggers. 'Androceles told me about the rescue when we dined together last evening. But he did not tell me that he had forced the sibyl's hand.'

'The sibyl has powers beyond ordinary mortals' understanding. She no doubt has her reasons,' Tullio said. 'It is not for me to question the will of the gods.'

Tullio's body was turned towards her aunt, but his gaze held a knowing gleam and seemed to pierce Helena's soul. He knew. But did he know that Kybele did not speak to her? That this whole was her fault? A mistake that she had yet to recover from? Helena felt the ice sink into her veins. If only she could replace the sands of time, she'd never ever have gone to the quayside. She'd have found another way. But for now, all she could do was to hope and to listen.

'Kybele has always taken the seafarers' part,' Captain Androceles drawled. He brushed a speck of dirt from his green cloak. 'Time and time again, Kybele has shown a coldness toward Rome. It is only natural the sibyl should want to protect her investment.'

'Gods can be notoriously fickle,' Tullio replied.

'As can Romans.'

A muscle in Tullio's jaw jumped, but he said nothing.

Helena struggled to breathe. In a few more sentences, Androceles would be accusing the temple of colluding with

Rome. Having been thwarted in stationing men here, he was attempting to use Zenobia to force the situation. The Roman was playing into his hands. She had to regain control of this interview. She had made another error. She possessed none of Aunt Flavia's unerring instinct for the best way to bend circumstances to her will.

'I have seen nothing to lead me to conclude that Kybele requires a change of allegiance. The sibyl even forgave the shipload of mouldy grain.' Helena stepped forward, making an expansive gesture with both her hands. 'It was your wish that the Romans be housed here, not the sibyl's. The sibyl relayed the conversation to me yesterday so that there would be no mistake on anyone's part. She has felt the goddess's call.'

She glanced at both Tullio and Androceles. Her answer should satisfy both of them. Tullio gave her a slight nod.

'As you say, my lady,' Captain Androceles murmured.

'Your words make me ashamed of my thoughts, but I know much of Roman treachery. My sole concern was for Flavia.' Zenobia drew her gown away from Androceles. Her lips curved upwards in a self-satisfied smile. 'These Romans would sell their own mothers if they felt they could get a good price for them.'

Helena ignored Androceles's laughter. She wanted to scream at Zenobia that she had glimpsed more humanity in the Romans than she had ever seen in the seafarers, but what good would it serve? She knew the temple did not have the resources to fight the combined force of the two major seafaring houses. However, for now she held the advantage. She had to make sure she used it and ended this interview on her terms.

'Aunt Zenobia.' Helena cleared her throat and waited a

heartbeat for silence to fall. 'Have you a boon that you wish the sibyl to consider? The temple does not run itself…'

'Flavia should have you make the final ritual, Helena,' Aunt Zenobia retorted and her voice could have been chipped from the snows of Mount Olympus itself. 'You will make a fine sibyl some day. You have Flavia's exact intonation down.'

'I will take that as a compliment.'

'Today appears to me to be as good as any for sooth-saying,' Androceles drawled. 'I trust the sibyl will not delay in answering Zenobia's question. Knucklebones simply do not give the answer required. We want to consult an expert.'

Soothsaying. That was it.

Not merely looking at entrails or rolling the four-sided knucklebones to see the future, but actual communication with the goddess. Entering her abode and returning unscathed to the land of the living. The ultimate test to indicate that the sibyl retained the goddess's favour.

Aunt Flavia had made her reputation on getting the prophecies correct. Helena's mind raced. She had to stall for time, and hope. If Aunt Flavia became better, maybe there would be a chance.

'And the question is?'

'I desire to know if Lichas's mission will succeed.' Zenobia snapped her mouth shut like a turtle closing in on a particularly juicy bug. She and Androceles exchanged knowing winks. Helena felt the knots in her stomach turn. Having failed to get her to confess to an open breach with the seafarers, they were trying for a new line of attack. Exactly what was Androceles plotting? 'Surely this is not too difficult a question for a seer of Flavia's standing.'

'Soothsaying is not so easy. It requires careful consideration and preparation,' Tullio said. 'In my humble experience.'

A weight seemed to roll off Helena's chest and she
could breathe again. Tullio had thrown her a lifeline, a
glimmer of an idea. Something she could use. 'The tribune
is quite right. To foresee the future is not a gift to be
rushed.'

'The tribune shows a marked knowledge of the temple's
affairs,' Zenobia remarked. Her expression had turned even
more sour.

Androceles leant over and whispered in Zenobia's ear. She
nodded back at him. Zenobia gave another of her trilling laughs.

'Do tell Flavia about our request. I truly wish to know what
the goddess thinks. It would be a dreadful thing for this island
if her powers started to desert her. Of course then, maybe
someone I know would take her place.'

They suspect something, Helena thought with a sudden
certainty. The reprieve was too easy. And Zenobia thinks I
will be a simpler sibyl to manipulate.

Who carried the intelligence to her aunt? One of the
guards? Could she really trust anyone? How long did she
have before they acted? Enough time for Aunt Flavia to
recover her health? She had to.

'You shall have your answer by the Ides. The sibyl needs
time to make her ritual preparations.'

'You impress me with your certainty, Helena. A quality to
be admired in a sibyl.' Androceles bowed low, with his green
cloak flowing behind him.

'I leave such things to my aunt. She is an extraordinary sibyl.'

'For now.'

Androceles's words sent an icy chill through Helena. She

wanted to sink to the floor and put her face in her hands, but she forced herself to remain upright.

'Helena has given you her answer. I suggest you heed it.'

Tullio crossed his arms over his massive chest as if he were one of her guards. Solid, steady and protective. The message was unmistakable. He knew and was trying to protect her. The temptation was there, but she needed more. She had to know she could count on him and Rome always. And she already knew the answer to that.

'You will have your answer by the Ides, Aunt Zenobia.' Helena held her head and met Zenobia's gaze. Zenobia was the first to look away.

'Six days, and tell Flavia I expect a clear message, not one of her usual obscure ones. Far too often she has been able to wriggle out of a situation with an interpretation after the fact.' Zenobia turned on her heel and with a click of her fingers left the chamber.

Helena's knees threatened to give way and she reached out a hand to steady herself. Instead of encountering the small stone altar, her hand brushed the wool of Tullio's tunic. The brief contact sent shock waves through her body. She hurriedly withdrew her fingers.

Why now? Why this man? No other man had sent these strange flickers through her body. One touch and she was ready to forget all her training. Was this how it had happened to her mother?

'Is something wrong, Helena?' His warm fingers grasped her elbow, steadying her. Warmth like the heat from a charcoal brazier on a cold day spread up her arm. 'Let me help. Trust me. We can work together. We are both suspicious of Androceles.'

He was so close she could see every eyelash that fringed his dark rich eyes. She could even see a small white scar on his right cheek. But what she really noticed was the compassion in his eyes.

She tried to tell her body that this was a Roman and Romans twisted words, but equally her mind reminded her of yesterday when he was ready to take another's punishment and last night when he sat by his man's bed for the sake of a promise. He had integrity. Maybe she could trust him. She wanted to believe he could help.

She put a hand to her throat, surprised that she could even think such thoughts. What had she started with her masquerade? The ripples in the seeing bowl that Aunt Flavia sometimes used would surely show a dark path ahead.

'Are you all right?' Tullio's voice came from a long way off. 'You should lie down. You have gone pale.'

'I believe I need some air. The incense hangs heavy in this room.' Helena forced her lips to smile. She had to hold on to everyday things.

'You need to rest. Let me escort you to your room.' His tone allowed no space for dissent.

'I'd prefer fresh air. A tour of the temple grounds would be pleasant, if you insist on accompanying me.' Helena forced her mind away from the thought of him in close proximity to her in her bedroom. Fresh air and outdoors was the answer. It would give her time to see if her instincts were correct. Time to decide if she could indeed make him an ally. 'You should have some idea of the lie of the land.'

A tour of the temple?

Tullio stared at Helena and did not try to hide his amazement. Everything about Helena, from the way her hand clutched the doorframe to the pinched look about her mouth proclaimed she wanted to flee. He had seen the same look in the eyes of his men before battle, a trapped helplessness, but with more than a hint of courage. Such a change from the confident woman who had demanded his soldiers behave properly.

He would go on this tour of inspection, rather than confront her directly. He had to make Helena understand that he wanted to help. She did not have to face Androceles and the Lady Zenobia alone. The temple and her influence could be useful to Rome. Rome would pay handsomely for a naval base. Tales about the sibyl's healing powers could be spread and pilgrims would return. It was easy. He'd seen it done before. But first, he needed her agreement.

'I look forward to learning more about your temple and grounds. You will find me an eager pupil.'

She gave a brief nod and glanced over her shoulder towards a closed ornately carved door as if seeking reassurance. Tullio longed to draw her into his arms, and tell her that, if she trusted him, he would do everything in his power to make sure she was protected. That would have to wait until her shoulders had relaxed and her face no longer wore its wary expression. He had to earn her trust.

He took one last glance at the reception room before they left. Here and there amongst the friezes and mosaics it was obvious that the chamber had been altered. Had this island always worshipped Kybele? Or was it fairly recent? When he had travelled with his mother, he did not think they had seen Kybele's aspect as a healing goddess and yet here she was. All the healing temples they visited were linked to Aesculapius with his motif of the twinned snakes. In the far right-hand corner, half-disguised as grape vines, were the twinned snakes.

The temple had belonged to Aesculapius once.

Tullio permitted himself a grim smile. Now he needed answers to his questions.

How and why had the temple changed allegiance? And what did the change have to do with the pirates?

'Slow down, you are walking as if the Furies are chasing you,' Tullio called out to Helena.

'We have a lot of ground to cover. The temple is more than its religious buildings.' She halted, her skirts swishing softly about her legs to reveal neat ankles. 'If your wound pains you too much, I can go slower or we can postpone the tour until another time.'

'My wound does not trouble me.' Tullio decided not to take the gamble on Helena repeating the offer.

'Very well, you know your body best.'

Helena's sandals struck the stone floor with quick impatient steps as she led the way past the small paved courtyard where his men sat in the sunshine, throwing knucklebones and counters, down a cool corridor and out into the large, immaculately kept vegetable garden.

Tullio tried to concentrate on anything but the curve of her hips and the swell of her firm bottom under her robes. He had to concentrate on who she was and what she could do for Rome. He could not afford a repeat of this morning, when she had rebuffed his mild flirtation. He had to remember what his primary purpose was and how he was going to achieve that. He could not let the hopes and fears of thousands be ignored in favour of the desires of his body.

If anything, the tour so far had shown him how powerful the temple was. Altars with inscriptions from kings and potentates around the Mediterranean filled every nook and cranny of the labyrinth of rooms and public spaces.

'And this is where the temple gets most of its fresh vegetables.'

A low hum of bees, and the smell of freshly tilled earth intermingled with the sweet scent of thyme and rosemary greeted him. The greenness of the fields contrasted sharply with yellowed hillsides that surrounded the temple. Several temple guards were hard at work with hoes, weeding.

At first glance, except for the glimmer of deep blue on the horizon, this place could be on any of his estates. Then, Tullio's eye began to notice the general shabbiness of the buildings, the half tumbled-down walls.

'All of this is yours?'

Helena paused on top of a small hillock. 'The fields to the sea are ours. My uncle's seafaring house owns the other ones.'

'You have fertile soil here. I am impressed with the way you keep your bees. They are spaced to prevent drifting and robbing of the nests.'

'My people know how to till the soil.' A sad smile played on her lips. 'It is a skill passed down through the generations. We honour good husbandry. Kybele is above all a goddess of the earth.'

'Now you do surprise me. I would have thought that your people would have been fishermen. That your gods would have been of the water.'

'The ways of the sea are hard. When men pray, they want more understanding gods.'

A faint breeze captured a lock of hair and blew it across her mouth. Tullio forced his fingers to resist the temptation to smooth it away. He had to concentrate on the administrator and not the woman. If he touched her, he would be tempted to draw her into his arms again.

'On land, crops fail. Animals get sick,' he said.

'Neptune is apt to turn angry at any time. We have always been farmers…in our souls. Some of greatest pleasure comes from working the land. You should taste the quality of our grapes.'

'You mean your people did not always fish?' Tullio leant forward. Perhaps there was an opening here. Romans were far more at home on land than on the sea.

She moved away from him, and drew her shawl tighter about her body.

'My people chose to support Carthage.' There was a bitter twist to her mouth now.

Tullio stared at Helena. There was such passion in her voice. Her eyes gleamed at old wrongs. She obviously believed in the truth of her story. Tullio pursed his lips. He knew of other stories, of the perfidy of Carthage and how Hannibal had crossed the Alps, living off the land, taking what he wanted. Even his family's northernmost villa sported a blackened doorway where Hannibal's fire had touched.

'And which would you rather they be—farmers or fishermen?'

'It is not a subject for discussion. Kybele has decreed what we are.' She dusted her hands on her gown and started off down another path.

Tullio caught her arm and turned her around so that he was looking directly into her eyes. 'I believe there is always a choice, Helena.'

There was something in her eyes—a mixture of hope and despair—something that was quickly masked. She pointedly removed his hand from her arm. 'You presume much, Roman.'

'You are right.' Tullio allowed his hand to fall to his side, silently cursing his impetuous act. 'I am a stranger, but I do wish to learn. Perhaps, if our people knew more about how much we were alike.'

Her smile flashed, echoing the sun after a thunderstorm. 'Come, see how the gods bless us. Neptune and Kybele approve of what we do. They refuse to let us starve, despite Rome's intentions.'

'Rome provides bread for its people. It cares about the welfare of its citizens.'

'For its people, but not for us.'

The scent of Eastern spices wafted on the light breeze. In the shadow of an olive tree, he could see a large number of amphorae clearly marked with Roman merchants' names, containing everything from olive oil to fish sauce and the grain—both the hard wheat, which was used for bread making, and soft wheat for pastry—being loaded into the warehouse. He thought of the people back in Rome who would have to pay inflated prices.

'What will you do with all this—sell it to Rome?' Tullio struggled to contain his anger at the pirates. First they stole, then they sold the goods at inflated prices because no grain reached Rome's markets.

'It is what the seafarers do.' Her voice was hard. 'We store their produce here until they have sold it on. Rome is their largest market, I believe. The sibyl prefers to keep the temple's tributes for her people. She refuses to let them starve. If we did not have the gifts from the sea, then my people would die, Tullio. My people want to live.'

'Pirates raid the Italian coast,' Tullio said bluntly. 'They kill innocent women and children, not caring about nationality. They seize what they can and burn the rest.'

'Not the seafaring houses who store their goods here. Aunt Flavia put a stop to that. On the sea, yes, the seafaring houses do what they have to, but they do not attack on land.'

She looked him directly in the eye. Tullio blinked. Either she was very good at lying or else she truly believed it. He saw the fervour in her eyes and decided it was innocence.

'How can you be certain?'

'My aunt banished two seafaring houses who attacked and murdered women and children.' Helena held both her hands out, palms towards the heavens. 'Our quarrel is not with them. She used her power with Kybele to curse them. Within six months, their kings had died, and their wealth scattered. Since then, the seafaring houses who store their goods in our warehouses have not attempted to raid the Italian coasts.'

'I know of pirate raids.' Tullio drew his mind away from the horror of six months ago and his subsequent vow to destroy those responsible. 'They have not stopped attacking the Italian coast. It is too ripe a plum.'

'They will not be from these houses.' She started away from the warehouse, shoulders square and a distinct edge to her voice. 'Rome makes war with many.'

'Yet you condone the attacking of ships and the confiscation of those goods.'

'It is a question of survival. Romans drove my people to this, and therefore we take what we can…from the sea.'

'If there was another way…' Tullio curled his fingers into a tight ball. He refused to lose his temper. He had to remember she had helped his men. And she seemed truly to believe that the pirates of these islands had not attacked the Italian coast. If that was the case, the sooner he spoke with the sibyl, the better. Perhaps together they could work to rid the seas. She had already taken the first step. 'If another way could be found for your people to survive, would they take it?'

'Do you know of another way? A way which would allow my people to live, to feed their children? Do tell me.' The flicker of hope in her face died almost before Tullio could register what it was. 'I thought not. Words are easy, but deeds are much harder. Others have made similar promises throughout the years, but always the same thing—the only thing we can truly count on is the sea.'

Tullio regarded the top of his right sandal, the one which Rufus had patched three days before they set sail. He had no alternative to offer Helena, only words. But for a people who did not shirk work and who loved the land, there had to be more than piracy.

'Your walls are precariously balanced,' he said, changing the subject. There was no point in arguing over what might or might not be. He had to do something practical. He had to show her that his words did have meaning. 'Your roofs need retiling. Let my men do some of the repairs.'

'Why? Why would you do this?' Helena's face showed her absolute amazement.

'To show you that Rome has good intentions,' Tullio replied smoothly. 'We wish to help those who aid us.'

'The temple has no need of favours from Rome.'

'This would be a repayment. You saved the life of my man last night. I am in your debt.'

'I will consider it and let you know my decision. But for

now, you had best rejoin your men.' She turned on her heel and left him standing by the sun-baked field.

Tullio smiled to himself. A small step forward. In time, he'd win her over—for Rome's sake.

Chapter Six

Tullio's men were now clustered in dispirited groups when he returned. Three or four played a quiet game of *latrunculi* with improvised pieces, but most simply sat, staring off into space, doing nothing, not even playing knucklebones.

Had one of the men accosted Helena's maid? Tullio wondered, recalling the conversation with Helena before Androcles and her aunt appeared.

Could one of them have broken the dictates of hospitality? He found it hard to believe. He knew his men—where they came from, who their sweethearts were and how many children they had. There were one or two other unpredictable like Quintus, perhaps, but they were Roman legionaries, fired in the same crucible. They knew what was expected of them.

At the sound of his sandals, the group struggled to their feet. Quintus smartly saluted him, bustled up, giving the impression of the ultra-efficient centurion. Tullio dismissed his earlier suspicions as unworthy. Quintus would never do anything to jeopardise the men.

'How are the men behaving?' Tullio asked Quintus in an undertone.

'Nothing I couldn't handle, but what I'd give to handle the woman who brought the medicine.' Quintus gave a distinct leer. 'A little older than the ones in Ostia, but what shape. She was taken with me. A few more encounters like the last one and she will be like fresh clay in my hands.'

'Did you make some comment to her? Something she might have found offensive?' Tullio struggled to keep a leash on his temper. He had given his word to Helena, and Quintus was bragging about his conquest.

'Me, sir? I complimented her on her dress and other things. I know how to talk to the women.' There was a distinct swagger to Quintus's posture. 'A regular honey pot, I am. Just being friendly-like, but the girls can't help themselves.'

A general guffaw erupted from the men. Tullio raised an eyebrow, and the room became silent.

Honey pot was not the term he'd use for the centurion. But he had to give Quintus the benefit of the doubt. He had not intended to upset the woman. And could he severely reprimand Quintus, when he himself had nearly stolen a kiss from Helena?

'The lady in question may not share the same opinion of your charms. Remember we're guests here. Their customs are different.'

'Are you trying to tell me something?' A worried frown appeared between Quintus's brow. His shoulders showed the slightest of hunches before righting themselves. 'She liked it. I could tell. I have a sixth sense about these things.'

Tullio hooked his thumbs through his belt and hoped his advice would be heeded. Quintus had only spoken a few words, tried a little coarse flattery. Nothing more.

'Watch your step, centurion. Do not let your desire outrun your common sense. We are guests here and must abide by the rules of hospitality. You could jeopardise everything we have worked for. There still might be an opportunity to save our mission. I refuse to allow any banter to put it at risk—not from anyone, especially not a highly decorated centurion who should know better.'

'My mind is always on my duty…to Rome.' Quintus stood to the strictest attention but Tullio could tell that he had taken the kindly meant words as a gross insult. 'It is not my fault that my mouth is not perfumed like a bath house. I ain't had no fancy education or nothing. But I am a Roman soldier, good and true.'

'Be careful, Mustius Quintus. Remember that there is more at stake than your personal desire.'

'It is never far from my mind.' Quintus tucked his chin into his neck. 'But still she was a pretty thing, not in the first blush of youth, mind. Mature, the way I like 'em. I fancy my chances.'

Tullio stared at Quintus. The centurion was close to insubordination. If they were on Roman territory, he would not hesitate to punish him, but out here he needed all the men he could get. Punishing Quintus would only inflame the situation and he didn't dare take the risk of allowing Quintus to apologise. The image was not a pretty one. His earlier apology to Helena would have to suffice.

'You will desist, centurion. That is a direct order.'

'Very good, Tribune.'

'The gods have granted us an opportunity and I for one intend to take it.

'What do you think this island is, Tribune?'

'It is an important staging post for the pirates' captured

goods. Helena showed me some of the warehouse complex.'
Tullio looked Quintus directly in the eye. 'There is a possibility of turning the temple towards Rome. Neither the sibyl
nor Helena appear to be overly enamoured with the pirates.'

'The sibyl is in with the pirates up to her pretty neck. You
remember that, Livius Tullio, next time you speak to that assistant of theirs.' Quintus's low voice just reached Tullio's
ears. 'Do you understand what that lady is mixed up with?
Think about that before you think about your nether regions.
Always one rule for the officers and another for the enlisted
men.'

Tullio advanced towards Quintus. His shoulders were
square and his footstep firm despite the pain in his leg. He
only knew that he had to reassert his authority or face more
insubordination. Quintus seemed determined to challenge his
leadership. He did not want to fight Quintus, but if he had to,
he would. 'Who is the tribune here, Quintus?'

The centurion took a step backwards. 'I was only joking,
Livius Tullio. Can't you take a joke?'

'We are in a very dangerous situation, Quintus. I have
looked into the jaws of Hades because of your mouth. You
will obey me in this matter. This is the Army, not the senate.'

Tullio stared at Quintus, daring him. The centurion looked
away. 'As you say, sir.'

'Very well, if there are no other objections, we shall play
this my way.'

Helena slammed her stylus down. She had hoped several
hours of hard work would clear her mind, but her thoughts
kept straying back to Tullio and his offer. Without a doubt,
the temple could use the manpower. The seafarers had first

pick of all the villagers and there were a thousand jobs that should have been done six months ago. But she had to beware of Romans bearing gifts.

Anything the Romans did to help the temple could be misinterpreted by Androceles. But all it would be was an excuse. He had made no secret of his desire to influence temple policy.

Helena pressed her fingers to the bridge of her nose, trying to will away the pain. She had never thought her simple masquerade would result in so many problems, force so many choices.

She rose and tapped on her aunt's door. Once she heard Galla's answering call, she entered, carefully closing the door behind her.

A single oil lamp burnt by the side of the bed. The familiar scent of cinnamon mingled with the less familiar one of alum creating a heady atmosphere that made Helena's head spin. Galla put her finger to her lips and shook her head, but Helena chose to ignore the maidservant. She walked over to the bed and touched her aunt's unlined hand.

At the touch, the sibyl's eyes fluttered open and her lips curved upwards. 'Helena?'

Helena's heart leapt. Her aunt had spoken. A whisper to be sure, but clear and unmistakable. Tears pricked her eyelids. Aunt Flavia had returned. She would recover…in time. She wanted to laugh out loud, but contented herself with clasping her hands together.

'You can speak. This is marvellous news, Aunt.'

'Hush, child, control yourself.' Her aunt's voice, although weak, held some of its old command. 'Dignity.'

Helena swallowed hard and stood up straighter. Her aunt

gave a small nod. 'Tell me everything. Galla tells me less than nothing.'

Helena hesitated, wondering how best to approach the problem. 'Aunt—'

'We had visitors,' Aunt Flavia said, cutting off Helena's words.

'The Lady Zenobia and Captain Androceles, but I answered their questions.' Helena forced her voice to sound light, as if it were a problem with fish sauce. A twinge of guilt passed through her. She knew she should say something about Androceles's request for a prophecy, but her aunt was too weak. She could barely sit up, let alone lift her arms for long. Helena had six days. When her aunt was stronger, maybe tomorrow, she would tell her and then they could decide together the best course of action. For now, her aunt had to recover.

'Together? Androceles and Zenobia? This is worrying, Helena.' Aunt Flavia struggled to sit up. 'Those two hate each other. Bad blood from childhood. Cilicians hang on to their grudges.'

'Androceles was stirring up mischief.' Helena rearranged the statues on the bedside table. She had to make her aunt understand the danger they faced. 'He twisted the story about how the Romans came to be here.'

'Typical. Sails close to the wind, that one.'

Aunt Flavia collapsed down on to the pillows and her head moved from side to side. Helena's heart contracted. Her aunt was not supposed to be like this. She was supposed to be the strong one. Galla pointedly cleared her throat. The interview needed to end.

Helena squeezed Aunt Flavia's hand. How much had she

understood last night? Did her aunt know that someone else had worn the gold mask?

'I need to go, Aunt. There are things that must be attended to.'

'Should never have let the Romans land.' Aunt Flavia's fingers reached for Helena. 'You should have woken me. You don't have the knowledge.'

Helena leant forward and brushed her lips against her aunt's forehead. Cool to the touch. No fever, thank the goddess for small mercies. She rocked back on her sandals and regarded the ornately carved bed. 'It was all my fault. I know that. I am doing my best to make it right.'

'It will be Kybele's will. Listen to what she says. Follow Kybele.'

Helena's throat constricted. She should confess now that Kybele did not speak to her. How could she trust the goddess, when she was given no clue as to how to proceed? All the hours she spent in prayer and ritual, but not a single sign, and with a mind that increasingly turned towards Tullio's legs.

Her aunt made everything sound so simple. She should tell Flavia the truth, but now was not the time. She refused to cause more distress.

'Sleep, Aunt Flavia. Get your strength back. The temple needs you.'

No response but a gentle snore.

Helena tiptoed out of the room.

Follow Kybele.

Helena was no clearer on what Aunt Flavia meant. She hugged her pile of tablets and scrolls to her chest. She had taken the long way round to avoid any possibility of encountering the Romans again. She'd ignore them, and the whole thing would begin to fade.

Helena stopped dead. Her mouth dropped open. Gradually she became aware she was staring, but she was powerless to do anything else.

Tullio's arms gleamed bronze in the sunlight. He had discarded his cloak at some point, Helena noticed, and was working in only his tunic and sandals. The tunic was short enough to reveal the entire length of his leg from thigh to calf as he positioned the next rock in place. The angry red mark on the limb had subsided, and he moved with more grace than she thought possible for someone who had been wounded. His tunic strained to contain the broadness of his back as he placed yet another stone on top of the wall.

She had not expected the Romans to be repairing a wall, let alone Tullio to be leading them. What was worse was that she found she was watching him not as a disinterested person, but as a woman.

There was a certain lithe grace in the way he moved. She had expected a Roman to be flabby and soft, unaccustomed to hard work, but his arms and legs were knotted with muscles. She wondered what the muscles would feel like under the palms of her hands. She drew in her breath sharply.

As if he sensed her presence, Tullio paused in his work, turned and his eyes locked with hers. Time stopped. Sounds faded. Helena glanced away first, then recovered.

'What are you doing?' She gestured towards the stone.

'Repairing tumbled-down walls.' He jumped down off the wall, wiped his hands against his tunic and nodded towards his men to continue.

'Who told you to repair it?'

'No one, but the stones had fallen, and we have hands and strong backs. I asked you earlier and you did not expressly forbid it.' He stared at her, his dark eyes meeting hers once again. 'My men need to work, Helena. Idle hands cause mischief. We are keeping within the bounds you gave us.'

Helena tried to think. She could not fault his logic. She had wanted that particular wall repaired for months, but there always seemed to be something more pressing to do. But what did he expect in return?

'You should have asked first.'

'The guards had no objection. They seemed to be quite pleased with the idea.'

'No doubt.' Helena rested a hand on her hip. The wall had collapsed during storms from two winters ago. Some of the capping stones now sported moss and grass. It was one of those little jobs she was going to have someone do, some day, when there was time. And there was never enough time.

She was not sure who she should be more annoyed at— the guards for allowing this to happen or at Tullio for simply going ahead and fixing something. All she knew was that she did not feel in control, and she had to be in control not only for her own sake but also for Aunt Flavia's. 'You should have consulted me first.'

He crossed the distance between them in three steps and stood so near her that she could see where sweat had soaked his tunic, turning it darker and making it cling to his body. A curl of warmth wound around her insides.

'I wanted to show you what we were capable of.' His voice soothed and caressed. She could feel its silken lures being cast out, urging her to agree with him.

'I know the destruction you are capable of,' Helena said, forcing her mind back to the stories that were told at the end of banquets, and the stories women told their children in whispers to keep them safe and quiet at night. 'I have heard tales of that.'

'But have you ever seen any? Has Rome ever attacked these shores?' His eyes narrowed. 'Or have you ever seen the aftermath of a pirate raid?'

'I told you before, none of the seafaring houses connected with this island make raids on Italy.'

His eyes seemed to probe deeply into her soul.

'I have seen the destruction, Helena. Recently.'

'Prove it was one of the five seafaring houses, and the sibyl will do something about it. We must have proof, not Roman rumours.'

Helena waited. He had to understand what sacrifices were made. If what he said was true, then it was all the more important that Aunt Flavia's condition was not known. The risks to the community were too great. She held her breath and waited to see what proof he would offer.

'Destruction is destruction whoever causes it.' He gave an elaborate shrug. 'The important thing is to build and to make the world a safer place for those who find it difficult to defend themselves.'

Helena heaved a sigh of relief. An open break with a seafaring house was not on the horizon. Her aunt would have time to recover before Tullio could find any concrete evidence.

'Do you always repair walls before obtaining permission?'

'The wall had fallen down.' A smile tugged at his lips. 'Walls, in my experience, are generally there for purpose. If you need them, they should be sound. If not, you should demolish them.'

'Your logic is flawless.'

'And sometimes, you only think you need walls.' He gestured towards the half-rebuilt wall with one hand. 'Which is it with this one? Demolish or repair?'

His face had such an intent look that Helena wondered if he was speaking about something more than this stone. 'This wall is supposed to help keep the sheep and goats out of the temple gardens.'

'Then it should have been rebuilt at once.'

Helena shifted once more in her sandals, hating the feeling of inadequacy. The legionaries, along with a thousand other problems, plagued her mind. There was no one to ask and everyone wanted an answer. Until now, she hadn't realised quite how much Aunt Flavia had done. Always there with a helpful word, or the correct ritual, Aunt Flavia had allowed Helena the illusion of control.

Repairing the temple benefits you as well, a traitorous voice whispered in the back of her mind.

'If you do work, you will not be paid for it. The amount of money you owe will still be the same. The seafarers took a great risk rescuing you.'

She watched his face. Only a muscle jumped briefly in his jaw. No other emotion was displayed.

'We would go faster if we had some proper tools to build with, and a guarantee of proper rations.'

'You eat what we eat. The temple makes no distinctions. Plain but enough to fill.' She hesitated. This was a delicate matter. She was under no illusion what a few men could do armed with hammers and hoes. If the Romans attempted to escape, there was little her guards could do to hold them. She had to trust that the display of strength had convinced the Romans and the seafarers alike. 'As for tools…'

'You can trust us. We have given our word as soldiers, as Romans.' His voice was low and intense. 'You need this work doing, why not put your faith in us?'

'As you have started, you might as well finish.'

'Thank you, my lady.'

Tullio returned to his men. Helena watched for a little while. To make sure they were fixing the wall properly, she told herself. It had nothing to do with the man directing them, or the temptation he presented.

Tullio kept an eye out for Helena the rest of that day, and the whole of the next, but she did not reappear. The only sign she might be softening towards them was a pile of tools and a wooden tablet listing the jobs she wanted doing. This temple and its list of repairs was worse than Hercules's encounter with the Augean stables.

Most of the men were glad to use their muscles during something other than training. Quintus, however, grumbled and moaned that they were being treated no better than slaves. But he had not disobeyed the direct order to work.

As Tullio and his men laboured in the sweltering heat, a crowd of villagers would often gather round. Most stood silently with hostile faces. One, a young girl dressed in a ragged tunic, held out a jug of water, which Tullio and his men took with grateful thanks. She gave a shy smile and then ran away. Tullio watched her go. A small start, but still a start.

After that, the faces appeared to be less hostile, the crowds not as large. The villagers were letting them get about their business. Not helping, but not hindering. With each passing hour, the faces grew watchful rather than suspicious.

Tullio put the final stone on the second boundary wall they had rebuilt that morning.

'You and your men work with admirable speed,' Helena said behind him.

Tullio wiped his hand on his tunic before he risked turning around and facing her. Who would he see this time? The woman or the administrator? He hated the way his blood jumped at the sound of her voice. He had to remember the stakes. Keep in mind his oath to Rome and his obligations. Quintus was correct. A dalliance could do more harm than good. But his breath quickened as he saw the way her gown hinted at her curves and the way her pearl-drop earrings drew attention to her long neck.

'My men and I are unafraid of hard work.'

'I can see that.' She paused, started to say something, but changed her mind. There was speculation, even admiration in her eyes. The tension eased slightly in Tullio's shoulders. It bothered him that he wanted her respect. 'I hope you've had little trouble from the villagers. They are not used to seeing Romans. Many have come with prayer requests for the sibyl, simply to get a better view of the legionaries.'

'They have been most kind. One in particular—a girl with big brown eyes and a ragged dress—brought a jug of cool water. She has become quite a favourite with the men and me.'

'When was this?'

'Earlier.' Tullio ran his hand through his hair. Was he now about be reprimanded for accepting a jug of water? 'She held out the jug. It seemed churlish not to accept. She then refilled it twice from the well, but would not speak. The sun is quite fierce and, while not as refreshing as the vinegar we normally drink, the water was welcome. Hopefully you have not received any bad reports.'

'No one has complained. I've heard nothing but praise.'

'I'm glad to hear it.' He leant forward slightly. 'I should like to thank the girl. It was an unexpected kindness. My men were parched. But she vanished before I had a chance to say anything.'

Helena's teeth caught her bottom lip for a heartbeat. Then she shrugged. 'Yes, that would be an idea. If you would follow me.'

Tullio motioned for Quintus to keep the men working on rebuilding the wall. Quintus grimaced, but moved to obey the order.

Helena led the way to a small pasture of rough grass where the young girl sat, stick in hand, tending geese. Catching sight of them, the girl gave a cry which sounded more birdlike than human. 'Is that the girl?'

'Yes, that is the girl. What is her name?'

'Niobe.' Helena made large gestures to the girl who started towards them. 'She lost the power of speech. She was a happy baby, toddling about, chatting to everyone and everybody. Then she caught a fever and fell silent. The villagers whispered that demons had stolen her soul and left a changeling. In desperation, her mother came to the sibyl. The sibyl decreed Kybele had touched Niobe. Her speech will return when the goddess decides. Since then we have provided a home for her, doing what we can. Her brother is our goatherd, Pius.'

The girl stopped, and stuck her thumb in her mouth. Her eyes grew round.

Without waiting for Helena to make any more introductions, Tullio knelt down. He hoped he could reassure the child that he came in peace. Having seen the pirates in action, he knew they would not be kind to the child. He held out his hands and kept his voice gentle and that his lips clearly formed each word.

'Greetings, Niobe. Do you look after the geese? They are very healthy and well fed. I wanted to thank you for the water you brought me and my men earlier. It was you, wasn't it?'

She returned his smile and nodded enthusiastically. She gave the imitation of a goose. Tullio attempted a honk and the girl burst out in a fit of giggles. She bowed several times and then raced off to rejoin her flock.

'You have made a friend.' The pinched look on Helena's face was gone. Her eyes held a new expression—as if he were some backward pupil who had just completed a difficult conjugation of a Greek verb.

'A little kindness never did anyone any harm.' Tullio concentrated on readjusting his cloak. Here was no heartless statue. Her concern for Niobe was real.

'The sibyl is of a similar mind.'

'The sibyl exercises great power.' Tullio stared after the now distant figure of Niobe, rather than at Helena's lips. The memories of the fights he had fought to protect his sister crowded in. 'No doubt there were many in the village who argued for the girl's destruction.'

'My aunt believes that the gods made each one of us. She has been a great force for good on this island and I intend to keep it that way.'

'But for how much longer?'

She gave him a panicked look and Tullio knew he had hit

a raw nerve. She was less sure about the temple's position than she pretended. 'What do you mean by that?'

'The pirates grow stronger in this region of the Mediterranean.' He leant forward and dropped his voice. 'How much longer until they decide they don't need your aunt or her portents? How long until they take what they need with force?'

Tullio watched her face intently to see if there was any sign that she was listening, that she understood. All he could hear was the distant honks of the geese.

'It is certainly something to consider.' She pointed back down the track. 'I believe your men will be waiting for you.'

Tullio started back. When he turned slightly she was standing there, the breeze whipping her gown about slim legs, a thoughtful expression on her face.

Could she trust him?

The question reverberated through Helena's mind as she walked back towards the sibyl's chambers.

Niobe, who hid when any strange man approached her, was not afraid of him.

His assessment of the situation was much the same as hers. As the seafarers grew bolder, their respect for the temple grew less.

How much longer before they decided to challenge the sibyl's authority with an attack on the mainland?

Or, worse, stopped paying tribute altogether?

The minor insults were clear to anyone who had eyes. Androcles was determined to challenge the sibyl's authority. Why Aunt Flavia had not chastised him when he first tried to deliver the mouldy grain, Helena had no idea. But each time, the house of Androcles dared that little bit further.

She hated the fact that Tullio had wakened these fears. She also hated the fact that she kept finding reasons to seek him out. She told herself that it was to make sure he and his men behaved properly but each time she saw them, it only served to show her how wrong she had been.

Lying on the table was another scroll from Androceles. Helena rapidly scanned it. Like the three that preceded it, Androceles respectfully reminded her of her promise. This time, he asked after the sibyl's health. A subtle hint that, like Tullio, he had realised Aunt Flavia was not well?

Helena's mouth went dry. He was guessing. He had to be. If he had solid proof, he'd have acted before now. But she had to do something.

'We have finished repairing the southern enclosure. What else would you like my men to do? The warehouse looks like its east wall is missing stone.'

Helena glanced up and saw Tullio standing there. His frame filled the doorway. The sun had tanned his skin to a deep bronze. His tunic touched the mid-point of his thighs. Solid, reassuring and something else that made her blood sing.

Helena became aware she was staring, and rapidly rearranged the tablets in front of her. He would have to appear when she was at her most vulnerable.

'The sibyl is grateful for what you and your men have done. She is relieved that you are obeying the rules of hospitality.'

'*We* are grateful to be given the chance.' His eyes seemed to bore into her. 'When the sibyl has a chance to inspect, I look forward to the opportunity of showing her all we have done.'

'When she has time,' Helena replied quickly. Too quickly.

She drew a breath. 'The demands on the sibyl are great at this time of year.'

'The loose stone is almost exhausted. I fear someone has found another use for it. The repairs to the southern granary need more stone if it is to withstand a fierce storm.'

'I already told you that is impossible.' Helena released a breath of air. She had to cope with this request. 'You and your men must stay within the confines of the temple. We must ensure your safety.'

'Our captivity, you mean.' Their eyes locked. Tullio crossed the room in three steps, and his warm hand covered hers. A tingle ran up Helena's arm. 'What is it, Helena? What are you frightened of? Confide in me.'

His whole being exuded strength and calm. Helena's hands trembled. Did she dare trust him? She had to trust someone. She had to speak with someone or lose her reason. She remembered how Niobe had turned to him. Her aunt always said that Niobe was the closest to the goddess, that she understood the goddess's will.

Was she being nudged towards the Romans?

The only thing she knew was that, if she stayed in this room, she'd be tempted. And this was not a burden she could share. However, she owed him more than a curt dismissal. The only thing to do was to take him to her refuge and hope the goddess offered more guidance.

'Come with me, please.'

Before Tullio had a chance to ask more or even consider why she might be reacting in this way, Helena had left the room and started down a corridor. She hurried along and then, when he thought they had reached a dead end, she pressed a hidden latch.

Tullio heard a click and a door swung open, revealing a passage hewn out of rock. He carefully noted where she had placed her fingers. Two indentations, so small he would have missed them if he had not known where to look. He tried to keep the rising sense of hope from bubbling over in him. The work he and his men had done had begun to bear fruit. This was his chance to bring her over to Rome's side. Silently, he wished that he was more of a silver-tongued senator than a blunt-speaking soldier. This might prove to be his best chance.

Helena put her foot on a small ledge. Tullio peered closer. Several narrow steps were cut in the rocks and she started to climb. Tullio caught the glimpse of a neatly turned ankle and the memory of her warm body from that first evening jolted him.

'Where are you taking me, Helena? I would have never found this track without you.' He asked only in an effort to turn his thoughts back to the present. He had to look towards what benefited Rome, rather than his own desires. He did not dare risk offending her inadvertently.

She didn't reply, but continued to climb the track. At several places, it levelled off, only to turn again and then begin to climb once more. In some places, his bulk was almost too big for the passage.

Tullio wondered briefly if this way could be used to escape and then rejected the idea when the path turned a final time and they came out on top of the tallest tower's roof. Below their feet, the entire complex lay spread out. Above them to the right, the stone-strewn mountain peak rose to meet the azure blue sky.

The view confirmed his earlier suspicion—the temple was virtually inaccessible, a perfect fortress for whoever controlled it. He wished Quintus could see it and then his grumbling about the need for escape plans would stop.

It was little wonder that the sibyl wielded so much power if her temple commanded the headland of the island. He could see what must be the palace of one of the seafaring houses further down the hill and then the harbour with its gaily coloured triremes, their prows painted with hawk's eyes—the better to see their prey—and fishing boats festooned with nets.

Tullio stroked his chin. He had given his word not to escape, but he had never said anything about regaining the tribute. He was determined that the pirates would not benefit from it. They would be punished and brought to justice.

The island expected an attack from the sea. The watch towers were positioned that way. Was there another route? Tullio turned and looked in the other direction. A sheer cliff dropped down to the sea. Small white waves played on the tiniest of shores. A possible anchorage? He lent over the parapet and tried to examine the shoreline closer—maybe a small boat.

A movement attracted his attention, made him forget all thoughts of the future and concentrate on the now.

Helena stood, her hands clinging on to the parapet so tightly that her knuckles shone white. The breeze whipped her gown about her ankles and flattened it against the curve of her breast. Gone was the self-confident priestess's assistant who had faced down the pirates and in her place was a young woman with wary eyes. Rome no longer mattered. Tullio longed to draw her into his arms and cradle her, whisper to her that he would take care of her troubles, fight her battles as long as it brought no dishonour to Rome.

'Is there any way to get down there?' he asked, his voice coming out as a rasp.

'The only way on or off the island is through the harbour. Remember that.' She gave a laugh, half-strangled and yet grateful, and turned to face him. 'There is a tale about a lover of a sibyl escaping down this cliff, but I think it is just a story. I searched and searched, but never discovered a path. Then the sibyl told me that the cave was bewitched and only those people who truly needed the path could find it. You can only go down, but never up.'

'Another one of the shadows and mirrors used to fool the unsuspecting.'

Her mouth formed a startled O and her shawl slipped slightly, revealing the creaminess of her throat.

Had she even realised that he knew about her trick with the bronze mirrors?

He ran his hand through his hair. If he was going to gain her trust, he would first have to tell her that he knew she was in trouble.

'You know about that?' Her hand plucked at her gown, twisting the folds and then smoothing them down. 'How?'

'My sister was ill like Niobe and my mother sought a cure. I have been to many temples, Helena. I have seen many tricks and sleights of hand.'

'The seafarers believed.'

He took a deep breath, and the same tightening of his belly that immediately preceded battle plagued him now. It was a risk, but one he had to take. He stared her directly in the eye and willed her to tell the truth.

'You are lacking men and the sibyl is gravely ill,' he said, choosing each word with care. His eyes were trained on Helena. The colour drained from her face and she swayed where she stood.

Chapter Seven

Helena gasped for air. Something to stop this terrible reeling, tilting feeling.

Tullio had guessed. That was all—a guess. He couldn't know for certain. Helena blinked. Her ears buzzed with the sound of a thousand bees. She would trust him a little bit, but not with the whole.

'The sibyl had trouble returning from Kybele's realm.' She forced her voice to sound even, measured, nothing to betray her inner turmoil. She would give no more information than she had to. 'She will recover in a few days. She needs complete peace and silence in which to heal.'

'You took her place on the quayside and at the daily rituals.' Tullio's face was hard, full of uncompromising planes and shadows.

'Somebody had to, it is expected.' Her hands twisted her belt in ever tighter turns. This was proving harder than she anticipated. 'The populace expects to see the sibyl when a pirate captain's ship enters the harbour, and I could not risk it.'

'Why?'

'Aunt Flavia will get well. Why should her position as sibyl be in any doubt?' She waited to see confirmation on his face that he understood the danger if the seafarers thought something was wrong at the temple. 'You've seen Niobe. Aunt Flavia uses her power wisely and well.'

'If I noticed, others will have as well, Helena.' His eyes softened. The shadows receded. His stance eased. 'Androceles has guessed. It is why he asked for the prophecy.'

'You may be right, but he is uncertain. When he gets the prophecy, he will be satisfied. All will be well.'

'How much longer do you think you can keep up this pretence? The Ides is in three days. If the sibyl is too ill now, will she be well enough?'

Helena's stomach knotted. It was one thing to have fears herself and quite another to hear them baldly stated like that. All her hopes and illusions tasted like ashes in her mouth. He was right. Aunt Flavia was not going to recover quickly enough. She would have to face Kybele and her cave alone, and the thought terrified her.

'The prophecy will be given.' A shiver ran down her back. She could see the gaping black hole of Kybele's home on earth before her, feel the cold seeping. The place haunted her dreams, but her duty was clear. To save the temple and protect Aunt Flavia, she had to enter the cave. 'I intend on keeping my word.'

'Can I help you? Is there something I or my men can do?' He leant forward. His hand brushed her shoulder. 'Tell me—if it is within my power, it shall be done.'

She gazed at the point where his tunic kissed the column of his throat. More than anything she wanted to turn to him and lay her head against his chest, and feel his arms about her, holding her. She only had to take one step closer and she'd be there, her body next to his, her hands entwined with his.

The image shocked her, made her hesitate. Her thoughts were not of a priestess in training but of a woman. Such thinking had led to her mother's downfall and disgrace.

She should despise him as her enemy, not be drawn to him. She wrapped her arms about her, refusing to give into the feeling.

'This is something I must face alone.'

'Has this ever happened before? Has she had trouble crossing over before?'

Helena risked a glimpse into his deep midnight-black eyes. Compassion, not condemnation. A lump grew in her throat. Someone wanted to share the burden with her.

'With Aunt Flavia?' Helena tilted her head. The memories of the other times Aunt Flavia had confronted the goddess, and how each time lately she had come back a little weaker, flooded her mind. 'She has been breathless before, and often takes to her bed for a little while. Galla makes her eat a dozen pyramid cakes. The goddess makes enormous demands on any who enter her lair, which is why she has always gone prepared.'

'But this time, it was different.' He reached out and touched her shoulder again. This time, the touch lingered. Warmth radiated outwards from his hand, soothing. 'It shows on your face, Helena, the way you hold your body. You are frightened for her.'

The pressure from his hand was gentle, as if he were trying to tame a wild creature. Helena found she had no strength to move away. The warmth grew within her. She wanted to stay. Her hands itched to touch his. She wanted to feel the strength of his arms.

'When she failed to return after the sand ran out, I began searching.' The words started slowly and came tumbling out. It was a relief to finally speak of it. 'Galla and I discovered her half in and half out of the deep hole at the bottom of the cave. I have no idea how long she had been there. Even a few breaths makes me dizzy, if I am not properly prepared. We had just laid her down on her bed, when Androceles's ship was sighted. I had no choice.'

'People fall ill all the time. Why did you not explain?'

Helena moved towards the parapet, away from the shelter of his arms. The triremes bobbed gently, their painted eyes a comfort as always. The distant shouts of the porters as they unloaded more cargo echoed up the valley. A scene she'd watched a thousand times before. Busy, but contented.

How could she explain that Aunt Flavia's illness was a signal that the sibyl's powers were fading? That it would intensify the rivalry between seafaring houses? All this could go. When Tullio returned to Rome, she had no doubt that he would use that information and any hope of peace would be gone.

'There was no need to alarm anyone. Despite the sibyl's illness, we continue to conduct the temple's business. She will get better and she will continue to command the respect of all the seafaring houses.'

'And if she finds it too difficult to continue, who will the people turn to? Who will stop the seafarers from raiding the coastline?'

'The next sibyl. Me.'

'How can you be sure of that? Lady Zenobia said that you had not made your final vows.'

'It is what I have been trained for.'

But as she said the words, Helena thought of the Lady Zenobia and her greedy fingers, of Captain Androceles and the way his tributes to the temple were increasingly on the light side. So many dangers. So much responsibility.

Helena pushed away thoughts about not having a response from Kybele when she put on the mask, about what had happened to her mother and about how, until last night, Aunt Flavia's skin had had a waxy tinge to it. She had seemed to be getting better and then had taken a turn for the worse. Aunt Flavia was not strong enough to face the prophecy cave and emerge alive.

Aunt Flavia needed time, and time was one thing she did not have. The miracle she prayed for was not going to happen. Not yet.

Was she ready for it? She could almost taste the rank smell in her mouth and hear the steady drip of the water. She wanted to run and hide in a corner as she had done the first time her aunt had taken her there. That was no longer an option.

She was not ready, but she had to be.

'Yes, I am certain of that.' She made her voice sound true and even. 'The people of the island have always looked to the sibyl for protection, and the next sibyl will not fail them.'

'And you will be the next sibyl.'

'If the goddess so chooses.'

The breeze ruffled Tullio's hair and his face turned pensive. He reached out and touched her cheek with gentle fingers, smoothing away a single lock of hair. From that one touch, her whole being was infused with warmth. Her lips ached with a sudden heaviness.

She gave into temptation and took the final step towards him. His hands drew her closer still until no more than a breath separated them. The heat of his body provided welcome relief from the chill of the breeze. She laid her head against his chest and listened to the rise and fall of his breath. His arms came around her and held her close. All her fears and worries faded away to nothing.

'Helena.' No more than a husky whisper, Tullio's voice did strange things to her insides, made her want something more than comfort. 'I want to thank you for all you have done.'

'I did what I felt was right.' She lifted her head and gazed into his eyes, deep pools of black. Not cold like the black marble of Kybele's high altar, but filled with flecks of warmth and promise. Her hand touched a lock of his hair, flicked off his forehead. 'You asked for the protection of Kybele, and it had to be given.'

'My men are alive today because of you and your actions.'

His lips were close, so close. If she lifted her mouth, she could touch them. A shiver of anticipation ran through her.

What did she know of this man and his life? Would he abandon her as her mother had been abandoned?

She took a step backwards and his arms loosened. Her hands rearranged her shawl so it covered her hair. A little gesture to hide her nerves from him.

'Hopefully no one will be pining for you.'

'My mother, my sisters and mayhap my dog.' His voice was a caress, pulling her back towards him, towards his mouth. 'My father will pay the ransom as we arranged before I departed. My wife divorced me two years ago.'

'I am sorry.' Helena saw the shadows in his eyes and heard the catch in his voice. Had his wife's defection hurt him that much? She examined her hands. She had seen the way he treated his men. How could anyone leave a good man?

'You must not be. We were not suited. It was a business decision on her part. We parted amicably enough.' Tullio gave a harsh laugh. 'She had already lined up her next conquest—a senator she had met at Baiae. A man more devoted to arguing in the courts than being a soldier or looking after his lands.'

'Baiae?' She tilted her head to one side.

'A resort near Naples where the wealthy go to relax. Perhaps both our expectations were wrong. I thought she understood that my duty came before pleasure. At least, she experienced some measure of happiness for a short while.'

'A short while?'

'She died six months ago.' His mouth took on a bitter twist. The pain increased in his eyes. The flecks of warmth had vanished.

'I'm sure it wasn't your fault.' She reached out her hand and touched the roughness of his cheek. Tingles ran up her fingers.

'It had nothing to do with me, but she didn't need to die. She was young and beautiful.'

'Sometimes the gods have reasons we mere mortals can not understand.'

'And why do you think the gods have brought me here?' His voice was no more than a ragged whisper.

'They have their reasons.'

Their eyes locked and she found it impossible to turn away. His hand reached out and drew her close. A single finger tilted her chin and he bent his head. His mouth brushed hers, feather light and then firm. She pressed closer.

Tullio's lips held the tang of the sea breeze.

Helena was surprised how soft and gentle his lips were and how her body rapidly filled with a warmth. She wanted to be closer to him. Her body pressed forward and her curves moulded to his body. His kiss increased in pressure and she opened her mouth. His tongue touched hers and retreated, then returned to touch again. Helena knew that, without the support of his arms, she'd sink to the floor.

How long they stood there, limbs and lips entwined, Helena could not say. Everything had ceased to exist except for this man.

Then it was over. He let go and stepped back. They stood facing each other, chests heaving. Her legs and arms trembled.

Helena found herself trying to concentrate on something other than his mouth, her aching lips and the feeling inside her that she had not experienced nearly enough. Her forefinger traced the outline of her mouth. His hand caught hers, held it there and then let go.

'You will keep my secret. You will tell no one.'

He raised an eyebrow then reached out towards her, but she backed away until the stone parapet touched the back of her thighs. 'If they are your secrets, they are not mine to tell. But if you need help, I and my men are here. We have no wish to see innocents suffer.'

A shout from the harbour, followed by a loud blast from a horn, brought her back to the present with a jolt. She shielded her eyes with her hands and stared at the purple-sailed ship with its hawk eyes. The mark of Androceles's house was clear even from this distance.

'I have to go. They will expect to see someone from the temple.'

'The sibyl?'

'No, it is Androceles's son. The sails of the Androceles's clan are distinctive. The sibyl only appears for the heads of the houses, the men who have proved their worth.'

Tullio let her go. The passion in the kiss surprised him. He had expected to offer comfort and found himself desiring more. He should be thanking Jupiter the pirate vessel appeared when it did and reminded him of who he was kissing and what she stood for.

He watched her rapidly disappearing figure as she descended, and followed her with his eyes as she crossed the courtyard. No doubt soon he'd see the lions emerge pulling the chariot and the whole charade would begin again.

How many had been captured this time?

Would she attempt to save them?

She held the fate of his men in her palm. There was more to her than curves and an attractive smile. He tried and failed to imagine a Roman woman holding the power of life and death like that. Perhaps a Vestal Virgin.

A shiver passed over him. He knew the penalties for toying with a Vestal Virgin. Did the followers of this sibyl expect the degree of purity?

Was he guilty of what Quintus had accused him? Of putting his desires before his loyalty to Rome?

He had meant to comfort her and had ended up plundering her mouth. Tullio raked his hand through his hair and knew that, despite the risk, he would do it again.

'Did you get the stone?' Quintus asked before Tullio could say a word.

The men were lounging by a rebuilt wall. Most wore satisfied expressions on their faces. Workmen rather than discontented prisoners or slaves, Tullio thought with approval.

'Something more important has happened. Another pirate ship has arrived.'

'Our tribute?' one legionary asked in a joyful voice. 'I didn't think it would be here before the end of the month. Thank the gods. We will be free men.'

Tullio held up his hand, silencing the general happy chorus. The men fell silent and then assembled into their formation. Their faces bore expressions of anticipation. Tullio hated he had to destroy that hope.

'Quintus, take the men back to the barracks. Immediately.'

'Is there some reason, Livius Tullio?'

'It is not the tribute ship. It is more than likely full of plunder.' He watched the men's faces sober. There was little point in offering soft words of comfort. The memory of the hold was too raw. 'I'm going to do everything in my power to make certain any Roman being held captive is brought here.'

'How are you going to do that, Tribune? What are our orders?'

'You men must be out of the way if the prisoners are brought here.' A grim determination filled Tullio. He longed for his sword and a chance to prove himself again in battle. 'I don't want any excuse for the pirates to station more guards.'

'What do you plan to do?' Quintus asked in an undertone.

'Wait,' Tullio replied. 'And hope.'

The late afternoon sun beat against Helena's back as she hurried across the deserted courtyard where her aunt grew her precious bee orchids. Only one had bloomed this year. Its purple petals danced in the slight breeze.

Usually Helena's mood lightened when she saw it, but now her skin crawled from her encounter with Androceles's son, Kimon.

When she arrived at the quayside, one of the guards reported a disagreement about how many amphorae the temple was set to receive. A few words with Kimon, and, to her horror, he casually offered to have the man whipped. At her protest, he bowed low, and eyed her lips as if he saw Tullio's kiss branded there.

She knew many of the village girls thought Kimon very handsome and admired his strong shoulders and athletic prowess. But Helena always saw the look of disdain he had for women and for the seafarers under his command. Such a difference from Tullio and the way he treated his men. His men followed him out of love rather than fear.

She knew which sort of man she'd rather choose.

Choose?

Helena shook her head. Where were her thoughts leading this afternoon? She was unlike other women. Her destiny was different, no matter how much she might long to be normal and have a husband and children. Her aunt had drilled that into her time and time again until her hand ached from copying the words out. Her first duty was to the temple and the people it served. There was no time left for the ordinary desires and passions of a woman.

My mother had the time. A little voice nagged at the back of her mind. *She had a lover, then she had me and the temple thrived.*

My mother died, brought down by the gods and her conceit.

Helena curled her fingers around her belt. The tiny emblem of Kybele dug into her palm. It reminded her of the lessons and her duties. With Kimon's arrival, there was a gathering of Androceles's clan. How many more triremes were drifting on the tide towards here?

She had run out of time.

With each day that passed, the whispering would grow and the temple's authority would start to ebb away. She had to brave Kybele's lair today. Her childish fears were unimportant beside the need to safeguard Aunt Flavia.

It was her only choice.

Something in the shadows shifted. Helena jumped. A gasp rose in her throat. Within a fraction of heartbeat, she knew without a word or sound, with the barest of outlines who it had to be. A bubble of excitement rose within her despite her resolutions of no more than thirty breaths ago.

Tullio stepped from the shadows into the light. The golden afternoon sun highlighted the planes of his face. The time he had spent working outside had coated his skin in a deep bronze, which the whiteness of his short tunic only highlighted.

'I disturbed you.'

'Disturbed me? No, no, I was thinking about…other things.'

Helena thought what a lie that was. Everything about him disturbed her, made her sense, feel alive. It bothered her that, in a few short days, he had succeeded in reconstructing this temple as it was when her mother was alive.

'Tell me your thoughts. A problem shared is a problem halved.' His eyes crinkled at the corners.

'They would bore you, I'm sure.' She forced a laugh from

her throat. She had to do this alone. She had already confided more than was wise. 'There are things I have to attend to. The temple is very busy.'

'I wanted to ask…' He paused. His eyes were unfathomable, the same colour as storm clouds ready to burst. 'Did the pirates, the seafarers, have any more Roman guests?'

His mouth curled around the word guest as if it were more unsavoury than *infamis* or a hundred other insults.

'Does it matter to you? Is it any of your concern?' Helena lifted an eyebrow. One kiss and he thought he could control her.

'I would like to plead for them to be housed here if at all possible.' The set of his jaw challenged her. 'I know what a pirate's hold is like. If you consider that impertinent, so be it, but I had to try. These are men, not animals.'

'These seafarers did not have the occasion to rescue anyone from the sea.'

She stared over his shoulder at the fresco of Kybele and her chariot. Thank the goddess, she had not had to make that decision. The risk of the seafarers insisting on guards was too great, but she remembered the dreadful condition of Tullio's men.

'Why have they landed?'

'They've grain destined for Rome's markets. It will be stored here safe and dry until they find a buyer. It is simple but effective arrangement.'

'How did they obtain that grain? Did they buy at the market in Alexandria?'

Tullio's face searched hers. She flinched. She had heard the whispers of how Kimon captured so much grain, the lengths he was prepared to go to.

'It is not my place to ask. We, the temple, and the seafarers have a long-standing agreement. It makes no difference to us where they get the grain.'

'It should.' A muscle in his cheek jumped. He crossed his arms in front of his chest.

'The merchants of Rome don't care. Why should the temple?' Helena gave a deliberate shrug of her shoulder. The situation was not straightforward. If he wanted to pretend that the Roman merchants who gleefully purchased grain, wine and even slaves from the seafarers were innocent, he could think again. 'Before you start to criticise this island, Rome should examine its own tablets.'

She watched Tullio run his hand through his hair. He reached out towards her, but she took a step backwards, knocking the orchid pot slightly.

'Can you tell me if you would have brought the Romans here, if they had been in the hold?'

'Only the sibyl can make that decision.' She turned her head and watched the drops fall from the fountain into the basin, making little ripples and waves. One tiny choice, like a drop of water, could affect so many different things. When she had put on that mask, she had thought any consequences would be for that day alone. Instead, there had been new expectations, more problems. 'And I am not her.'

'But you did go down as the sibyl. You're the acting sibyl.'

She shook her head, cutting him off. She had to think clearly, difficult when he was so near and she simply wanted to lay her head against the firm wall of his chest and be comforted. She had no desire to dismiss his ideas with a polite laugh. The feelings inside her were too new and raw for that. She wanted him to think well of her. She had to make him understand. As he did, she lived in a well-ordered society, one bound by rules and regulations. She'd not chosen to masquerade as the sibyl on a whim. She had done so out of necessity.

The temple and the island worked because everyone knew what was expected of them and when to expect it. And she knew as well. Her aunt had drummed everything into her head until it ached. She knew the traditions, from the proper way to light the ritual lamps to the number of pyramid cakes the sibyl had to eat.

He understood nothing about their way of life.

'Our customs are different from yours. The sibyl only appears when the occasion demands it. Captain Androceles is a chief—a king, if you will—and he had to be accorded a royal welcome. His son is merely a captain.'

'Then it was good fortune a chief captured my men and me.' The words were lightly said, but Helena could see the deep seriousness in his eyes, and the shadows of what could have been.

'I suppose it was.' Helena prodded a paving stone with the toe of her sandal.

The state of his men when they arrived—ill kempt, injured, starved to the point of exhaustion—was clear in her memory. She refused to think about what might have happened, and indeed what must have happened to the others because her aunt insisted on keeping Romans in the holds of ships. When her aunt recovered, Helena would argue hard for guests to be held in the temple.

'Rome's and my gratitude is great.'

'I did what the ritual required me to do. You left me no choice.'

He captured her hand. A tremor ran through Helena before common sense reasserted itself and she withdrew her hand.

'We value friendship…wherever it is offered.' His face held an eager expression.

Helena examined the point of her sandal, rather than continue to look into his eyes. She knew what his words were. A code. An offer for her to openly condemn the seafarers and align the temple with Rome. That would never happen. It was impossible. The very fact she was even considering it and how best to respond astonished her. He had shown her that Romans were no different from the people who inhabited this island. They were not monsters. They were civilised.

She might be able to ensure fair treatment of prisoners, but they were at war with Rome. She was not a traitor and she could guess the price Rome would exact for its friendship. But what if the seafarers were plotting to overthrow the temple—what then?

Helena wished for the simpler days when all she had to worry about was whether or not the incense burners were filled. She did not have the power to make that sort of decision, even if she wanted to. She drew her breath inwards. But he deserved to know the truth.

'I—'

'Helena, the grain has been unloaded and is ready for inspection.' Kimon's high-pitched voice interrupted her and drowned out the reply.

She had never thought to be grateful to Kimon, but she was.

Chapter Eight

~~~

Tullio stared at the pirate striding across the courtyard, his dark green cloak billowing in the breeze. His high-laced sandals made a metallic sound. He lifted a hand and pushed his slightly too-long locks back. A shaft of sunlight caught the eagle tattoo and three gold rings with blue stones. The emblem of a lion fighting an eagle was clearly visible on one.

Blood pounded in Tullio's ears.

A coincidence. It had to be.

There was no guarantee that this was the pirate responsible for his ex-wife's murder six months ago. But there was the signet ring that she wore, complete with the chip on the eagle's wing. He had to keep calm, and not let his temper get the better of him. But he knew the ring and on whose hand he had last seen it—the final encounter with Marcia where they had reached a certain peace.

He had wished her well in her new life. She had laughed, and confided that she enjoyed being the wife of a senator much more than being the wife of an Army officer. Ten days later, he heard of her and her husband's murder in a pirate raid on the Italian coast, as well as the description of the pirate captain who had carried it out, and who, according to Marcia's tire-woman, had performed the actual killing.

After he attended Marcia's funeral, Tullio vowed to track down the pirate responsible. Now it appeared the gods had delivered the man to him.

Tullio pressed his lips together. Patience. He had waited this long, and he would have a chance to avenge the deaths. He had a face and a name. He was no longer chasing shadows.

Half-dazed, he listened to Helena and the pirate discuss the grain storage arrangements. Helena was wrong. The seafarers who used this port did raid Italy. They were not frightened of the sibyl's curse.

'Zenobia was correct,' the pirate drawled. 'You are offering a safe haven to Roman scum. Whatever is this world coming to if the temple can not be trusted?'

'The sibyl has extended us a welcome while we wait for the ransom demanded after an unprovoked attack.' Tullio moved forward, positioning himself between Helena and the pirate. He held on to his temper by the thinnest of threads.

The pirate flicked his fingers under his chin and sent a deliberate stream of spittle, narrowly missing Tullio's sandal. The insult was unmistakable. Tullio crouched on the balls of his feet. His belt hung with the three bronzes he had won for inter-cohort wrestling. He had even spent a time at Olympus, perfecting his skills. The pirate would not rise, but where to land the first blow?

The pirate's eyes gleamed. He made a slight beckoning motion with his hand, a hint of a grin played on his features. Drawing on all his military training, Tullio froze. A faint movement in the shadows caused Tullio to glance to his right.

Seven seafarers were in the shadows, bristling with menace. He might reach the pirate captain, but not even a single punch would land.

Everything he had worked so hard for over the past week would be wasted in a display of temper. Tullio pursed his lips. He would not throw away the gains so easily.

Tullio drummed his fingers against his thigh and waited. He hated this impotence. It went against his nature. He wanted to strike and strike first, but he had others to think about. His men were more important than the satisfaction of avenging an insult.

'By the shade of my ancestor, Alexander, my father grows soft, allowing Romans to dictate terms.' The pirate's eyes narrowed, giving him a hawklike appearance. 'Helena, you take too many chances. You know the reputation Romans have. You must allow me to station guards here. I insist.'

'The temple has everything under control, I assure you, Kimon.' Helena inclined her head, half-covering it with her shawl, but Tullio could see the strain about her lips. 'When we need help, we shall ask for it. In the hour of our dire need, Neptune will answer our call. It has been foretold.'

'They might try to escape.' The pirate stroked his chin. 'For your own safety, Helena, I beg you to consider my offer. My men will be only too delighted to serve the temple in this fashion.'

The pirate wore a smug smile as if the request was a mere formality, and Helena had already agreed. Tullio willed her to pause and to think. Once before she had rebuffed the pirates. She had to do it again. He forced every muscle, every sinew in his body to remain still but ready. If she needed his help, he'd give it.

'Your father has already had my answer.' Helena's head-dress quivered. 'Why should it change now?'

'You have spent several days with the scum. Surely you must see how untrustworthy and prone to lying they are,' Kimon replied. 'I beg you, Helena, for the sake of the temple—reconsider.'

'The Romans have behaved honourably.'

'Romans and honour do not go together, Helena. You know that.'

'I have given my word as a Roman and an officer,' Tullio said between gritted teeth. He had to keep control of his temper. He was tempted to ask what right a thief and murderer had to judge honour, but refrained.

'Who exactly are you?' There was a curl to the pirate's lip. 'I have known many Romans and few keep their word unless paid sufficiently.'

'Marcus Livius Tullio.'

'I have heard of the family.' The pirate gave a loud grunt. 'My father gets paid one way or the other.'

'What precisely do you mean, Kimon? You arrive at the temple, speaking in riddles.' Helena had crossed her arms and her tapping foot made a noisy tattoo. 'If you have some proof that the tribute will not be paid, out with it.'

The courtyard crackled with tension. The pirate's eyes grew crafty. He tapped the side of his nose.

'No proof, just a feeling in my gut. The same sickening feeling I get every time I see a Roman. The same feeling every decent person should have.'

'Unless you have proof, our business has concluded, Kimon, son of Androceles.' Helena drew herself to her full height. 'Next time I will take it ill if you attempt to tell me how the temple should conduct its business.'

The pirate's eyes hardened. He looked ready to strike

Helena. Tullio's muscles tensed. Powerful man or not, if he took one step towards Helena, raised his hand, Tullio would act. He would not have a woman abused in front of him.

'As you wish, Helena.' The pirate clicked his heels together. 'You cannot say you were not warned. When you have trouble, you have only yourself to blame. And my father sends his regards. I, too, wait for the sibyl's prophecy.'

He strode off, stopping only to crush a fragile flower deliberately between his fingers. Tullio watched Helena. She kept her figure rigid until the pirate disappeared out of sight. Then and only then did she drop to her knees and gather the crushed flower petals together.

'The sibyl's favourite—a bee orchid,' she said with a rueful smile. 'We get only one bloom a year from this plant and he destroys it. Typical.'

Tullio walked over and placed his hand on her arm. Her warm skin radiated heat throughout his body. He wanted to draw her to him and tell her that it would be all right, but until he had weapons and more men he could make no assurances beyond mere words.

'Would you trust such a man to protect Niobe?'

Helena stared at the shredded bits of the purple petal. She longed to agree with Tullio, to tell him everything she thought about Kimon, but she had already revealed too much. To speak against one of the seafarers would send her down a road she was not ready to take. 'Crushing an orchid does not make anyone evil, Tullio.'

'That is not what I asked.'

'Kimon, son of Androceles, has been a good friend to the temple. He has brought in more goods than most of the recent seafarers.' Helena stared at the wall. Prejudice blinded both men. Without inconvertible proof, she refused to act. 'The rings he wears are a gift from his father to commemorate the amount of grain he brought last year.'

The line between Tullio's brows increased. He tilted his head to one side. 'From his father?'

'Kimon worships his father. Did you not notice they even sport the same tattoo? The emblem of Alexander? Kimon is Androceles's heir apparent.' Helena's words came out in a rush.

'Do you know how Androceles came by the rings? I thought I recognised them from somewhere. They are of Roman design.'

'I have no idea. Androceles has many contacts in Rome. Is it important?' Helena took a closer look at him. His face had become shadowed. She reached out a hand and risked touching his shoulder. No response. 'Is something wrong?'

'It may be nothing.' He moved away from her hand and bowed stiffly. 'I have tarried here too long. I need to get back to my men.'

'Tullio, I—' Helena stopped and forced the words back down her throat. She had nearly given into impulse and confided her fears about the cave, and the task she had before her. But not when he was like this. This was one journey she had to make herself. She knew she was ready for it. She had seen Aunt Flavia prepare herself often enough. But why did she wish she had confided in Tullio when she had had the chance? Especially now, after the encounter with Kimon.

'Is something the matter, Helena?' he asked, but his face was unyielding, the face of a Roman tribune.

'No, I was pleased we didn't have any more guests. May the goddess go with you, Tullio.'

She straightened her shoulders. She was the sibyl's assistant, the one who would take over. She knew what had to be done. She was no clinging vine. She would stand on her own two feet. Face Kybele and survive. She would save the temple on her own.

Helena stood and watched him until he turned the corner. She shivered despite the heat and pulled her shawl tighter around her shoulders. One of the purple petals drifted out of her fingers and landed on the stone, reminding her of her task. She had delayed long enough.

She took an involuntary step towards Tullio's retreating figure and forced herself to stop. She could not ask him for help. She swallowed hard and turned her footsteps towards the beginning stage in her plan—the ritual cleansing.

Tullio rejoined his men in a sombre mood. The dark circles under Helena's eyes and the slight trembling of her rose-coloured lips haunted him. It had taken all of his hard-won self-control not to demand she tell him what it was that truly bothered her. Androceles's son had unsettled her. More so than when they were on the turret.

Patience. Easy to preach, but difficult to exercise. He had to wait and let her turn to him. If he pushed too hard, he risked losing any foothold that Rome might have gained. He had to earn her trust. He had to show he was different from the pirates and that the pirates had resumed their raids. He had to have that final bit of proof.

'And—?' Quintus jerked his head towards the direction of the town.

'The ship only carried plunder. Grain.'

'The bastards,' Quintus replied.

There was no need to say anything more. Silently, Tullio

regarded the men. They were engaged in a mock battle with bits of wood.

'You approve, Livius Tullio?' Quintus gestured towards the men. 'Not exactly legion wooden swords and wicker shields, but they will do.'

'I gave the order that the men were supposed to go back to barracks. Not engage in behaviour that might be threatening. Helena has indicated the temple is not a drill hall.'

'It is only a bit of fun. Something to keep their spirits up.' Quintus wiped the sweat from his brow. ''Sides, if there were t'have been more soldiers, I wanted to give them hope, so to speak.'

'Your hope would have caused the pirates to station men here. Did you think about that?' Tullio glared at the centurion, who glanced away. Tullio rubbed a hand across the back of his neck. He was being too hard on the man. 'How did you get the sticks?'

'There was some wood left over from the repair job we did on the warehouse, and I asked Galla, who agreed.'

Tullio noticed there was a slight hesitation in the way the hardened soldier had said 'Galla' and there was a faint rosy hue to his cheeks. Had Cupid's arrow found the centurion?

A richly spiced aroma wafted into the yard, and the men hastily dropped their weapons. Galla entered, carrying a tray of honey cakes. Quintus hurried over and relieved her of the burden. Both sets of cheeks flamed to the same hue.

'Galla has brought us some refreshments, lads,' Quintus called, his mouth full of the small cakes, 'in thanks for the reconstruction job we did on the goat sheds.'

'It appears you have worked out a system of payment.' Tullio walked over and casually took one of the cakes. Honey and cinnamon teased his senses. A most welcome change from barley soup.

'An army needs to eat as well. It would be folly to refuse such a gift.' Quintus sheltered his mouth behind his hand. 'Your idea about sweet talking worked. We have been trading bread recipes. All those years as the cohort's baker, who'd have thought it? My tongue may not be smooth, but I can get things done.'

'I'm glad to hear it.' There appeared to be a distinct change in Quintus. Tullio hoped it was due to genuine feelings for the maid, rather than a desire to use her.

'The sibyl is most grateful that you and your men have contributed to the well being of the temple.' Galla came over to stand next to Quintus, her face wreathed in smiles.

'It is our pleasure, I assure you.' Tullio sketched a bow. The maid's reaction was balm after his encounter with the pirate. It was proof his idea was working. Given time, he would be able to convince the temple to side with Rome. He had to believe that. 'These cakes, then, are from the sibyl, and not Helena.'

'The cakes are from me to thank these men.' The maid adjusted her shawl more firmly about her head. 'It is not something I wanted to trouble the sibyl with, or Helena for that matter. I am the mistress of my own kitchen.'

'My mistake. I merely wanted to express my appreciation for such a gift.'

The woman harrumphed at the flattery, but Tullio noticed her cheeks were an even brighter hue, and she had a distinct twinkle in her. She rearranged her shawl, and her face sobered.

'There is another reason I am here,' she said 'The sibyl has requested an interview with you.'

Tullio felt his second honey cake begin to slip from his hand. Perhaps Helena was correct and the sibyl would recover. Where would it leave him? 'When?'

'As soon as you can spare the time. She has much that she wants to discuss with you.'

A thousand questions buzzed through Tullio's brain, but he was careful not let his face show anything beyond courtesy.

'My time is at the sibyl's disposal.'

Helena contemplated the range of herbs laid out on the bed before her. She pushed away the fears that were more suited to a child, not a grown woman who had seen more than twenty summers. She had watched her aunt complete the cleansing ritual many times. She felt she could do this blind-folded.

The cleansing part had been easy. She had oiled her body with olive oil from the first pressing, and then had carefully scraped it with a new *strigil*. She had finally rinsed her body in the sacred spring that bubbled up beneath the sibyl's chambers.

With each step, she became more certain that this was the way to proceed. When she was with Tullio, she had suffered doubts, but now, having cleansed her body, and donned the snow-white robes, she knew that she was doing the correct thing. It was the only thing. And, more importantly, she was equal to the task that lay ahead of her.

She would take the herbs, but she would not take a bird for companionship, Helena decided, mixing the powder with a bit of wine. The collecting of the dove would only bring her intended journey to everyone's notice. And then she'd have to explain about the sibyl's incapacity.

Helena fastened the gold-lion brooches on her shoulders and tied the gold belt about her hips.

She was ready.

Kybele would speak to her. Kybele would understand that her actions were to protect the temple.

The goddess *had* to speak to her.

Helena slipped her feet into the sandals and started off towards the grotto. Now was the time, while everyone would be breaking bread for supper and Galla was otherwise occupied. She had no doubt that Galla would argue that she should wait.

The combination of Androceles, Kimon and the Lady Zenobia required a robust response. Each day she delayed, the power of the temple ebbed away. If Aunt Flavia was well, she would have braved Kybele's lair before now. She never hesitated where that was concerned.

She glanced over her shoulder, hoping to see the reassuring bulk of Tullio. Nothing, not even the shadow of the temple's cat. She shook her head. After she finished with the cave, then she'd decide what to do about Tullio. She had to concentrate.

Her footsteps rang out as she crossed the empty temple courtyard, towards the smaller, more private sanctuary of the sibyl. Solitary and alone.

Beside a small stone altar, she stopped and said a prayer that her mission might be successful, that Kybele would understand.

Her hand hovered by a pile of unlit torches. Her aunt always used one, but Helena knew the torches would be counted. If she failed, and Kybele did not speak to her, she wanted to leave no trace. Helena swallowed hard. Her hand trembled.

If she failed…

It was unthinkable. She had to succeed.

At the concealed entrance to the grotto, Helena paused one final time. Her mind went blank. What were the final rituals? Did her aunt do anything, say anything that she had forgotten? Anything important?

The frigid air from the cave contrasted sharply with the hot sun that was beating down on her back. The cold prickle of sweat moulded her gown to her back.

Helena tightened her belt about her hips and tried not think about Tullio and the way his arms had held her. She had felt a sort of peace there, something she had not thought to ever feel. She pressed her lips together. How could she be thinking of Tullio at a time like this? Her mind should be full of pure thoughts. What happened on the parapet would never happen again. She was different from her mother.

She bent down and undid her sandals. She carefully placed them on the small altar as she had seen her aunt do.

She muttered one last prayer to Kybele as she allowed her eyes to adjust to the gloom and started off down the track.

'Kybele, I have come in peace and harmony to speak with you.'

'At last we meet, Sibyl,' Tullio said, striding towards the fragile figure in the centre of the elaborate bed.

The room smelt strongly of incense intermingled with cinnamon and myrrh and brought Tullio back to his youth with a jolt. It reminded him of other sanctuaries that he had visited. Same smell, same hushed atmosphere, same authority.

He peered more closely at the grey-haired figure and could see the resemblance to her niece.

'Indeed, Roman.' She held out a hand. Her voice had the same bell-like quality of Helena's, but he could also hear the note of a person used to command.

'I must thank you for the temple's generous hospitality.' Tullio shifted on his feet. He wondered if the sibyl knew of Helena's confession to him.

'The goddess moves in mysterious ways, Roman.' Her deep green eyes seemed to pierce into his soul. She nodded briefly as if what she found there satisfied her. Then she looked tired, as if she knew her time was ending. 'It would not have been my choice.'

'Rome is grateful, none the less. Rome always prefers the hand of friendship.'

'Rome's friendship is tied to Rome's interests.'

'Isn't everyone's? Would the pirates—I'm sorry—the sea-faring houses be as friendly if you did not provide them with a safe haven?' He waited to see her reaction.

The sibyl gave a hearty laugh, the laugh of a woman used to power. 'You are clever, Roman. I like a forthright man. Kybele has chosen well.'

'What do you mean? My coming here has nothing to do with the goddess.' Tullio bit back the words condemning religious practices as mere shams for the priests. He needed this woman and her power.

'Nothing escapes the goddess. She has brought you here for a purpose. What purpose, I do not know yet.'

'My sole purpose and concern is to get my men back to Roman territory.' As Tullio spoke the words, he knew them to be false. His purpose had altered. He wanted to save Helena and her people from the ferocity of the pirates. He had no doubt they would turn on the island once they realised how ill the sibyl was. After seeing her, and considering his earlier encounter with Androceles's son, he could understand why Helena had taken such a risk.

'You do know and your heart understands, even if your mind will not recognise it yet.' The elderly woman's lips curved upwards in the merest hint of a smile.

'I have no idea what you are talking about.' The incense was beginning to work on his brain. He forced himself to focus. This woman might be holy, but he refused to allow the combination of smoke and ritual to befuddle him.

'May you find what you seek, Roman.'

The sibyl's eyes fluttered closed, her breathing became regular and her hand relaxed on the coverlet.

The interview was over.

Outside the room, he breathed deeply, cleansing his mind of the woolly feeling. He gave a wry smile. Even the most straightforward interview with a sibyl was cloaked in riddles. He should have learnt that by now.

He would have to dissect her meaning, and most times he knew there were only words and no meaning. It was what the listener heard that was important. Words only had power if you let them.

As he came around the corner, he collided with a small body. Tullio reached down and set Niobe back on her feet. 'I should look where I am going.'

The mute girl flashed a smile. Then her small hand tugged at his tunic, indicating he should go with her in the opposite direction to where he was quartered.

'But I need to return to my comrades, dinner is about to served. My stomach is rumbling. Tomorrow, tomorrow I will go with you. We can pick flowers. My mother taught me how to make a crown.' Tullio mimed picking flowers and twisting them into a garland. 'Shall I make one for you?'

Niobe shook her head, stamped her dusty foot in frustration and tried again. This time, she pulled his hand.

Tullio crouched down. 'Is something wrong? Something I can help with?'

The girl nodded vigorously.

'Is it one of your geese?'

A quick shake of the head. Tullio ran his hand through his hair and wished Helena were there. She always seemed to understand what Niobe wanted.

'Has something happened to my men?'

The girl tilted her head to one side. She shrugged.

'Are the pirates, Androceles's men, massing to attack the temple?'

Niobe's eyes grew big and she shook her head. Tears of frustration appeared in the corners of her eyes.

'Who then? What has happened?' But as the words fell from his lips, Tullio knew who. He knew who would cause Niobe concern. Something had happened to Helena. His heart skipped a beat.

He forced his voice to remain calm. His hands gripped Niobe's shoulders. 'Is it Helena? You must tell me quickly.'

The girl nodded and looked distressed. Her face became white. She mimed walking with her hand and then falling.

What had Helena done?

Tullio offered a prayer up to Jupiter or any god that might be listening that he was not too late. That somehow Niobe had got it wrong and Helena was fine.

'Shall we go there now?'

But as he followed Niobe through the labyrinth of passageways, he started to fear the worst. He urged her to walk faster, even though she was practically at a run.

Niobe paused at a half-concealed entrance to a cave. From the symbols outside the cave and the small stone altar with a simple offering of broken bread and incense, everything proclaimed it was a sacred spot. Tullio hesitated. His mother's superstitions returned. He had no wish to despoil a holy place. The vengeance of the gods could be swift.

The entrance gaped black.

'Are you certain that Helena is there? That she is in trouble?'

Niobe began to pull him towards the cave's mouth.

'But there are no guards, no one to help her.' Tullio bent down, retrieved an oil lamp, lit it and then peered in the dark empty space.

The moment he stepped in to the cave, he detected a strong, unpleasant odour of sulphur and something else to make his knees feel weak. He could remember tales of miners who delved deep in the ground and who were overcome by the demons of the mine.

Was something similar happening here? Exactly how did the sibyl communicate with Kybele? What was down in that hidden cave, deep in the bowels of the earth?

'Helena!'

The echo returned his voice to him, a hundred times over. How large, how deep was this cave?

He waited, but there was no answering sound. Only silence and a distant dripping of water. His heart constricted. Where was she? He willed her to appear, but nothing. Glancing over his shoulder, he saw Niobe's face crumple. She sank to her knees, her face pleading with him.

'I will find her. She is bound to be communicating with the goddess. Safe.' He hoped his words were true.

Covering his face with a corner of his tunic, Tullio took another step forward. Nothing. The cave was deserted. Whoever had been here had left a long time ago. He turned to go.

A pale form made him stop. At the far side of the cave, a white-robed body lay in a crumpled heap.

Chapter Nine

A black swirling mist enveloped Helena, holding her in its grip, preventing her from moving.

She knew she should go. The goddess had not spoken to her, ignoring all the entreaties. But her feet were heavy as if they had turned to lead. She tried lifting one foot, but it stayed stubbornly attached to the cave floor.

The icy mist pressed closer.

Helena knelt and began to crawl towards the entrance. One knee, then the other. A piece of sharp rock cut into her palm. She stopped and brought her hand to her mouth, licking away the faint trace of blood.

No blood. Never leave any blood. That was the first lesson her aunt taught her. She should stand up, but that took too much effort.

The mouth of the cave with its shimmering light was further away than ever. It swayed and changed. Helena wiped a hand across her forehead and felt the sticky sweat.

The black mist curled around her ankles, cold and damp. She attempted to move her right leg, then her left. Each time, it seemed to take more effort and the light never got any closer.

The black mist covered the entrance, plunging everything into darkness.

A thousand voices screamed, reverberating, echoing in her mind until she knew her own voice was being torn from her.

At the sound, the mist came down more firmly, pressing on her chest, sucking her breath from her lungs, pushing her to the ground.

Air.

She had to get more air. Her lungs burned with the need.

Helena concentrated on inhaling. Each time she tried, the mist pressed more heavily against her, squeezing the last drop of breath out of her.

The ground that had felt so sharp before became soft like feathers. She'd lie down for a little while, then, when she had the strength, she'd try again.

Her final thought was that she had failed, she was unworthy. Her pride had led her to this and Kybele punished pride. No one knew she was there, no one would help here.

Still the mist pressed on her, seeping into her very core, making her lungs feel as if they were on fire.

Unable to fight back any longer, she allowed her body to succumb.

A voice penetrated the darkness, calling her name.

Tullio?

Not here. He couldn't be.

It was forbidden. She had to warn him to keep away. He must not be here.

She opened her eyes, and forced a breath through her lips.

She tried to lift her head and answer, but no sound emerged. It took too much effort to keep her eyes open.

The mist pressed heavy once more. She wanted to close them and to sleep for ever.

Please.

Then suddenly she was floating, moving, and her head no longer rested against the cold hard stone. She could feel instead the unyielding softness of muscle, the rough rasp of wool, the steady heartbeat.

Tullio?

It had to be him. She knew it was him.

Tullio had found her? But how?

She wanted to ask, but her mind refused to supply the words. Did it matter? He was here and the black mist was receding.

She drew a deep breath, expecting the burning sensation to come back—but nothing.

Her lungs began to fill with clean air. One breath. Two.

She gagged and was set down. Without the arms about her, she felt cold, a cold that seeped to her bones. She wanted to stand but her limbs refused to obey her. The horror from the cave returned. She lashed out with her hands, pushing it away.

A cup was pressed to her lips.

'Drink this,' Tullio's voice commanded.

She opened her mouth. Several drops of fresh water trickled down the back of her throat. Bliss. She tilted her head back and allowed the cool liquid to run down her throat, cleansing her, making her stronger.

She blinked and his face swam in front of her. A sigh escaped from her mouth.

Tullio said something. Not to her. To someone else.

Helena shook her head to clear the ringing noise from her ears. She tried to rise. This time, she made it to her knees.

His arms went round her again and lifted her up. She turned her head and listened to the reassuring steady thump of his heart.

Her mind seemed to drift and then she felt herself fall. The arms were abruptly withdrawn. Helena shivered and tried to turn again towards the security and the warmth of his body. His heartbeat resounded in her ears.

Had it been a dream?

She had gone to the cave. She knew that much. The mortar and pestle she used to pound the herbs lay by her side.

She rubbed her eyes and saw Tullio standing at the foot of her bed, a crease between his eyebrows. It was all too easy to remember how his arms felt.

A dream, surely.

Her mind swam as the questions buzzed about her head. She raised herself on her elbows, then tried to sit up, but had to collapse back down as the room tilted. She saw the swift look of concern on his face as he started forward, grabbed her elbows and pushed her back against the pillows.

She wanted to lay her head on his chest. His scent filled her nostrils. Warm, spicy, as if he had eaten honey cakes. She reached out her hand.

What if someone saw her like this? She'd have to explain, and then…

She glanced over and saw the door was firmly shut. At least she was shielded from any passer-by's gaze. Her hand fell back and knocked the statuette of Kybele that stood on her bedside table crashing to the floor.

Tullio bent down and righted it, placed it back so Kybele's all-knowing eyes stared directly at her.

Helena turned her head away.

'You are awake. I will leave. They will be releasing the lions soon.' Tullio's voice was low and pleasant. Her fingers reached out and touched his warmth. 'Sleep. Your strength will come back.'

How long had he been here, watching her?

She remembered nothing beyond the suffocating pitch blackness of the cave. She was sure she had been there, and had tried to face the goddess. There had been nothing in reply, nothing but blackness. Blackness pushing at her.

The vague memory of being carried stirred.

'Stay with me,' she croaked between parched lips, and longed for water. Her mouth felt stuffed with old rags. 'I need...honey water.'

'I won't leave you, if you need me.' He smiled. Then he reached over, poured her a cup of water and held it out to her.

As she took the cup, their fingers touched, and a searing bolt of heat went up her arm. She nearly dropped the cup in surprise, but recovered enough to take a few sips of honey water. Each sip brought more and more strength. She found it impossible to remember when she had been as thirsty. She held out the cup and he refilled it.

When she had drained it for a third time, he took the cup from her and set it down on the small bedside table, next to Kybele. 'It is here if you need more.'

Helena watched his chest rise and fall. He had rescued her, but she had no idea how he had found her.

How could he have discovered the cave? Kybele's sacred place? So well hidden she had not known it was there until her tenth birthday. It was sacrilege for any but the anointed ones to go there. Whoever did faced a certain death, but he had lived. Without him, she would have died. She passed a hand over her eyes. The trembling in her limbs started again and she swallowed hard.

'How did you know I was in danger?'

'Niobe saw you go into the cave, and came to fetch me. I discovered you lying on the cave's floor.'

'Where is Niobe?' Helena looked wildly about her, but the room was empty save for Tullio. She started to sit up, the linen coverlet slipping down to reveal her under-tunic and nothing else. With a wild grab, she clutched it to her shoulders. 'Did anyone see you…carry me?'

'Niobe returned to her geese. She waited until you were back here, then honked loudly. We encountered no one on the way back to your room. Niobe knows all the hidden passages in this temple.'

Tullio leant forward and his hand firmly pushed her back down on to the mattress. His face was so close she could see the faint bristles on his chin, and the different flecks of colour in his eyes. How many colours did his eyes have? He had impossibly long lashes for a man.

'You must rest. Lie back. The air was bad in that cave. It will have sapped your strength.'

'What do you mean?' Helena propped herself up on her elbows and stared at him in disbelief. Her head felt stuffed with unpicked wool. Tullio seemed to know so much about the dangers of the cave and she, who had lived in the temple all her life, so little. 'The air there is the same as anywhere.'

'It smelt strongly of rotten eggs. I found it difficult to breathe.' Tullio's face grew grave. 'This is why you collapsed.

If you had remained there much longer, you would not have recovered. My uncle owned mines, and had to be careful. He had no wish to lose slaves unnecessarily. When was the last time the cave was used?'

'When I found Aunt Flavia.'

'It could explain why your aunt suffered as well.'

Helena wanted to believe Tullio's words. Was it a case of bad air? She too had heard of problems in mines. She bit her lip and straightened her shoulders, ignored the weakness in her arms.

She knew the truth.

It had nothing to do with the air in the cave and everything to do with Kybele's favour. She and Aunt Flavia—maybe the whole island—had done something to displease the goddess. This was the goddess's revenge. Her way of telling the whole world she needed a new anointed one. Humiliation washed over Helena. She had thought she was the goddess's chosen one, but she wasn't. The goddess had no use for her.

She reached out and turned the statue face down again. This time when Tullio reached out to right it, she placed her hand on his wrist. His hand gave hers a brief squeeze, but he left the statuette where it lay.

'Kybele protects her own.' Helena fought to keep her voice steady. 'I did everything right. I took the herbs. I washed in the sacred spring. I should have been safe. It was Kybele's choice. It had nothing to do with air—bad or otherwise. If Kybele had desired it, I would have emerged unscathed as I have seen my aunt do countless times.'

The unspoken words hung about them. Helena regarded the frieze of grapes that ran around the top of the ceiling.

If he said the words, it would make it easier to hate him.

To forget in her despair she had called out for him. Called out for a Roman and not for Kybele. And he came, her unruly mind whispered. He saved her from the fate Kybele decreed. She owed him a life-debt.

'I have seen people suffer from underground sickness before. I know what it looks like.' His voice cut through her as if it were a ritual knife with the sharpest edge. 'It is not a question of the gods' favour, but of being sensible, of not taking risks, of not staying where the air is bad. Truly, Helena.'

He reached out and touched her lips with a gentle finger. The tingles from that one touch infused her whole body with warmth. She wanted to believe his words. Like his touch, they filled her with a warmth. Maybe it wasn't a judgement. Maybe it was something else.

'Was there nothing the sibyl does that you didn't do?' he asked. 'Is it possible you forgot some small detail?'

'She brings a bird, a dove, but I did not want to call attention to myself. The birds tend to let out a loud cry and all would have come running.' Helena tapped a finger against her mouth. She tried to keep relief from flooding. Was there a possibility that she had not displeased the goddess? That she had not preformed the ritual correctly and so the goddess never came to protect her? 'And the sibyl always takes a lit torch, but I did not see the need. I see well in the dark.'

A shiver ran through her as she recalled the absolute blackness of the cave. She had wanted a light, but it was too late, and the air had begun to move with a rustle of a thousand wings. Then the black mist descended, choking her. The thoughts sucked out the relief she felt and left in its place a great emptiness, a well that needed to be filled. Tullio's fingers tightened around her hand.

She withdrew it and he let her go.

'You think there was a reason for such things?' Helena tilted her head. She had thought them theatrical trappings for her aunt. 'A true believer who is pure of heart should have nothing to fear from the goddess.'

'In my experience, there is always a practical reason for such things, although sometimes it is lost in the mists of time.' A dimple showed in his cheek when he said the words. 'It sounds to me as if the air is bad in that cave and your aunt quite sensibly took precautions.'

'But she is known for the accuracy of her prophecies. The goddess should protect her.'

'A good priest or priestess uses everything at his or her disposal. Not to do so is to refuse a gift of the gods. The rituals are there for a purpose.'

Helena shifted uncomfortably. Was that what she done? Refused Kybele's gift? Had she been too proud, as Zenobia accused her of being? All she knew was that the thought of the cave now terrified her. She had to get her mind away from there. Something, anything that was not about the cave.

'You seem very knowledgeable about the religious craft and practice.'

'As I said before, my mother visited practically every priest, soothsayer and charlatan in Italy, searching for a cure for my sister's speechlessness.' Tullio ruffled his hair. He gave a wry smile that made Helena's heart turn over. 'She dragged me along until I was old enough to protest. In the end, my sister spoke when she thought my mother was in danger of falling. She made her own miracle.'

'People expect bells and incense. It is faith that counts. Surely it was your mother and sister's belief that caused the miracle.'

His face loomed close to hers. The bristles from his shaved-this-morning chin were clearly visible. She ran her tongue over her lips and tried to concentrate on his words, not on the feelings building up inside, clamouring to be heard. She wanted him to touch her. She wanted to feel his skin against hers.

'Torches and birds are more than smoke and mirrors, Helena.'

'I…I knew what I was doing.' She twisted the edge of the blanket around her fingers. 'Maybe I took a risk but it was for the good of the temple.'

'Do you put the temple's needs above your own?'

'You put your men's needs above your own when you put yourself forward for punishment instead of your centurion.'

'I did what I had to.'

'As did I.' Stung, Helena sat bolt upright.

The coverlet slithered to the floor.

It lay there, unheeded.

Her under-tunic gaped open and she knew from the flicker in Tullio's eyes the swell of her breast was revealed. Neither moved. Her heartbeat resounded in her ears, so loud she thought he must have heard. Her hand touched the neck of the under-tunic, pulling it higher.

He reached down and picked up the coverlet, tucking it back firmly into place. All she could do was watch him and long for his touch.

His fingers trailed along the side of her jaw. The gesture of a friend? She wanted more than friendship. She wanted… A burning consumed her, made her long for more than gentle touches. She had been cold before, but now her body was alive with sensation pulsing through her.

'You are important to the temple in other ways, Helena.

You must not risk your life like that.' His voice held a husky note. 'Without you, the temple would suffer.'

'I wasn't risking my life,' she whispered. His lips hung over her, tantalisingly close. A deep longing swept over her. She wanted to experience the soaring feeling she had felt up on the turret.

'I ought to go.' He made no move towards the door, and continued to look at her as if he were a starving man. A muscle in his cheek twitched. 'My men will need me. You are safe now.'

The memory of the black mist welled up within her. Would it reclaim her once he had gone? Already she could feel it gathering around the edges of her mind. What if this was all a dream and she woke to find herself in that dark grotto where the only sound was the endless echo of her voice calling?

'Stay. I don't want to be alone. Please stay for a little while longer. You said you would stay…if I asked.'

Her hand reached up and touched his cheek. His skin shivered under the pads of her fingers, but he made no move towards her. Instead he stood as if he had been turned to marble. Helena ran her hand down his arm, feeling the warmth of his hard muscle, but he did not move, not even when her palm touched his.

She swallowed hard, and knew he would go because he had said he would. He did not feel the way she did.

'Helena.'

One word, but enough. He was going. A terrible longing swept over her and her eyes traced his features, hoping to make a memory. When she was old, she wanted to take it out and remember that this was the man who had saved her from the black mist. She reached out again.

Her lips parted.

His forefinger touched her bottom lip, the briefest of touches. Her whole being stilled.

'Hush now. You are safe. Sleep well.'

He started to turn.

Then she knew she needed more, much more. A deep longing swept over her. She refused to let him go, like this. She had to know.

Her fingers interlaced with his, pulling him down. She lifted her face towards his, brushed his mouth with hers and heard his muffled groan.

His mouth came down and captured hers, a far more seeking kiss than any they had shared before. Her lips parted and she tasted his mouth. Warm, wet and inviting. She drowned herself in the kiss.

An ache started to grow between her legs, driving her forward, building within her. She wanted more. Her body demanded more. She was alive, gloriously alive.

Her tongue entered his mouth and then retreated. Another groan passed his lips and he pulled her closer.

Helena's body arched forward and her breast brushed the firm wall of his chest. Her skin sought his and the heat of him inflamed the fire building within her.

The coverlet slipped unnoticed to the floor and she pressed her body closer, seeking the solid reassurance of him.

His mouth left hers and travelled down the length of her throat, making a fiery trail as he eased her back amongst the cushions of her bed. The bed sagged as he moved next to her. To give him more room, she shifted on to her side and felt the plaster wall against her back. He watched her with deep black eyes, propped up on one elbow, but he made no attempt to draw her into his arms.

His eyes traced her mouth, and she knew he was thinking about the kiss they had just shared.

She smiled and he returned the smile, making her heart beat faster, too fast.

She touched his bronzed muscles, glorying in their hardness, in their warmth. They were not sculpted from marble, but were flesh and blood. These arms had carried her.

His hand trapped hers, held it there against the warm flesh. Helena could feel the black mist of the cave retreating as his assault on her senses continued.

He lowered his mouth to hers again and she welcomed his tongue as it teased and tormented hers.

His fingers moved the material of her gown and he pressed a kiss at the base of her throat. She glanced up and saw a question in his eyes.

'What is it?'

'Do you know what you are doing to me?'

'I think so.'

Her hand smoothed back the lock of hair that had fallen over his forehead. It was soft to the touch, softer than the wings of the white doves. Her fingers, having touched one lock, seemed to wander of their own volition over his head, burying themselves in the springing curls. Her forefingers traced the outline of his ear and then his jaw where the beginning of soft bristles grew.

She wished she knew more about what she was doing, if she was doing it right. She wanted him to feel the way she felt.

'Am I behaving properly?' She had to know and waited for his response.

'What is that you want?' he asked, his voice little more than a rasp against her lips.

'You.'

The word came from deep inside her. And as she said it, she knew it was true. Nothing else mattered but the feel of his skin against hers. It was if she were encased in a bubble outside time. And yet she knew she was born for this, that she had never been truly alive before. She never wanted to be anywhere but his arms. Her hand snaked up around his neck, pulling his head closer to hers until her breath mingled with his.

'I want you.'

He groaned and recaptured her lips with a fierce swiftness, his tongue entering her mouth, teasing and tormenting her until her whole body was infused with heat.

Mere kisses were not enough. She longed to see him. She had to see all of him. Her hands moved down his broad back and pulled at the hem of his tunic.

'My lady is bold.'

'Please, Tullio.'

The dimple at the corner of his mouth deepened. In a heartbeat the short tunic was gone. The firm line of his broad shoulders and the sweep of his chest held her vision. Never had she seen skin of such a hue. She ran her hand down his back and felt the strength ripping under her fingertips.

He was a statue come to life. His golden skin contrasted with the whiteness of the loincloth he wore. She refused to look lower and instead feasted her eyes on the sculpted muscles of his chest. Smooth and firm. Bronze except for the dusky rose of his nipples.

She tentatively reached out a hand to brush his nipples and then drew back.

A swift intake of breath.

From her? From him?

The sensation of touching his skin made her knees go weak and an ache developed inside her, and a deep hunger that longed to be satisfied. The urge to experience more drove her on. She reached forward again and pressed her palms against his puckered nipples. His heart seemed to be beating at the same time as hers—faster and faster. She started to move her hands and his hands covered hers, holding them there.

It seemed to her that she had never experienced anything like this before. She knew that perhaps she should stop, that she should consider her duty. But the warm ache in her body made other demands. It was if Helena with her concerns was some other person, watching from far away. And she was being made new for this man.

He caught her fingers, bringing them to his lips, tasting each one, suckling them, sending fresh waves of sensation through her. His other hand eased her under-tunic over her shoulders, pushed it down past her breast band. A delicious shiver passed over her as his hands encircled her breast over the band. His thumb and forefinger rolled her nipples under the cloth until they contracted so tightly that a new aching filled her.

His tongue followed his fingers, lazily drawing circles on her skin and on the cloth. But he made no move towards removing the band that bound her breasts. She raised her hand, and unfastened the cloth, dropped it on the floor, and allowed him to see her rosy-tipped breasts.

She wondered at his response.

Would it affect him as deeply as seeing his chest had done her? Did he experience this aching in his loins as well?

He lowered his lips and captured a breast. His mouth tugged and pulled, and a stream of stars shot through her mind. Her body bucked and she felt his weight come down on her. She felt the hard maleness of him press into her belly and knew she wanted him inside her.

A tiny voice in the back of her mind issued a warning. This was not her destiny. She was about to throw away all that she had worked for, all that she had dreamt about since she was a child—and for what? For a Roman? She silenced it. Why should such things be forbidden?

Helena gasped at each new sensation. Each time a thrill went through her, her body demanded more. But was it right? Was she doing everything correctly?

Her hand stilled.

'Tullio, is it supposed to be like this?' she asked. 'I want to make sure you experience pleasure.'

He raised himself on his elbow again, his eyes tender. One hand traced circles on her breast. 'Like what?'

'Like this? I feel as if I am floating on a sea of air. Everything in my body is alive in a way it has never been before. Is it just me? Please, I have to know.'

A crease appeared between his eyebrows and his face changed, became harder. He rolled off her and stared up at the ceiling, expelling a deep breath of air.

'How do you feel?'

'Out of control. Burning with a fire. My head is spinning with it.'

He made no move to touch her. The distance between them increased.

Helena shivered. What had she done wrong? Tentatively she reached out a hand, stroked his arm, but his muscles did not ripple as they had done before. She felt the tension in them as if he were holding back from something.

He turned his head towards her. With one hand, he smoothed curls off of her forehead. 'You said earlier that you took herbs before you went into the cave.'

'I did. A mixture to ward off the chill and to make communication with the goddess easier.'

The bed creaked and he stood up. He reached down and retrieved his discarded tunic.

'Where are you going, Tullio?'

Tullio stared down at Helena's body. Her dark hair was splayed out over the white pillow. She had recovered the sheet and draped it about her and the cloth clung to the soft swell of her bosom. His manhood was hard to the point of pain.

This was one of the toughest things he had ever done—leaving.

His body called for him to continue, but he could not take the chance. He could not allow Helena the opportunity to throw his actions back in his face. Too much depended on him and his actions. He couldn't just take his pleasure.

He took one lingering last look at the curves, then lifted the blanket to her chin and tucked it around her as if she were a child. His lips brushed her forehead.

A friend's kiss. A brotherly kiss. He felt anything like that. The merest touch and his body ached.

'If I stay, Helena, I will make love to you. And I refuse to do that while you are recovering from your ordeal.'

'And what would be the harm in that?' Her voice sound normal, but he could see the dilation of her pupils. He had no idea what she had taken. He had heard stories of the way sibyls acted after their communication with the gods, how some needed to slake their body's hunger with any man. And he was proud enough to want her to want *him*, not just any man.

'In the morning, you might regret it—when the herbs' influence wears off.'

'I won't.' Her bottom lip stuck out, giving her the appearance of a girl barely older than Niobe.

Tullio forced his eyes to look at the lip and not the curve in her neck, the point where he could see the rapid beating of her heart.

'Some day we will make love, Helena, but not to banish the horrors of that cave, and not when you can say that I took advantage of the situation.'

He touched her shoulder with the lightest touch and the flesh quivered. It took all of his self-control not to crush her again in his arms and make her his own.

'I suppose you will say you have been in charge of the situation.'

'It was not something I planned.'

'Go, please go.' She hid her face in her pillows. 'It is obvious you don't want me.'

Tullio restrained from slamming his fist into the wall. It took every ounce of his strength not to go to her and kiss her. Instead, he would go back to his men, using the passage that Niobe had shown him earlier.

'We can be lovers, Helena, but I want your friendship more,' he whispered, but she gave no sign she had heard him. He closed the door behind him with a click.

Chapter Ten

The late afternoon sun kissed the back of Helena's neck as she sat, combing the wool smooth. A simple task, and one she normally left to Galla or one of the other servants, but it was all she felt able to do. Her limbs were weak and none of the other chores held any interest. She'd examine the lists tomorrow. Everything could be done tomorrow.

She had spent yesterday and most of the morning asleep, then had woken with a start—embarrassment flooding over her.

Had she actually begged Tullio to make love to her?

Her mouth twisted at the memory. She should be grateful he had refused. The terrible thing was that even now she hungered for his touch. She wanted him to desire her. She wanted him to think her attractive, even though Aunt Flavia had warned often of the fleetingness of beauty.

It was the inside that counted.

She had taken trouble with her dress and hair. A flattering rose pink, but nothing flashy or showy. Her hair was caught up in a simple style and twisted at the base of her neck. Her shawl had slipped down and now lay discarded at her side.

Helena forced the comb through another tangle in the wool, picking out the clot of dirt with practised fingers.

She needed to stop thinking about Tullio and his Roman ways. The temple's allies were the seafarers. They were the ones who would guarantee the villagers' survival, not a Roman tribune with crinkles in the corner of his eyes when he smiled, and a powerful grip.

A seafarer would never have rescued her from the cave.

Helena silenced the traitorous voice in the back of her mind.

'Have you given a thought as to how you are going to answer Androceles? Today is the Ides,' Galla asked, breaking Helena's musing.

The maid was swathed in cream cloth from head to foot and her face was slightly perspiring from the heat. She stood in front of Helena, hands on hips.

'That is my province, Galla.'

'Flavia is not strong enough, Helena, you know that. You will need to inform Androceles of her illness. You should have done so before.'

The implication hung in the air between them. Galla seemed to trust that the seafarers would give them time and not demand concessions. Helena could not afford to listen. She had made her decision. She would stick by it.

'It is under control. I...I have had an answer from Kybele.'

'You?' The maid's eyes widened as the full implications of what Helena had said sunk in. She made a sign warding off evil spirits. 'You didn't? Your illness begins to make sense. And here, I thought it a headache brought on by overwork. Helena, you took an awful risk. You foolish girl, you should have told me.'

'Why? What could you have done?'

'Kept a watch out for you.' Galla pushed the basket of wool aside and sat down next to Helena. She put an arm about the younger woman's shoulders as she had done when Helena was small and frightened from one of her aunt's tests. 'That cave is dangerous, child. Even my lady says so. You don't know what you are playing with.'

'I am here. I survived.'

Helena kept her face resolutely turned away from Galla. She was no longer a baby who hid her face in Galla's skirts when the rituals frightened her. She was a grown woman who had to consider what was best for everyone under her care. Her own fear did not play a part. Responsibility came before fear. A shiver ran down her back.

A lump came into her throat as she saw the worry lines in Galla's face. She had no idea that Galla knew so much or cared. Maybe she should have approached the maid for advice, instead of trying to brave the cave on her own. Her mouth twisted. Had she taken Galla's advice, Tullio never would have been there to rescue her.

'There is a prophecy now. It remains to be seen what the seafarers will do with it.'

'But still—' Galla's clucking subsided. 'You must not take chances, Helena. People depend on you. The temple depends on you.'

Helena kept her head down and concentrated on the wool. She picked apart a tangle and ran the wool through her fingers. People depended on her. Sometimes, she wished they didn't. Sometimes she wished she was an ordinary person with ordinary desires and a family.

All the girls she had grown up with had children hanging on to their skirts—married for five years or more. She had aided her aunt at a few of the more difficult births. Her aunt made a point of showing her the horror, but she had also seen the pleasure of a mother's face when she first beheld her child and heard the shared laughter of a man and woman.

It was folly, she knew, but she couldn't help longing for something like that in the quiet spaces of her mind.

Helena pinched the skin between her eyebrows. Her life could never be full of an ordinary woman's pleasures. She knew her duty. It was one of the reasons that her desire for Tullio was impossible. It made her long for things that were best left to others.

'I have sent a scroll with the answer. Lichas will arrive in a black mist.' Helena shifted uneasily. It was what the black mist meant. It had to be. She couldn't have gone through the ordeal for nothing. Kybele may not have spoken to her directly, but she had experienced something. She had no idea who it was meant for, but it was all she had.

Her lips turned up in a wry smile. With her luck lately, Uncle Lichas would arrive in bright blue sky and Aunt Flavia would have to reinterpret the portents. But she had bought some time.

'Does Flavia know? Did she give her permission? Does she agree with the exact wording? The wording is important.'

Helena stared at her hands. 'It is my responsibility. She needs to get well. I will explain when she is better.'

'What happens next?'

Helena's hands stilled. She had no desire to think about that. 'We wait to see what Zenobia and Androceles do. If they are sensible, they will accept the answer.'

'I pray they do.' Galla took some wool from the basket and started to comb it. 'I used to be afraid of the Romans, and what they could do, but now I fear the seafarers more. Androceles's son has been calling at the temple twice a day since he returned, demanding to see Flavia or you.'

'And what did you say?'

'That there was more to running a temple than being at a seafarer's beck and call. Quintus told me what to say. I asked him when he gave me his recipe for fig bread.'

Helena gave Galla a sharp look. A tell-tale pink appeared on Galla's cheek, but before Helena could question her further, the maid rose and hurried towards the kitchen, shawls quivering.

Helena pursed her lips.

What exactly had been going on while she lay sleeping? Soft words for Romans from Galla? She'd never have expected that.

She tapped a finger against her mouth.

Galla had not mentioned any more unruly incidents. She wondered... Then Helena dismissed the thought from her mind. She was seeing romance behind every bush. There was probably a much more simple explanation. Galla had become flustered and had asked the first person she saw.

Helena attacked the pile of wool with renewed vigour.

A shadow loomed over Helena, blocking out the rays of the sun. Her eyes travelled up the bronzed legs and white tunic of Tullio to his strong throat and square chin. Their gazes locked and all she could do was stare.

'The sibyl's assistant has returned.'

She ducked her head and tried to pay attention to the wool, to ignore the desire to touch him. She placed the comb down and picked up a distaff.

'The effects of the drugs and the cave have worn off, if that is what you mean.'

'And...?'

Without waiting for an invitation, he sat down next to her. His bare leg casually pressed into her gown. The faint breeze ruffled his hair. The faint stubble on his chin was just as vivid as it had been in her memory.

She swallowed hard as the memory of his mouth against hers threatened to swamp her. His gentle touch against her skin. She shut her eyes tightly and then opened them. She was not going to remember and she most certainly was not going to beg for another touch.

'And nothing. I have recovered.'

She stared across the courtyard, rather than at his face. If she concentrated on breathing normally, maybe he wouldn't hear her heart pounding, maybe the curl of warmth growing in her belly would vanish. She moved the basket of wool so that it formed a barrier between them. She risked a glance upwards. A half-smile appeared on his lips as if he knew exactly why she had done that.

'You were right,' she said to fill the silence. 'The experience made me react in an unaccustomed way. There is much to be done in the temple.'

'Do those duties include venturing into Kybele's lair again?' His voice became stern.

'Are you forbidding it?' Anger surged through her. Typically Roman. He was a prisoner and yet he wanted to control how she did things. 'What right do you have?'

'The right of someone who rescued you from certain death.' He raked his hand through his hair, making the locks spring upright. 'I'm not in a position to forbid anything. You know that, Helena. But don't let my rescue be in vain. Next time, take the proper precaution. Use the rituals. They are there for a purpose.'

Helena regarded the pile of wool. She had to say something.

'The cave is not used very often,' she whispered.

'That is probably a good thing.'

Helena picked up a spindle and gave it a vicious twist to set it spinning. Too hard because the thread caught on her finger and broke, sending the spindle rolling on the ground. Tullio bent and retrieved it. Helena carefully took the top of the spindle with two fingers, avoiding all contact with him. She made a show of re-attaching the wool and starting the spindle again. This time, the thread twisted smoothly.

'My aunt should recover before the cave is next needed,' Helena said to fill the silence. 'She is rapidly regaining her health.'

'I spoke to the sibyl.'

Helena stopped the spindle, not caring that the thread doubled up, and placed it down. A simple action, but necessary. No doubt Galla would sigh in annoyance at a good spool of thread wasted.

'You never mentioned it. You should have said something.' Helena strove for a natural tone.

Why had he spoken to Aunt Flavia? Why had he gone behind her back to arrange an interview? How much had he told her?

'I am saying something now.' Tullio caught her hand and gave her fingers a squeeze. 'She summoned me. When I was leaving her apartments, Niobe found me and led me to you. From then on, certain other things became more important. You were in no shape to discuss your aunt's health or anything else.'

A queer warm fluttering filled Helena. She wanted to think that somehow her welfare had mattered to him. That he had

come to save her because he cared about her. But then he
moved and she caught sight of his Army belt, hung with a
number of bronzes. Medals won in service of the Senate and
the people of Rome.

She had to remember Tullio had his own reasons, just as
surely as Androceles had his. His concern was not for her as
a person, but as someone who could do something for him.
His sole interest was her ability to deliver the temple to Rome.
That was all. Her heart protested at this bitter thought, but
Helena knew it had to be true.

She listened to Tullio recount his interview. When he had
finished, Helena stood up and walked to where the fountain
bubbled and gurgled. She pressed her hands against the basin.
She had to explain. She had to tell him how powerless she
really was. She could not…she could never take sides against
the seafarers. She turned and he was looking at her with an
expectant expression on his face.

'Now you know,' she said, 'it was a mistake, an error of
judgement. I'd never intended to allow you to disembark. The
sibyl is implacable in her hatred of all things Roman.'

'The goddess moves in mysterious ways, according to
your aunt. It may not have been her intention to have me and
my men housed here, but we are, and we have a part to play.
I know that for a fact. She did not order us out of the temple.'

'I'll need to speak to Aunt Flavia about this.' Helena
adjusted her shawl, hiding her face in its depths. She hated
this feeling of being in charge, everyone coming to her with
their problems and expecting her to solve them, blaming her
when it was not right. 'Her guidance is paramount.'

He crossed the courtyard in a few impatient steps. 'Speak to
your aunt, and you will see. The Fates saved you for a purpose.'

'Save me from what?' Helena drew her eyebrows together. From Kybele's lair? Or from begging him to initiate her into the arts of love? A few more heartbeats and she'd have been more wanton than the priestesses of Aphrodite, the ones who were rumoured to take coin for their favours.

Tullio stood close enough to touch if she put out her hand even the slightest bit. His red cloak brushed her gown and his finger reached out to touch her cheek. It took all her will-power not to turn her face into the palm of his hand, but to stand there unmoving. A quick touch. A lover's touch? Helena's mind shied away from the possibility.

His arm dropped to his side. He cocked an eyebrow as if he knew exactly how rigidly she was holding her body and why.

Warmth crept through her. She should move away, but her feet refused to obey her. He leant forward and his lips touched hers.

The kiss lasted no longer than a butterfly visiting a flower, but a thrill ran throughout her body and set her limbs trembling. The ache from yesterday afternoon returned as if it had never been gone.

'What did you save me from?'

'I think you know what I saved you from.' His voice was all male and doing strange things to her insides. 'I made a promise to you and I intend to keep it.'

'You were right when you said that I was suffering from the after-effects of the herbs. I have a wish to forget my behaviour.'

His fingers lifted her chin and her eyes stared into deep unfathomable pools. 'Who is speaking here—the acolyte or the woman?'

'They are the same person.'

'I wonder. I also wonder if I should try an experiment?' His hand gripped her elbows and pulled her close. She could feel his hard muscles through the material of his tunic. Her hands came up on his chest. She knew she should push him away. Modesty demanded that, but her hands refused to obey and his arms tightened around her. His mouth swooped down and reclaimed hers. At its pressure, her lips opened and she tasted him. She gave a small sigh and surrendered herself to the latest onslaught on her senses.

A pricking at the back of her neck warned her. She jumped back and his arms fell to his side just as the sound of approaching sandals reverberated throughout the courtyard. Helena moved to the other side of the fountain and tried to compose her thoughts.

What next? Her stomach turned over at the thought of being discovered like that. She should feel more alarmed, but all she could think about was his kiss. She tucked a pin more firmly into her hair and avoided catching Tullio's eye.

Androceles burst in the courtyard, closely followed by his son, the Lady Zenobia and various retainers. His lip curled as he saw who the other occupants of the courtyard were.

'It appears the Roman takes the notion of guest quite literally.'

'Helena and I were discussing temple procedure.' Tullio gave an ironic bow. 'I'm a student of religion and religious practices around the Mediterranean. Did you know that libation bowls differ from Spain to Antioch? In Dianium, they are shallower than in Ascalon. Why do you think that is?'

'Libation bowls?' Androceles's mouth hung open and then

shut, giving an impression of a fish. 'Indeed. How fascinating.'

Helena's stomach knotted when she thought how close she had come to being discovered. It must never happen again. To do so, would be to force her to choose. Her hand touched her amulet.

Was it Tullio's intention to make her choose? Was that why he wore a smug expression? She tapped her fingers against the side of her gown.

She offered up a small prayer, then took a deep breath. She would never allow such a situation to arise again. She refused to be used like that, to have her own desires used against her. How like a Roman. His seduction would not work. Whatever else she did, she did not intend to become a traitor to her people.

'Captain Androceles, to what do we owe the pleasure?'

'We seek further interpretation of the Sibyl's prophecy,' the Lady Zenobia said.

'An audience, if that is not too much trouble or disruption to the temple's routine,' Androceles added.

'You should know the sibyl never explains anything.' Helena crossed her arms. She was on firmer ground. She knew where she stood and the proper responses to counter this attack.

'Always her prophecies have been clear, but this one…' Androceles tapped the scroll against his teeth.

'Prophecies are not something you can pick and choose, Captain. Prophecies simply are.'

'Which means, Father,' Kimon broke in, 'she does not intend to explain. You are better off asking the wind than getting one of the temple to clarify. You have said this often enough to me.'

Helena started. She had not expected any help from

Kimon. She thought he would make the same demands as his father. She gave a wary nod.

'But I don't understand this black mist and a thousand voices crying out,' Zenobia whined, her face contorting to an ugly grimace. 'Is this a bad or good omen for me? Is Lichas in danger?'

'Which do you want it to be?' Helena held out both her hands to Zenobia, palms upwards. 'The sibyl only reports her visions. She cannot be held responsible for what you do with them.'

Zenobia sniffed—a loud and long sniff. 'I should have known you would take Flavia's part, Helena. This was not a good idea, Androceles. I thought so at the time. Flavia never gives anything away. She is worse than the oracle at Delphi.'

'Personally I would take it as an omen that Rome will destroy those who attack the mainland,' Tullio drawled. Helena could see the steely glint in his eyes.

'The seafarers don't attack the mainland,' Helena retorted, but she noticed Androceles's slightly uneasy shifting. A shiver passed through her, chilling her to the core for a heartbeat. 'The sibyl has cursed any who might.'

'It is not what the scrolls say.' Zenobia gave Androceles an uneasy glance and drew her skirt away from him. 'There is not a word about Rome in here. And, well…Lichas has nothing to do with those raids. He promised me. He is too frightened of his sister's power.'

Helena felt her mouth go dry. Tullio's guess had some merit. She could see the looks that passed between Androceles, Zenobia and Kimon. Panic from Zenobia, unease from Androceles, but a positively smug expression from Kimon.

What exactly had the House of Androceles been involved in? What if they had begun raiding again? What then?

There were recent whispers in the taverns and among the village women that Androceles and his sons no longer took any notice of the sibyl and her injunction against raiding. They were confident that their donations of grain and other goods would protect them.

All in good time, Helena, was Aunt Flavia's standard answer. Kybele will deal with any who cross her in her own time. Not ours.

She swallowed hard and avoided Tullio's gaze. She had to do something, but not until she had proof. Not until Aunt Flavia had regained her health. Until then she had to hope that it was some ghastly misunderstanding. Her hands smoothed the folds of her gown.

'Is there anything else you want, Captain?'

'I wish to speak with you again about stationing some of my men here.' Androceles dropped his voice and tapped the side of his nose. 'Rumours of the temple staff being molested have reached me.'

'Molested? In what way?' Helena tilted her head, and looked up at the captain through her eyelashes. Someone in the temple was speaking to the seafarers. She needed to find out how much they knew. Or was it, like Tullio's statement, a guess? She could not react. 'Pray tell me.'

'One hears things, Helena.' Androceles bowed. 'Perhaps it would be more appropriate if we spoke without the Roman being present.'

'I think I should hear the accusations against me and my men.' Tullio's voice was quiet. He stepped so he was chest to chest with the seafarer, making the seafarer look small and insignificant. 'Tell me what have we done to dishonour our word.'

'You are Roman and Romans never keep their word.' Androceles picked a piece of thread from the corner of his gold-shot purple cloak. 'Many times, I have heard, the great dictator Sulla spoke out against me and my house, but he never objected to my money helping to fund his election campaigns. He was quite happy to trade with me and purchase my goods. Welcome profit was his motto.'

'Sulla has been dead for these past three years, and little you say about the former dictator would surprise me. He did keep unsavoury friends. I would ask to be judged by a better standard than his.'

'You were acquainted with the man?'

'We were acquainted.'

Androceles sucked his teeth, but said nothing. The pirate captain was deliberately baiting Tullio, but to what purpose? She had to put an end to this.

'Will that be all, Captain? There are rituals to prepare.' Helena placed a hand on her hip. 'I have already tarried here discussing libation bowls for far too long.'

'Perhaps there is more to you than meets the eye. Do give our regards to your aunt. I wait to see if this prophecy proves correct. Black mists in the summer sunshine, indeed!'

With a flourish of cloaks and a stamping of sandals, the company departed. Helena turned towards the hospital and safety.

'There was another reason for his visit.' Tullio's fingers caught her elbow, preventing her from moving. His face had a hard uncompromising look to it. 'Androceles is playing a game. Surely you must see that he is playing the sibyl and the temple as fools.'

'What would you have me do—declare for Rome?'

'Yes.'

The single word fell from his lips and hung in the air between them. Helena's heart shattered. She had thought him different from Kimon or Androceles, but in his own way he sought to control the temple through her.

'That is what this is all about, isn't it?'

His hand released her elbow. Helena thought she detected a slight paling of his features.

'What are you saying, Helena? What precisely are you accusing me of?'

'There are many unanswered questions, Tullio. But Androceles has proved a true friend for many years to this temple. He is a very powerful man. He has the interests of the temple in his heart. His offerings are always large.'

'Androceles is only interested in one thing—himself.'

Helena pushed away the thoughts of the mouldy grain he had foisted on the temple the last time. She had to remember who Tullio was and what he represented. She had come close to forgetting that. She intended to keep it uppermost in her mind from now on.

'You think to lecture me now on my allies?'

'I merely seek to warn you.'

'And he seeks to warn me about you and your intentions. Of the pair, who has proved a better friend to the temple? The seafarer who has brought much needed food and supplies? Or the Roman soldier who is being held here against his will?'

'I believe you should ask your heart why you trusted me with your secret.' His voice was low.

Helena spun around on her heel. 'I panicked. I needed someone to speak to. I made a mistake.'

Tullio's eyes glittered with some suppressed emotion, hard

and uncompromising. 'I suppose you intend to deny I rescued you. I saved your life, Helena.'

Helena wrapped her arms about her waist and bit her lip. She had made another mistake. She should have remembered her aunt's maxim that Romans always require payment. She had thought his soft words were for her alone, but they were for the temple. Her only use to him was the temple. She had wanted to be a woman and he only needed the acolyte.

'You have my gratitude, but you must understand the temple is greater than one person. I have other things to consider. We depend on the seafarers.'

'Give Rome a chance to prove its worth to this sanctuary.' His hand caught her elbow and turned her to him. The intent look in his eyes seemed to pierce her soul. She moved her arm and he released his hand, almost as if it had burnt him. 'We can do much together.'

'You ask too high a price.'

'Very well, my lady, as long as we know who you can trust.' Tullio gave a low bow and was gone.

Helena stared after him. She tried to tell herself that everything would go back to as it had been before, but even that thought did not make her heart lift.

Her only course was to ensure they were never alone again.

Since the encounter in the courtyard, Tullio had seen little of Helena. He tried to tell himself that he was not looking out for her, but he knew he was. He also knew he had allowed his temper to get the better of him. He had been so sure that she was close to declaring for Rome.

She had to see the danger Androceles posed. Danger not only to the temple but to herself. When the pirates discovered the deception, they were bound to react with fury. The only way she could save herself was to ally with Rome. Why did she refuse to see that?

By Jupiter's thunderbolt, he had not saved her from Kybele's lair for her to throw her life away so easily.

It rankled that, whenever he entered a courtyard, she departed without a word. He could not complain that the treatment of his men became worse. It was far better than he could have hoped for. But he missed Helena's rippling laugh and her smile. Although the pirates did nothing, he felt it was the calm before the storm, waiting for Lichas's ship to return.

With each passing day, more and more pirates found an excuse to be in the temple.

'I fear a tempest is brewing, Livius Tullio,' Quintus said three mornings after the courtyard's encounter, when the air felt heavy and sticky. The oppressive heat reflected Tullio's mood.

'Tell me something useful. My tunic has been stuck to my back since I woke this morning.'

'If it is a large storm, then perhaps we should take a chance and make a break for it. The islanders would be otherwise occupied and we could steal a boat...'

Tullio regarded the centurion with distaste. 'We gave our word.'

'A word given to a pirate or his priestess is not worth the breath you waste. Do you think they intend to keep their promises?'

'What do you think will happen to this temple if we try to escape?'

Quintus shrugged. 'It is not my concern.'

'I thought you were sweet on that maid—Galla. You seem to spend a long time chatting about bread-making.'

'My first duty is to Rome,' Quintus blustered. 'While you've been concentrating on the men, I've been discovering how the temple operates. Who really holds power…'

'And have you found out anything useful?'

'The temple revolves around your girlfriend, the sibyl's assistant. She makes all the decisions. Lately she has broken with tradition and is not allowing anyone to have an audience with the sibyl.'

Tullio ground his teeth. Had his interest in Helena been that transparent? He thought he had been discreet. 'I would hold my tongue if I were you, Quintus. You appear to be seeing ghosts where there are none.'

'I was teasing you.' The large soldier clapped his hand against Tullio's shoulder. 'I thought she had possibilities at first, what with you having to see her and all, but lately you have only been concerned with drilling the men. Helena is an attractive woman.'

'There is nothing between us, Quintus,' Tullio said a little more forcefully than necessary. 'There never could be.'

'If I were in your sandals, I'd pursue her.' Quintus rocked backward, looking inordinately pleased with himself.

Belatedly, Tullio remembered the centurion's reputation for practical jokes.

'What did you really want to discuss with me?'

'Our escape plan.'

'We're not escaping, Quintus, not without a map or a compass. Not all the men would make it and I refuse to leave any behind. We have been over and over this. Nothing has happened to change my mind.'

'If you were General Pompey, he'd do it. Why, even young Caesar would have the balls for the task.'

Tullio hooked his thumbs around his belt. He would not rise to the bait. By invoking his rival tribune, Tullio knew Quintus was trying a very crude attempt at manipulation. He felt a muscle jump in his jaw and knew Quintus had nearly succeeded. He hated this inactivity as much as Quintus, if not more.

'I thank the gods that I am not either man, Mustius Quintus. I trust my own judgement. Invoking that glory-hound Pompey or that young upstart Caesar will not move me. And I will remind you that you renewed your oath before we set sail.'

'I know that.' Quintus stood at attention. 'It was my great pleasure to take it for the entire cohort.'

'An oath such as that is not soon tossed away.'

Tullio strode back towards his abandoned game. He felt sorry for the centurion. Captivity was not easy…for anyone. But certain conventions and rules had to be obeyed. None of his men would be left to rot in a pirate's prison while the others made a futile gesture of escape. He wanted his men alive, not massacred.

'If you would just see, sir.' Quintus stepped in front of Tullio. His face took on a wheedling expression. 'I'm positive that it'll be a simple task to work our way down to the harbour. By Jupiter, I am. It will give us a chance to regain our lost honour.'

Honour. There wasn't a breath when that particular virtue was far from his mind. They had lost much honour, but this was not the way to recapture it.

'Do you think the seafarers will let us march down to the docks and commandeer one of their ships?'

'The men are getting restive. It has been nearly two weeks since we arrived on this rock and all we have done is strengthen the temple. We're helping the pirates out. When the time comes, we'll have provided an impenetrable place for their last stand.'

'Are you questioning my judgement, Quintus?' Tullio drew himself up to his full height, towering over the smaller man. Their eyes locked until Quintus looked away.

'Not questioning it exactly, but confused.' The centurion scratched his head. 'I say if I'm right and Neptune brews up a storm with his trident, at the first sign of Jupiter's lightning bolt, we break out through the warehouse and head for the harbour. The seafarers will all run for cover. We take a trireme and are out of here before the seafarers can mount a counter-attack.'

'Have you ever piloted a trireme before? Have the other men? Can you read the stars?' Tullio asked between gritted teeth.

'No, but—'

'Then leave the thinking to me. Your job is to obey orders and get the men ready. When the time comes, we will recapture the standard. I promise you on our sacred Rome.' Tullio pulled his cloak tighter around his body. He glanced up at the thick, ever-blackening clouds. 'Let's get the men under cover. A north wind is starting to pick up. The storm looks about ready to hit.'

Chapter Eleven

'**W**here's Niobe, my Lady Helena? Please, have you seen my sister?'

Helena paused in her examination of wine amphorae and looked up at Niobe's brother, Pius, who was standing in the doorway, wringing his cap with his hands. Her back ached from bending over the amphorae. She needed to determine if any of the cork bungs had started to leak. A job she found difficult to entrust to anyone else, like so many other jobs. And now it was one more thing to add to her hectic day. It was at times like these that Helena vaguely wished she did not have responsibility, that she was an ordinary person without any cares or worries about other people and their problems.

'Niobe will be tending the geese, as she always does.'

'There's a storm brewing, and you know how she hates storms. Last time, she disappeared for two days and I discovered her crouched in a cave, hands over her ears.'

Helena rose and dusted the storeroom dirt off her gown. She pushed an errant lock of hair behind her ear and glanced out of the narrow slit of a window.

When she had arrived at the warehouse, the sky had been a brilliant blue, but now huge dark clouds rolled. She shivered and picked up her discarded shawl and tucked it firmly about her head and shoulders. She wished she had opted for a heavier garment. This one was good for keeping off the sun, but did little to provide any warmth.

The sky had blackened. Helena lit an oil lamp, taking her fire stone from her hanging purse to produce a spark. The lamp flared and provided a golden glow, helping to drive away the storm's darkness. Storms always brought back the memory of that fateful day with her mother.

'Where's that storm blown up from?' She wrinkled her nose and cursed herself for being so unobservant. Steps had to be taken to make the temple safe from a ferocious battering. Last storm but one was when they lost the roof off the goat shed. She tried to think of all the things that had to be accomplished before a storm hit. 'There's so much that needs to be done. Why did no one inform me? Have the guards been alerted?'

'Neptune is not happy with us.' Pius held out his hands. Tears shone in his big eyes. Given his size, it was easy to forget that Pius was closer to being a boy than a man. 'You will help me find my sister, won't you? She worships you, has done ever since you bandaged her prize goose's wing. Even if she is hidden away in one of those caves, she will come out if you call.'

Helena hesitated. She should be supervising the men, but they did know their jobs. Niobe's quick thinking had saved her life. The least she could do was to return the favour.

'We had best check the temple grounds first.'

'She won't be there. I saw her on the way up the mountain

earlier.' Pius twisted his cap. His face wore a pleading, whee-dling expression. 'What will I tell our mother if she is missing again? What will I tell the sibyl? She told me to take extra-special care of Niobe as she was precious to Kybele.'

'It does no harm to look. She might have returned.' Helena placed a hand on Pius's shoulder. 'Don't worry, we'll find her.'

After making sure the guards were doing their duty, Helena began looking for Niobe. She was not in any of her usual places, but some of the geese were milling about. Helena lifted the latch and let them back into the pen. They rushed in with a great honking. She called out, but Niobe did not appear. She glanced up the mountain and thought she saw a red shawl flapping in the distance.

Niobe, it had to be.

The low rumble of thunder resounded in her ears. Helena bit her lip, torn with indecision. Everyone was busy. but what if she asked one of the Romans for help? They were soldiers, surely they would be used to searching for people.

She made a face. It was an excuse—like all the other excuses she had thought up to see Tullio again. She had to stop this. It was simply a sickness that would be cured by time. She had to remember what Captain Androceles had said and what he was capable of doing. No good ever came from being friends with a Roman. The only thing Tullio wanted from her was the one thing she dared not give—the temple's allegiance to Rome.

The red shawl appeared to have stopped, no longer flut-tering in the breeze, urging her onwards.

'Niobe, wait there! I am coming.'

If she hurried, Helena was certain that she could reach

Niobe, and lead her back to the temple's safety before the heavy downpour of rain started. For Niobe, she would brave the mountain during a storm.

This was one problem she'd solve without Tullio's help.

'Have you seen Helena?' Galla asked from the doorway.

Tullio turned from the game of *latrunculi* he was playing with Rufus to look at Galla. He had finally manoeuvred his glass soldiers to within a striking position of Rufus's king. The pieces might not be conventional, but the game was no less intriguing for that. Above all, it occupied his mind.

Quintus and the other men stood about in groups, playing knucklebones, swapping impossibly tall tales, but behaving themselves.

The maidservant had a worried expression on her face. He pushed back his stool and crossed the stone floor to her. Quintus was only a few steps behind him.

'Is there some problem, Galla?' Tullio asked.

'Neptune is brewing a terrible storm with his trident and the sibyl is asking for Helena.' Galla wrung her hands. 'She wants to know if all the preparations have been made. Last time there was a storm, Helena forgot to instruct the guards to remove the statues of Kybele from the courtyard, and one of them toppled. Unlike Helena to leave like this. She should have told someone where she was going.'

Tullio laid a hand on her shoulder and felt the tension reverberate through the maid. Something was wrong with Helena. His insides twisted. Too clearly he remembered her body on the cave floor. A little while longer and he might have been too late.

Had she attempted to contact the goddess again? Surely she was not so foolish. She had barely recovered from the last time.

'Have any more questions been asked of the sibyl?'

She shook her head slowly. 'It would not matter if they had. Helena has nothing to do with the sibyl's communications with Kybele. She deals only with the day-to-day running of the temple.'

Who did this woman think sent the prophecy to Androceles?

It angered him that Helena's contribution was so little acknowledged. She ran the temple, answering questions, making sure the food was there for those villagers, and the sibyl simply sat in her room and communed with the goddess. Without Helena, this temple would be nothing. However, it was not worth an argument. Instead, he nodded. 'It does relieve me to hear that.'

'Ever since she was a child, Helena has hated thunderstorms.' Galla cast him a sharp look. 'She used to wake, screaming and bathed in sweat at the slightest rumble. It would take hours, and sometimes the sibyl would be woken.'

'Have you checked everywhere?' Tullio fought to keep his irritation under control. Helena needed more than begrudging comfort. She deserved more than that. She was a person, not a machine to help the temple function better. 'Is there somewhere else she could have gone?'

'I have looked everywhere I can think of, from the kitchen to the store rooms and even the sacred places of the temple. I thought perhaps she might have come to see the patients. Helena takes her duties seriously.'

'We are all well recovered now,' Rufus broke in, 'thanks to her ministrations. Once we get more stone, I'm joining the work detail.'

'We will discuss that later, Rufus.' Tullio laid a hand on

his old friend's shoulder. Now was not the time to be pressing their demands. 'Helena appears to be missing.'

The older woman's face crumpled and a sigh escaped her throat. Quintus moved quickly and led her to a stool. She leant her head against Quintus's shoulder and Tullio wondered if there was more to Quintus's interest in her than simply exchanging recipes for fig bread.

'I am worried that some harm has befallen her. The sibyl was most insistent…'

'Would you like us to search for her?' Tullio knelt down so that his face was on the same level as the maid's. He took her hand in his and made sure his voice was even. The ice cold from her palm seeped up his fingers. 'Where should we start?'

'The guards and I searched within the grounds.'

'But what about outside the grounds? She may have gone to the harbour. My men and I could check.'

'I can't let you do that. Helena gave the order that you remain within the temple's ground.' Galla withdrew her hand and stood up. She paced the room. Tears sparkled in her eyes.

Quintus patted her awkwardly on her shoulder. Tullio had never seen his centurion look so helpless or uncomfortable. The man who had led the last charge against the pirates felled by the possibility of a few tears.

'Is there any reason why she might have gone down to the village?' Tullio asked.

'The captain of the guard would have seen her go. I asked and no one has seen her since midday.' Galla gave a glance over her shoulder before dropping her voice. 'I'm so afraid that she has gone up the mountain and something has happened to her. They say that is how her mother perished—

hit by Jupiter's lightning bolt when Helena was naught but a wee thing.'

'Knowledge of that caused her fear?'

'Oh, no. She was discovered next to her mother. The tree that crushed the Lady Lydia also crushed Helena's little finger, so the captain of the guard told me.'

Tullio's stomach tightened. After experiencing that, all Helena had was grudging sympathy. No wonder she tried to stand alone. He wanted to make sure she knew that she no longer had to. She could turn to him for comfort. He would protect her if he could, as he had done when he discovered her in the cave.

'Did you question Niobe? The little goose girl seems always to know where Helena is.' Tullio forced his mind away from the memory of carrying Helena's nearly lifeless body. 'If anyone knows, it will be Niobe.'

'Niobe is at home today with her mother. I already had the captain of the guards check. Her brother thought the girl missing, but discovered her making pastry.'

Tullio pressed his fingertips together. Here might be a way to turn Quintus's thoughts from escape. He could amuse Galla for a short while Tullio discovered where Helena had gone. A neat solution to the problem. 'Will you permit me to go search for Helena? Leaving my men here as a guarantee.'

He heard protesting noises from the men, in particular Quintus, but silenced them with a look. He refused to have discipline slip. It was a chance to prove his worth to Galla, Helena and the sibyl.

'Would you do that? Would you really do that?' Galla's eyes shone. 'Because of the Lady Lydia's death, no one dares brave the mountain during a storm unless they are forced to.'

'Without hesitation.' Tullio tried to ignore the fear growing in his belly. The memory of Helena's white-robed body in the prophecy cave was too vivid. He needed to find her and convince himself that she was safe. He wanted to discover why she had taken a chance like this, why she had taken the risk. 'If she is on the mountain, I'll find Helena and bring her back unharmed.'

'Then find her.' Galla clasped his hand with a tight grip. 'Find Helena and bring her back here safely. May Kybele and the rest of the gods go with you.'

'Niobe! It's me, Helena. Come out and we will go to your mother. Niobe, I am here to help you!'

The first large drops of rain splattered Helena's face. She paused in her climb up the mountain to readjust her shawl more firmly about her head and shoulders. Sweat plastered her hair against her forehead. The temple complex below her looked like a collection of statuettes. She had climbed far and fast, but still no Niobe.

Niobe's beloved red shawl had clung to a thorn bush halfway up the mountain, fluttering in the breeze, but there was no sign of the goose girl. Helena tried to keep the worry from rising as she scrambled across a dry stream bed. At least, she did not have to be concerned about Niobe being swept away. The rain had not begun to fall, and Niobe was sensible. She knew how swiftly the streams became torrents.

She had to think. No one had ever just disappeared on the island. They were safe from the kidnappings that plagued other communities. The seafarers respected the sanctity of this place. Niobe was somewhere on this mountain.

The wind whipped her shawl across Helena's mouth. With

impatient fingers, she pushed it away. She had to find Niobe before the storm broke. She refused to leave the girl out here defenceless.

The sky had turned an inky black now, making it seem more like the late evening rather than mid-afternoon. Helena knew how the gods disliked anyone to be on the mountain during a storm.

Perhaps Niobe had returned to the temple by another way. Helena put her hands on her knees and drew another breath.

Her throat ached from calling Niobe's name. She tried once more but there was no answer.

Helena struggled through two thorn bushes to reach the small trickle of water in another stream bed. She scooped up some water and quenched her thirst. The ice-cold water restored some small measure of calm.

Helena rocked back on her ankles, trying to think logically. Niobe had never come to any harm on the mountain, even when she disappeared during that storm. Aunt Flavia had said it was because she had Kybele's special protection.

She had to be somewhere, waiting for the worst of the storm to pass. Helena stood up and took one last look around. No sign of any living creature.

The rain started to fall in earnest, coming down in a sheet of water. Helena readjusted her shawl so that her head was better covered. She could feel the cold drops as they seeped through her gown.

No doubt Galla would fuss and force her to drink a cup of hot mulsum wine when she returned. She could almost taste the honey-sweetened drink now and feel how good the warm cup would be in her hands.

Niobe's quick thinking had saved her a few days ago, and Helena needed to repay the favour. She had to keep looking. Just one more circuit of the hillside…

A large clap of thunder resounded overhead as a bolt of lightning sliced through the sky, throwing everything into a queer white brilliance.

Helena froze.

The memory of the black mist from Kybele's lair crept over her and she wished she was not alone. It was dark. Too dark. It was easy to imagine the Harpies and Furies rising in their chariots, looking for souls to snatch.

The chill she remembered from the cave began to curl its way around her insides again. She felt its weight pressing down on her.

Helena shook her head to clear it. She locked her hands together and then released them. The action restored some small measure of calm. She was not in the cave. What had caused her to faint then was bad air. The air was clear and fresh here.

She filled her lungs and then expelled a long breath.

She was safe in the open.

Ahead of her was the twisted pine tree, the one half-burnt from a lightning strike years ago. The black charred remains had weathered to a silver grey. Memories of the last time she had been caught out in a thunderstorm swamped her. It became difficult to put one foot in front of the other without thinking about what had happened, and her mother's screams.

She glanced back at the temple. Its tiled roof and white building were hardly visible through the driving rain.

It was at least a mile away now, and there was very little likelihood that Jupiter's next thunderbolt would miss.

Jupiter never missed his targets—humans who thought they could consort with gods. Humans like her mother.

Her hand clutched her throat as she sought to control the rising sense of panic. She couldn't stay out in the open. She had to shelter away from the storm and then she'd return to the temple. When sunlight returned, her fancies would fade.

Niobe would understand.

Helena scrambled a few hundred yards more up the mountain to a shallow cave. The bushes in front of the cave provided some measure of protection. Gratefully she sank to the dry ground and wrapped her arms about her knees, trying not to wince at the rumbles of thunder, trying not to think about what had happened the last time she was out in a thunderstorm.

She blew on her hands and shook the raindrops from her shawl. She gathered a few bits of dry wood and leaves and stared at the meagre pile. The fuel would last barely an hour and then she'd be forced to go out into the storm to gather more wood.

She'd wait until the fire became a necessity rather than a convenience. In the meantime, she'd recite the first six rituals of Kybele as well as going over the duties she'd need to carry out when she arrived back at the temple. Her hand grasped her set of knucklebones and she threw them three times out of habit. Would Kybele grant her a perfect Venus?

Helena gave a wry smile. All of the throws had come up dogs. What more could she expect—playing *tali* with her forecasting stones?

She pocketed the four pieces of rock crystal and concentrated instead on the tasks she'd have to do when she returned. She had finished with the amphorae, but there was still the incense to see to. Little things to keep her busy… But her eyes kept straying back to the mouth of the cave and the flashes of lightning she could see as Jupiter threw each one.

What had this island done to deserve Jupiter's wrath?

'Helena! Helena!'

At first, Helena ignored the shouts, dismissing it as no more than the wind through the trees working on her over-active imagination.

Who could be calling her out in the wind and the rain? No one knew she was here, and no one would look for her. The fear of the storm Furies ran deep within the island. Every child had heard the whispered tales. Three shepherds were taken in a storm last winter, swept away on a sudden flash flood.

Would anyone care that she was out here? Alone? Had anyone even noticed?

She swallowed hard at the thought.

A tiny voice in the back of her mind whispered—liar.

She remembered how Tullio had rescued her from Kybele's sacred space the other day. He had not hesitated then. She gave a half-smile. Only a lovesick fool would imagine such a thing, and she was anything but that. She sat still and willed the wind's voice to go away.

She tossed the knucklebones one more time. Venus.

The voice came closer and she realised with a start that it was Tullio. She heard him call her name again and moved closer to the entrance, peering out through the rain. The wind whipped her hair in front of her face. Impatiently, she pushed it away. He should be back in the temple, not ranging the mountain. She had given orders and he had ignored them. She stepped out into the storm.

Tullio had paused about four hundred yards down the slope, sandalled feet planted between two rocks. The rain had plastered his dark hair to his head. His tunic and cloak dripped with water. He looked so real and solid that Helena's heart skipped a beat. She called his name, but he gave no sign of having heard her.

He raised his hands to his mouth and called her name again.

At the same instant, the sky became white-blue with a lightning bolt. She heard the deafening crack of thunder and saw the forked tree that had been set ablaze only a few feet from where Tullio stood.

Tullio paled, but he did not run or cower. He called her name again, more loudly this time so that the very rocks rang with it.

Helena grabbed the side of the cave and refused to panic. She started forward until she was no more than a few yards above him, separated by a slope and the small stream bed.

'Tullio, up here. I'm up here.'

She waited and watched as he seemed not to notice. He half-turned to go back down the mountain and called her name once more. She could hear the longing in it.

Helena summoned all her strength. She made her voice carry and prepared herself to run to him if necessary.

'Tullio, here I am. Helena.'

This time, he heard her, waved to her and started to climb towards her. He stepped into the disused stream bed, bending his head to avoid an overhanging sapling.

Thunder reverberated above them as a bolt of lightning struck the ground.

Helena heard a roaring sound and screamed a warning.

She rushed forward in time to see him lose his footing as the muddy waters broke through a barrier of sticks and rock. He reached up, made a grab for the saplings and found a handhold, clinging on. The tree bent double from the combination of Tullio and the dark swirling water.

Helena scrambled down the bank, half-walking, half-falling as the rain lashed with cold tendrils across her face. Her hand closed on a large branch and she held it out to him.

It didn't quite reach and Helena uttered a curse.

The water foamed and swirled white against brown in the darkened world. Tullio's cloak flowed behind him, a thick black on the water. She could see the veins sticking out on his forearms as he struggled to keep hold. The sound of the rushing water filled her ears.

The sapling he clutched bent under his weight, becoming ready to snap. There was a distinct creak of wood. Then it was gone. Tullio flailed his arms, and grasped another sapling a few hundred yards away.

Helena raced along the bank. He was closer this time. She lay flat on the bank, and held out the branch as close as she dared. If he would lunge forward, she knew she could save him.

She refused to think about the men who had been swept to their death in the last flash flood. Kybele's judgement, her aunt said.

'Here, grab this.'

He gave her a furious look. He gestured with his head, not releasing his grip on the tree. The water kept rising.

'Get back. The bank could go.'

'I'm not leaving.' She braced her feet against two rocks and leaned further out. This time, the branch touched his shoulder. 'If you take this, I can pull you to safety.'

'You will be swept away with me.'

'Tullio, you must try.'

Time slowed.

She watched as he let go of the tree with one hand and she felt his weight burden the branch. So heavy, she nearly dropped her end.

She grasped it with both hands and tried to pull backwards. Nothing.

'Hang on, Helena.'

'Oh, Tullio, I can't.'

Her hands started to slip on the wet wood. The rain grew thicker. A bolt of lightning sliced through the sky and showed Tullio's white face as he battled for footing. Her arms screamed with pain and exhaustion.

She had to hang on.

Her shoulders ached until she thought she'd have to let go. The branch started to slip from her grasp. Hand over hand, Tullio climbed forward.

Suddenly, the branch felt light and Tullio dropped beside her. His curly black hair was plastered against his head. Rain and river water dripped off his body, but he was alive.

Helena collapsed against the rock. He was alive. She wanted to touch to make sure he was real, but she didn't dare. There was too much between them. She contented herself with allowing her eyes to devour him.

When the rain started dripping off her nose, she became aware that she should do something, say something. They could not stay here for ever, staring at each other.

'What are you doing here?'

'Looking for you.'

Tullio moved within touching distance of Helena, his eyes

feasting on the way her wet gown moulded to her curves. He didn't want to think how close he had come to being swept away.

She had risked her own life to save his. He tried and failed to think of another woman who would have done that.

The damp had made her hair curl and little ringlets framed her face. He had spent the last hour imagining her injured or worse and she was fine. He wanted to crush her to him and throttle her at the same time. She could have been the one caught in the water. She could have been swept to her death or hit with one of Jupiter's bolts. How dare she go off without telling anyone? Particularly after what had happened back at the temple.

'Is this another one of your duties? What do you think you are doing?' The words were out of his mouth before he had time to think. A sharp intake of breath showed his remark had struck a raw nerve.

'I have just rescued you,' Helena replied. 'The very least I expected was a word of thanks.'

'Thank you.' Tullio wiped the wet strands off his forehead. 'Galla is frantic with worry. I volunteered to search the mountain for you.'

'I went looking for Niobe. She is lost.' She placed her hands on her hips. 'Someone had to find her and the guards were too busy making the temple safe. Galla should know I can take care of myself.'

'You could have come to me,' he said quietly. 'My men and I would have helped.'

'There wasn't time.' She held out a red shawl. He could see the frightened look in her eyes. 'I spotted this blowing in the wind. I wanted to catch her before she wandered further away.

But I can't find her anywhere. I went in circles, calling until my voice was hoarse. Then the full force of the storm hit and I had to take shelter. I only hope she is safe and dry. Not out there.'

She nodded towards the flooded river, running in full spate.

'She is with her mother. One of the guards found her and brought her back. Last seen, she was happily making pastry.'

'You do not know how much that means to me. I was so…so worried.'

Her shoulders sagged with relief and a small smile tugged at the corner of her mouth. Tullio forced his hands to curl around his belt, rather than pull her into his arms.

'All this could have been avoided if you had consulted with someone,' he said, watching her rearrange her sodden shawl.

'How did you know where to look for me?'

He shrugged, and tore his mind from his frantic scrambling over the rocks. His legs bore bloody scratches from thorn bushes. Tomorrow they would itch and he would curse, but now nothing mattered except Helena was safe. 'Instinct. Galla was frightened for you.'

'She worries too much. I can take care of myself.' Helena's laugh sounded hollow and Tullio wondered who she was trying to convince. 'No one should be scared of a little thunder and lightning.'

'I have known grown men to cower in their beds when Jupiter becomes angry and starts to throw his lightning bolts.'

Another thunderclap reverberated overhead. Helena jumped and wrapped her arms about her middle. 'I was once caught in a storm.'

Tullio resisted the urge to draw her into his arms. If she

was to trust him, she had to turn to him. His ex-wife's accusation of being too ready to fight other people's battles still rang in his ears. Before he acted, he needed Helena's trust. 'Was the storm as bad as this?'

Chapter Twelve

Helena stared at the rain striking the swollen river rather than looking at Tullio's face. It mattered that he had not laughed at her or tried to make her forget her fear with false jollity. Long years of practice and her aunts' attitude towards her mother made her wary, but she had to explain.

'My mother and I were out walking, and the thunder came. My mother had been laughing about something, I remember that.' The words came haltingly at first, but picked up speed as she went on. 'She let go of my hand so I could pick some flowers, the tiny white ones you find dotted among the rocks. She was going to make me a crown. Then there was a flash of bright light. Later I learnt a lightning bolt hit my mother. She died instantly. They said it was divine retribution for her misdeeds.'

'What misdeeds?' He had not moved, but she could see the droplets of water gathering on his tunic. 'Is that why the temple changed allegiance to Kybele?'

'You know that!' Helena stared open mouthed. Sometimes Tullio appeared to be in communication with the gods.

'I notice things.' He gave a half-smile. 'The friezes with the snakes on the hospital walls, the statues with their inscriptions altered and the sibyl's reputation as a healer. Not difficult to figure out. Twinned snakes belong to one god—Aesculapius. Why did it happen? The usual story of the god deserting the island, not answering prayers?'

'My mother had me and the god Aesculapius stopped speaking to her,' Helena said in a small voice. 'She was supposed to be leading her people, but she had me.'

'And this is a crime? I think any mother would be proud to have a daughter as clever and quick thinking as you.'

'Not always, but Zenobia claimed she had lost her powers, brought disgrace on this island. She had a great reputation as a healer and she threw it all away for the sake of a man who deserted her and the child she bore. Zenobia demanded we worship her goddess, and Aunt Flavia agreed. In a dream, Kybele came to her and she started to prophesy. That is what the Lady Zenobia told me. Aunt Flavia refuses to discuss it.'

'Is there somewhere dry we can speak of this?' Tullio sneezed and then gave a rueful smile. 'We should take cover.'

'There is a dry cave a little way from here. I was waiting there when I heard you call. The river is too high to cross. It should have subsided in the morning.'

They walked along in silence for a while. Every now and then Helena risked a glance at Tullio, but his face gave no clue. She wondered if he'd draw away. Those who heard her mother's story always did. She could clearly remember the taunts of Zenobia's daughters until Aunt Flavia silenced them. When she stumbled, his fingers, warm and firm despite the rain, caught her elbow and held her upright.

'Did you ever see your father?' Tullio asked as they ducked inside the cave.

'When he found out my mother was pregnant, he left.' Helena flinched as she remembered the day Zenobia told her the story, her eighth birthday, the gleam of triumph in the older woman's eyes and the giggles from her cousins. 'My birth caused disaster for the island.'

'But your aunt, the sibyl, took you in. If she had felt that way, she would never have had you for her assistant.'

'Aunt Flavia made a promise to my mother.' Helena ignored the sudden lump in her throat. It was hard to speak of such things, but she felt Tullio needed to understand. 'Aunt Flavia always keeps her word. She has endured many things for that pledge.'

'Whatever the sibyl has done, you have given back a thousandfold. My men and I will long remember your kindness and your courage.'

Helena grasped her Kybele amulet. She should make a joking remark, something light, but the words died on her lips as she saw his intent face.

She heard her breath go in and out several times as she stared at him.

Tullio moved towards her. His hand traced the line of her jaw, sending tingles along it. Helena shivered, but not from the cold. His hand captured hers and brought it to his lips. The coldness of the rainwater contrasted with their warmth.

Out here she had felt so alone, but now she knew, within his arms, there would be a measure of peace. It did not matter that this man was supposed to be her enemy. It only mattered that he was here, with her, now.

He made no move to touch her further, but stood still and

upright. A muscle jumped in his cheek as her hand stroked it. She gave into temptation and laid her head against his chest. Immediately his arms came around her and held her tight.

'Thank you for coming to rescue me, even if I didn't know I needed rescuing.'

'And thank you for rescuing me. I didn't fancy spending a night clinging to a branch.' His fingers lifted her chin so that she stared into his deep brown eyes. 'I wanted to make sure you were safe. I needed to know you were safe. Do you understand that?'

'Yes.'

He crushed her to him as if he were afraid that she would somehow vanish in the rain, or disappear with the next clap of thunder. The strength in his arms caused her heart to soar. He had come searching for her. He knew the risk and he had still come. Maybe he did care about her. More likely he was worried without her, the seafarers would control the temple.

Helena broke away from his grasp. 'You're wet. I should start a fire.'

'That is one possibility.'

'It is you who will take harm from the cold. You could have drowned in that flood.'

'But I didn't. Someone has to look out for you, Helena.'

She busied her hands with the twigs and bits of branches she had collected for a fire. Then she struck one of her fire stones, created a spark and the old wood burst into flame. She sat back on her heels. She didn't always look after other people. He made it sound as if there was something wrong with that.

'There was no need,' she said around the lump in her

throat. 'As you can see, I am perfectly capable of looking after myself. I've done so for years.'

'There was every need, Helena.' His hand reached out and touched her shoulder. Brief, gentle, but filling her with warmth. 'You spend so much time sorting out other people's problems that I wonder if you ever see the danger you are in.'

'I'm not in any danger.' Helena pushed away the thoughts of Androceles and his designs on the temple. These were problems she'd think about tomorrow, concerns she refused to share with Tullio. 'Not any physical danger.'

'I had to be sure.'

He put both his hands on either side of her face, not with any force, but a gentle caress. A caress that sent a deepening warmth throughout her body.

All she could do was nod and hope he understood.

He lowered his face to hers and their lips touched. He kissed her forehead, her eyes, back to her mouth. Helena forgot everything—all her thoughts about the temple, the problems with the pirates, the storm—everything but the sensation of his lips.

She shivered. He pulled back. His eyebrows drew together in frown and he eased the shawl from her shoulders.

'You will catch a cold.'

'It doesn't matter, the damp makes no difference,' she said with a smile and pressed closer. She ran her hands down the length of his arm, feeling his strength under the pads of her fingers.

'Let me take off my cloak and yours.'

With one movement, the heavy woollen cloaks dropped to the ground. He stood in front of her, dressed in his damp tunic that hugged his skin. He reached down and undid his sandals, revealing the full length of his muscular leg. Helena feasted her eyes.

It seemed as if he were holding himself in check.

'Do you understand what you are saying, Helena? If we continue, I might not be able to stop.'

Stop? She had no desire for him to stop. She wanted to feel the sensations that had coursed through her after he rescued her from the black mist. To make sure he was real and here with her. She knew she had lied to herself that those things were unimportant.

'I do.' Her hand curled around his neck and brought his face level to hers. 'Indeed I do.'

Their lips met, clung. She brought her hands around his body. Her breasts pressed against the wall of his chest. She could feel the hard length of him against her.

When she moved slightly, it grew harder. His hands cupped around her buttocks, travelled up to her waist and pulled her more firmly against him. Sensations of warmth radiated out from her centre, hotter than the fire that crackled behind them.

A hunger within her grew, fuelled by the sensations racking her body. She heard him groan in the back of his throat. His lips travelled down her neck, making lines of fire to the hollow of her throat. His hand went to her shoulder and moved her gown, one finger running along the length of her collarbone. He caught a drop of water from the hollow of her throat and brought it to his lips.

'My dreams have been full of you,' he rasped.

Then his hands ran lightly over her gown, shaping her curves, pausing to encircle and tease her breasts, and all the while, the hardness of him pressed against the apex of her legs.

How long they stood, his hand drawing circles on her back, she didn't know. All she knew was the wonderful sense of warmth radiating out all over her.

Her gown felt heavy, the rain running off it to make puddles at her feet. Her hand plucked at the brooches that held her gown, undid them and she allowed the gown to drop to the floor of the cave to join the cloaks with a soft whoosh. He eased the under-tunic off her shoulders and that fell to the ground as well.

Now she was only clothed in her breast band.

She paused, uncertain of his reaction, but his eyes lit a renewed fire.

His hands ran down her body, caressing her skin as if she was made of the most precious glass, drawing circles of fire on it. Where his fingers went, his lips and tongue followed.

No one had said that the touch of a man would do this to her insides. Helena remembered the gossip of the village girls and her cousins—how they said that this was something to be feared. She felt no fear.

The lashing of the rain and the intermittent rumble of thunder no longer scared her. It seemed to urge her onwards, towards this man and her destiny. This was what she was born for—to feel his touch, breath his scent and taste his mouth.

Her hand touched his belt, hesitated.

Would he think her too bold?

Would he withdraw as he had done after the cave? She couldn't bear rejection a second time.

He pulled away and looked at her with gleaming passion-filled eyes. Helena knew she should blush, lower her head, but she found she didn't want to. She wanted to look on him as he looked on her. She wanted to see the ripples of muscles and the faint dusting of hair on his chest that went to a single line, pointing ever downwards towards the essence of him.

'Do you understand what you are doing to me?'

'Please, Tullio.'

She felt her knees tremble and knew she could no longer stand. To steady herself, her hands reached out and grasped his tunic. She had no wish to be a clinging vine to his oak, but she had no choice. Her legs threatened to give way.

He eased her back down on to the discarded clothes.

She watched him loom over her. Large, masculine, but moving with an easy, almost lazy grace. He discarded his tunic, allowed it to fall to the ground, then his loincloth. His naked body was fully revealed for her. The light from the embers cast shadows on the golden skin. It was how she remembered him. Sculpted like marble, yet wonderfully alive and warm. She glanced down and saw him, proud and hard. Beautiful.

Her tongue moistened her lips.

He was looking at her with a question in his eyes. She nodded, reached up towards him and it seemed to satisfy him.

His hands went to her breast band and pushed down, unravelling it until the tight rose-tipped buds of her nipples were revealed. He bent his head and lapped at each one. Fresh sensations washed through her. She was new made for him. Her body arched and cried out for his tongue. She wanted to feel his skin against hers.

His knee parted her legs and her body bucked against the firm muscle. She wanted to feel all of him, needed to feel him. She moaned in the back of her throat and her head thrashed from side to side.

Overhead, a huge crash of thunder.

She cried out, and felt his finger slip inside her, giving her some relief. In and out. Not enough. The fire within her grew wilder with each touch, consuming her being.

More. Her hands pulled him upwards, and she felt his full body against hers. Her hips lifted as the tip of him nudged the summit of her thighs, hot and hard, pushing them apart.

She stiffened, drew back. How could she tell him of her sudden fear?

Without saying anything, he seemed to understand. He stroked her hair, smoothing it back from her forehead. His lips brushed her skin. A light feathery touch, but enough to make her hips drive upwards, longing for him to make her feel as if she were a part of something.

'It will hurt for but an instant, then there will be pleasure. You will see. I will go as gently as I can.'

She nodded, not really understanding. Her body demanded more. She wanted to be one with him.

She gasped as he entered her. Pain coursed through her, sudden and unexpected in its sharpness. She stiffened, but her insides stretched, grew to accommodate the length of him. He lay still, embedded in her, a very masculine smile on his face. His hand smoothed the hair off her forehead.

'No more pain now.'

She hesitated, uncertain if she should believe him. He was inside her. She wanted more. Her body was driving her onwards.

He began to move gently at first. She opened her legs, longing to feel him deeper and then her hips began to move with an age-old instinct.

Slowly, then faster, until the world around her exploded in a rain of stars.

* * *

A shaft of sunlight pierced Helena's eyes. She wrinkled her nose and tried to move away from the bright light. Only then did she realise that she was not lying in her comfortable bed, but that her ear was pressed against Tullio's massive chest, the steady drum of his heart filled her hearing and her legs were entwined with his.

Cautiously, she opened her eyes and lifted her head. The cool morning air fanned her face.

'Good morning.' His voice rumbled in her ear. His hand ran down her back, sending pleasant tingles throughout her body. 'Surely you don't have to get up yet. You can rest a while longer.'

'The temple will be waking. They will be wondering where I am.'

'There is that.' He laced his hands through her hair, drawing it down, making a curtain between them.

Helena raised herself up and instantly his arms released her. She shivered and reached for her discarded clothes.

'I think it best if I get back. There will be storm damage. Someone will need to be responsible.'

'As my lady wishes.' He made no move from the make-shift pallet. She wished he'd say something more, but he merely looked at her with a raised eyebrow.

A faint ache was between her thighs when she moved. She swallowed hard, remembering his words of last night.

No more pain. How wrong he was. How typically Roman.

Roman—the word resounded in her mind, reminding her that he would not stay for ever, and that Roman promises had never done any of her people any good.

How could she have forgotten?

If the seafarers knew, they would see her liaison with Tullio as a betrayal. She would be branded a traitor. But she had betrayed nothing, except her heart.

Thoughts buzzed through her brain as a swarm of bees might circle the garden on a hot June day, filling the air with their wing beats.

How long had he been awake? How long had he been watching her? Had he liked what he had seen? Had he enjoyed their time together? He had said that he was divorced, unattached. However, nothing approaching love had been spoken between them. They had never discussed the future. What did he think of her?

Her hands stilled on her breast band. It bothered her that she needed his approval. It made her feel vulnerable, exposed.

She finished dressing quickly, hardly daring to look at his glorious body. If she took one peep, she'd be back in his arms, begging for his kiss.

Had she spent the night in his arms? Their passion seemed to be something out of time. Her mouth tasted bitter. There could be no hope for them. How could there be? Aunt Flavia might excuse one night of passion, but any more and she'd have to leave the temple. She'd be an outcast among her people.

If a child should result from last night? Helena swallowed hard. There were ways of preventing a womb from quickening. She had never thought of using them. She'd have to drink raspberry leaf tea from now until her next menses and hope.

Aunt Flavia had a raspberry bush brought from Greece for such a purpose ten years ago. Helena could still remember Zenobia's scandalised intake of breath, but even she had to admit the berries were sweet.

Helena rubbed the back of her neck. She had deluded herself before about Tullio. Too many obstacles lay between them.

'So that is it. You are leaving without kissing me good morning.'

Helena forced her fingers to finish fastening her brooch before she turned back.

Tullio was half-raised on an elbow. His magnificent chest where she had rested her head was uncovered. The only concession to modesty was his loin cloth draped over his lower half. Helena's knees weakened and she longed to sink back down, to taste his rain-soaked skin again. She drew on all her training to resist.

'I have duties to attend to. Morning is the temple's busiest time.'

With one fluid movement, he stood up, filling the cave. His fingers caught her arm, turned her towards him and his eyes searched her face. Helena forced her features to remain impassive.

'Is that all—you have duties to attend to?'

'What do you want me to say? What passed between us was very instructive.'

'Instructive?' He gave a short laugh. 'I have heard it called many things in my life, but instructive is new.'

'What would you call it?'

His fingers traced the line of her jaw, sending sharp tingles radiating outwards, making her want to turn her face towards him and to experience that intense moment of pleasure again.

The harsh outline of his mouth softened. Helena swayed towards him. Her lips felt full, her eyelids heavy. A half-smile appeared on his face, his eyes assessing as if he knew her words were but a defence.

'I expect you are correct. Instructive is as good a word as any.'

Helena stared out at the azure blue sky, a sky so bright, it hurt her eyes. 'It appears there is sunlight after the storm.'

'If you wait, I will come with you.'

'You don't need to do that. I am perfectly capable of finding my own way back to the temple.'

She wanted to go back to that time not so very long ago when she had listened to the thudding of his heart and felt safe. It all seemed wrong now. Unsettled.

'I know you can find your way back there. I simply wanted to go with you.'

'Why?'

'To make sure you didn't stumble.' His tone was light and his eyes twinkled as if they were sharing some intimate joke.

'Or to make sure somehow you bound me to Rome?' The words slipped out of her lips and hung between them.

His face became hard. Gone was the lover and in his place was the Roman tribune, a man used to command. 'What passed between us last night passed between two people, Helena, not two countries. There was no one there but you and I. Maybe some day you will learn the difference.'

Helena clamped her mouth shut. She started off down the mountainside, with short sharp strides, not caring if the thorn bushes bit into her ankles or not.

Tullio let Helena go, despite the temptation to hold her back. He watched her dark hair stream down her back as she picked her way among the rocks and bracken. The storm of yesterday had cleared the air and, despite the hour, he could already feel the heat beginning to hang heavy, drying the puddles of water. She missed her footing on a rock and he was by her side before she could fully right herself. His fingers touched her elbow, steadying her. If she'd have pulled away again, he'd have let her go, but she didn't move. She stared at his fingers.

'When I need your help, I'll ask for it. I am perfectly capable of walking down this slope on my own.'

'Sometimes, everyone needs a little help from their friends.'

'You are not my friend.'

A stab of disappointment coursed through Tullio.

'Your lover, then.'

There was a sharp intake of breath. He wondered if she'd deny that as well. He knew the sigh of pleasure he had heard after they made love was genuine, but he wanted to hear her say it. He needed to hear her confess that she had experienced delight. That she would do so again.

'That was a mistake.' The colour rose even higher in her cheeks, but she made no attempt to move her arm. 'It should never have happened.'

'If you think…' Tullio said, changing the pressure on her elbow slightly so it became a caress. The skin under his fingers prickled with pleasure. Her body wanted his touch, but he wanted more than that. 'If you think grinding out a few sentences between gritted teeth about how this was a mistake means that we are finished, you are wrong. We have barely begun. There is nothing wrong with what we did, Helena.'

She pulled away, opening and closing her mouth several times, but no sound issued forth. He waited, listening to her breathing and to the early morning chorus of birds.

'I have to get back to my people, see what damage the storm wrought.' Her hands combed through her sleep-tousled hair, straightening it. Her face took on an earnest expression. 'I need to see if my aunt was disturbed. The last storm caused the roof of the temple to blow off.'

'If you need any help, you only have to ask.' He looped his fingers through his belt.

'I know.' She made no move to go, but rearranged her shawl. 'What happened back there…it has no bearing on my future.'

Tullio refrained from answering. If he had anything to do about it, it would, but for now he'd play a waiting game. The time for Helena to choose was not now. It bothered him that her choice should matter, but it did. He wanted to give her the opportunity to make the right decision for both her and her people.

He caught her fingers with his hand and she did not pull away, rather her fingers tightened around his. They walked down the slope together, slowly. Somehow, he swore, he would find a way to make this woman his own not just for the night, but for ever.

At the bottom of the slope, Galla stood, wringing her hands and wiping her face with the end of her shawl. The lines of her face seemed more pronounced than ever. Every so often she glanced over her shoulder with an increasingly worried expression. Helena quickened her footsteps and called out.

When Galla saw them, she started forward with a cry. Helena dropped his hand and ran towards her. They met halfway and Galla hugged Helena fiercely.

'As you can see, I've returned Helena safe and well.'

Galla turned towards Tullio, her eyes shining with tears. 'Thank you for keeping your promise. Helena is very precious to this temple. I don't know how we would have survived without her quick thinking.'

'You are only saying that because I have not stolen any honey cakes lately.' Helena's eyes danced. 'You are not nearly so complimentary then.'

Something twisted in Tullio's stomach. Precious to the temple. Useful to the temple, but did they really care about what happened to the woman?

He knew how important the temple was to Helena, but he could not rid himself of a niggling suspicion that her life did not matter very much to them. With great difficulty, he managed to keep hold of his temper.

'Where did you spend the night? The wind whistled so. The sibyl was worried about you.' Galla linked her arm with Helena's.

'I found a cave to rest in.' Helena glanced over her shoulder at him and smiled. 'Jupiter was quite fierce last night. Once the storm started in earnest, I did not dare brave the lightning. The other half of the cypress tree was struck.'

Galla made a ticking noise in the back of her throat. 'Whatever possessed you to go off like that?'

'The reason does not matter now.' Tullio moved to the other side of Helena. 'She is safe and well, and that is all that counts.'

'The demons of the mountain have not stolen my voice, Tullio.' Helena's lips curved into a sweet smile. 'I went to find Niobe, but I understand she had already made her way home. Then the storm was too fierce for me to venture back.'

'And nothing happened?' Galla stopped. Her sharp eyes went from Helena to Tullio and back again. 'You were gone all night.'

'Whatever can you mean, Galla?' Helena moved away from the maid. Her stomach churned. She forced a breath through her lips. She had to remain calm. 'Did anything happen here? How many ships were lost? Did the new roof on the warehouse hold?'

'Androceles craves an interview with you. It is about your uncle. He has returned.'

'My uncle? Uncle Lichas has arrived back?' Helena fought to keep her voice steady.

'Last night.'

'Oh.' Helena took a small step backwards. Her face became as white as the newly cut marble on Jupiter's temple in Rome.

Galla jerked her head towards the main temple.

'Since the first light, Androceles and his men have been there, waiting. I dare not wake the sibyl. She spent a restless night, only sleeping once the storm abated.'

Tullio moved so he was positioned at Helena's elbow. Now was the time to make his offer. She had to understand that he wanted to protect her. He and his men would do whatever was in their power to save the temple from the pirates. She had to trust him.

'I am here if you need anything. I can help. Rome can help,' he said in an undertone.

'Haven't you done enough?' she replied with stricken eyes.

Chapter Thirteen

Helena forced her feet to walk steadily across the court-yard towards the high altar where Androceles and his entourage waited. Behind him, his bodyguard bristled with menace, their heavily tattooed forearms crossed in front of their chests. Helena's shoulders eased when she saw they weren't wearing their swords. They still respected the sanctity of the temple. They had not come to occupy it.

She paused and glanced over her shoulder. Tullio remained in the courtyard. He gave the briefest of nods as if to encourage her. Helena straightened her back and forced her face to be stern.

Androceles must not guess where she had spent the night. What had passed between her and Tullio had no bearing on the future. It had been some sort of madness in her blood. Now it was over. Her heart constricted at the thought but she forced it to be still. She had to be the acolyte and not the woman.

Helena pushed an errant lock of hair behind her ear and wished she'd had the time to put on a fresh gown and her cap of red and white ribbons.

Androceles and the captain of the guard broke off their discussion as she approached.

'There was a time when the sibyl or her representative would have been here to greet me before I could even unbuckle my sword.' Androceles ostentatiously glanced at his portable sun dial. A gesture designed as much to emphasise his wealth and power as to reinforce how long he had been waiting. 'It has been nearly an hour by my clock.'

'Captain Androceles.' Helena inclined her head. She drew on her years of training to keep her voice steady and sure. She had no need of the outward trappings of the sibyl's assistant. She knew who she was and what power she held. 'To what do we owe this early morning visit? We suffered much damage in the storm last night. There is much to be done. However, I'm assured that the warehouses survived the storm. Your goods are safe.'

'Your uncle's ship arrived into the harbour at the height of the storm, when the sky was at its blackest.' Androceles swiftly knelt in front of Kybele's statue.

Helena forced her body to stay still. Everything seemed to slow down. Her words took an age to say. 'Is my uncle in good health?'

'Lightning struck the mast as his trireme pulled into port. Everyone who watched cried out with one voice.' He bowed his head. 'I asked Kybele for a vision and refused to believe it. He lies in his palace as if dead.'

'I should go to him.' All other thoughts vanished. The only thing Helena could think about was her uncle.

'Zenobia has her Greek doctor caring for him. No doubt she will send for the sibyl if need be.'

Helena felt a weight pressing down on her chest. Uncle

Lichas had always been a voice of support for the temple. Now he was cut off from Aunt Flavia.

'Kybele speaks very powerfully through the sibyl,' Androceles said as if he were discussing the time of day, but his eyes watched her with the intentness of a hawk.

Helena crossed her arms to hide their trembling. What would he say if he knew the prophecy had not come from the sibyl, but from her? She had to get her mind away from danger. Everything was about to come tumbling out, if she was not careful. Mundane things. She had to talk about the little things, and get Androceles away from the sibyl.

'I trust it will not take long to repair my uncle's ship.' She gestured about the courtyard where fallen statues lay intermingled with bits of masonry and tree branches. 'I regret that I cannot offer any men. My first priority must be the temple.'

'Of course, of course, there has never been any suggestion otherwise.' Androceles's lips curved in a cruel smile. 'You are a most able administrator, Helena. I predict you will go far. A pity you were busy last night. Where exactly were you?'

The feeling of cold pervaded Helena. That oblique smile and the quick flick of the eyes. Did Androceles know, or had he guessed?

Her stomach knotted as she realised the danger she had put the temple in. It had been a test from the goddess and she had failed miserably. Worse, she knew if faced with an identical test, she would react in exactly the same way again. But her desire for Tullio in no way affected her loyalty towards the temple and more importantly her people.

'The temple has a history of good relations with the seafarers.' Helena chose to ignore the question. 'No doubt this will continue long after your Romans have left.'

She waited to see if Androceles would challenge the statement and repeat his question. He rocked back on his sandals and sucked his teeth. His hand stroked his chin.

All of Helena's muscles tightened. She prayed that Tullio would not speak or draw attention to himself. He had to know how dangerous this situation was. This was not about them but about the very survival of the temple.

'When all the repairs are complete, the Lady Zenobia wants the sibyl to perform the blessing of the boats. She failed to do that last time.'

Helena allowed a small smile to appear at the corner of her lips. Androceles had accepted her words. She had won. She had crossed the danger point. They could now discuss ordinary temple business.

'I'm sure the sibyl will be delighted to appear, if the proper tribute is paid.' Helena made an expansive gesture with her hands. She'd worry about how and when the sibyl appeared when she knew more. 'The sibyl does expect something in return. Zenobia preferred a new Tyrean purple robe instead of paying the sibyl her proper due, if I recall correctly.'

'You dare much,' Androceles blustered.

'I dare because the villagers need grain. Roofs will have been blown off buildings. The seafarers will look to their boats, but who will look after the temple?'

Androceles shrugged a shoulder, leant forward and tapped his nose. 'Zenobia assures me that you will not have trouble. Neptune blessed your uncle on this voyage. Grain, olive oil and some of the finest *liquamen* sauce I have seen for years. The sibyl will have to give her opinion on it. Is her taste in fish sauce as discerning as her palate for wine?'

'The sibyl does enjoy her fish sauce,' Helena replied cautiously.

'I shall send over an amphora of my Falerian wine as gratitude for her prophecy.'

Helena regarded her sandals rather than look at Tullio. The seafarer made it seem that Aunt Flavia was as corrupt as Androceles and his son. Aunt Flavia might enjoy the good life. She received tributes from around the Mediterranean, but the people came first. Always. 'It's not necessary.'

'As long as your aunt appears at the ceremony, I'm sure there will be no problems.'

Helena tilted her head, listening for hidden meaning. A shiver ran down her back. Then she gave her mind a shake. She refused to worry about that now. Some day, everything would be back to the way it should be and she'd be able to stop pretending.

'Of course the sibyl will be there to perform the ceremony,' Helena said with much more confidence than she felt. How long would it take to fix a mast?

'I'd wondered. Word reached your uncle about his sister's bout of ill health.' Androceles's eyes glittered. 'She has served as sibyl for these past twenty years.'

'There are always rumours.' Helena's head began to pound in earnest. Why had the gods chosen last night for her uncle's arrival? There was always the possibility that someone would confide in him about his sister's well-being.

'When the sibyl last spoke with me, she appeared to be very strong.' Tullio stepped forward and his eyes seemed to challenge Androceles. Helena's knees sagged with relief. Rescued again.

Androceles turned as crimson as Tullio's cloak. He raised an eyebrow.

'Marcus Livius Tullio and I were discussing the repairs to

the temple when Galla found me,' Helena said. 'No doubt you've spotted the work he and his men have already completed. Romans are excellent engineers.'

Helena waited for Androceles until she released the next breath. Would he see it for the lie it was? But she couldn't tell the truth. Androceles grunted, but did not pursue the matter.

She signalled to the captain of the guard. 'Please escort the tribune back to his men. Our interview is over.'

Without protesting, Tullio followed the guard. Helena heaved a sigh of relief. He had shown sense. Without his intervention, the interview might have gone badly wrong.

'It does surprise me, Helena, that you allow a Roman so much freedom. After the trouble they cause the seafarers…'

'What trouble was that, Androceles?' Helena crossed her arms. 'You have obviously overcome your reluctance to trade with them. I see little reason why the temple should not fulfil its proper role.'

Androceles's face grew even redder. She could see his hands shake with rage. But he was not yet certain enough to act on it. The sudden knowledge gave her hope.

'If you are so concerned about my uncle, perhaps I should see him.'

'Perhaps you should.' Androceles signalled to his men. 'There is no time like the present.'

Helena pressed her lips together and wished she had not made the statement. She had neatly boxed herself in. There was no way she could refuse without losing face.

'I'm ready whenever you are.'

The barracks was quiet, much quieter than Tullio had expected. His men should be up and bustling about, but there was little sign of any activity, not even the clicking of knuck-lebones or stones. From where he stood in the doorway, he could see three distinct lumps where men still lay on their pallets. The rest were sitting around in dispirited groups, muttering. Quintus should have had the men out rebuilding long before now.

Tullio rubbed the back of his neck. In a way he was glad, it would give him an excuse to yell, to do something to relieve the frustration he felt.

Watching Helena's interview with Androceles, he had felt increasingly powerless. Twice he had come close to intervening, but had held his tongue.

He wore no armour, spoke with no authority.

The only thing that pirates understood was force. The puffed-up pompous pirate had his day of reckoning coming. His house would be the first to fall.

The most important thing Tullio had learnt in the army was the necessity of picking his ground. If he was going to fight—and he knew that it would come to a fight—he wanted to ensure all the odds were on his side. He was not sure how the addition of another pirate captain would affect things, but he was certain that when the time came, his men would win. Their dedication and training gave them superiority, if the ground was correct.

Before that he wanted to give Helena the opportunity to pick the correct side. She had to see the difference between the pirates and Rome. He wanted to make sure she made the correct choice.

After last night, it meant a great deal to him. She was more than a symbol. She was Helena, the woman he wanted to spend the rest of his life with.

'Mustius Quintus, why are the men lazing about? There is work to be done. Quintus!' he bellowed, but there was no answering shout.

Tullio frowned. One night away and already his men's discipline was gone. The problems with Quintus had been brewing for a long time and he would have to take action. No army could function with two commanders.

'Mustius Quintus, when I call, I expect an answer.'

Silence. He saw the others line up smartly, shoulders back. One legionary glanced at the three still sleeping on the floor. Tullio's heart sank. Three of his men could not be dead. He had been so sure that everything was going his way, that he was winning Helena over to his side, and that his men would be healthy enough when the tribute arrived to mount an attack against the pirates.

'Sir, Quintus is not here. He's gone.' There was a distinct tremor in the legionary's voice.

'Not here? What do you mean?' Tullio's mind raced through the possibilities. Had Androceles come to claim some of the legionaries for sport? And had the temple guards let them because Helena was not there to stop them? There were so many things he'd put at risk by giving into his desire. Tullio winced.

Rufus walked over to him and motioned for Tullio to follow him into the corridor. Rufus twisted his belt around his hand and shifted from one foot to the other.

'Out with it, man, what has happened?' Tullio instinctively put his hand to where his sword should be, and then inwardly cursed. 'There may still be time to rescue them.'

'He and two others, members of his old cohort, left, Livius Tullio, last night at the height of the storm.'

He stared at Rufus, not quite believing his ears.

'Left? Where did they go? Under whose orders?' Tullio curled his hand into a fist, but resisted hitting the stone wall. 'I seem to recall leaving strict orders that you men were to stay here in barracks, out of trouble. I gave my word, man.'

Rufus's cheeks flushed. He tugged at the neckline of his tunic. 'He saw his chance and took it.'

Tullio cursed loud and long. He threw open the door, marched over to where Quintus's pallet lay and saw the crudely piled-up bundle, something that would fool no one for more time than it took to blink an eye.

The other two missing men were young legionaries, men who had looked up to Quintus, worshipped him almost as a god. Tullio's stomach felt as if it were doubly punched.

'I gave orders for him to stay.'

'He said that it was his duty as a Roman soldier to escape.'

'It was his duty to obey orders!'

How could he begin to explain to Helena what had happened? He had given his word. How would she ever trust him again?

He had been so close. Everything had been within his grasp. He stared at the rough plastered wall, mastering his temper before he turned towards Rufus. 'Why didn't you stop him?'

'The man saved my life,' Rufus replied quietly. 'He saved the life of every man here. We owed him a life-debt.'

Tullio gazed around the room. The men's faces were white in the gloom. The last thing he needed was this complication. Helena had trusted him; now, through the actions of someone else, a man under his command, all that trust was about to be destroyed. She would have to offer them up to the pirates, and retribution would be swift and sure.

'He has put every man's life in danger. How do you think the pirates will react when they discover his escape? We have no weapons, nothing.'

'We are important to them. They want the tribute money,' a legionary piped up.

'How important to them will the money be when they discover that they have been duped? Yes, money is important, but what price pride?' Tullio ground out between his teeth. 'Did he think beyond his own skin?'

'Maybe Quintus thought your friendship with Helena would protect us.'

Tullio turned incredulously towards Rufus. The man backed away with hands held out in front of his face.

'It is just a thought,' Rufus said. 'Not a very good one, but you could always explain the situation to her.'

'Do you know what is at stake here? Do you realise what Quintus has thrown away? Have I ever let you down before?'

Tullio started towards the door. He needed to breathe clean air, to be away from the fetid atmosphere of this room. There had to be a solution to this mess. He had to think clearly and not to panic. All his exertions, all the groundwork he had laid, gone because one of his men had decided to act on his own.

He refused to think about what this would mean for his relationship with Helena. A pain stabbed through his heart. There had to be something he could do.

Rufus caught his arm.

'You have to give him a chance to get away,' he pleaded. 'To do his duty as he sees it. You cannot betray a fellow soldier to the pirates. Maybe he will get down to the harbour and see you were correct after all. He might return. If you go to anyone now, it will be the worse for us. For the sake of our long association, wait. Let Quintus prove what type of man he is.'

His men ringed around him, healthier than when they had arrived on this island, but still captives. Tullio pressed his lips together. His first duty had to be to the men who remained. He had to find a way to protect their lives.

'How long has he been gone? Six? Seven hours?'

'Quintus and the others went when the storm was at its height and the guards were distracted.'

Tullio ran a hand through his hair. He wanted to believe that Quintus had somehow changed his mind and decided against this suicidal escape attempt. He had no doubt they would be caught and tortured. The pirates would show no mercy.

'I will give him an hour to return, but after that may the gods protect him. I certainly won't.'

Did she look any different?

Helena regarded her face in the small bronze mirror as she sat on her stool in front of her dressing table. The pots and jars filled with make-up and scent were placed in neat and tidy rows.

Everything where it should be.

Everything as she had left it yesterday morning. The only thing that had changed was her.

Or had she? The same face with its green eyes and over-generous mouth stared back at her.

The interview with her uncle had been short and unpleasant. The Lady Zenobia hovered at her elbow. Her uncle drifted in and out of consciousness. She had leant forward and his fragile fingers squeezed one of her hands. Then, at Zenobia's nod, she had left the room. No one seemed to have guessed her relationship with Tullio.

Helena placed the mirror down with a thump.

In the cold clear light of day, she regretted what had happened in the cave. She should never have clung to him in that way or given into the temptation. When faced with a test, she had made the wrong choice. She had chosen to be a woman.

He was the same as her uncle or any number of pirates, worse because he was Roman, but her heart kept whispering she could trust him. She tried to keep from making plans. He had said nothing about the future.

She knew he could leave when the tribute arrived, but hadn't something passed between them last night?

Other sibyls had taken lovers. Why shouldn't she? She had not taken her final vows, and there was no reason why she couldn't leave. It seemed incredible that she should even be thinking such thoughts. Helena pulled the folds of her gown straighter. What would it be like to be a Roman lady?

A sharp rap at the door startled her. Another interruption. She should be grateful for it, but she wanted time to think. She rose, re-adjusted her shawl and opened the door.

Tullio's frame filled the doorway. He had changed his tunic. This one was baggier, as if it belonged to a bigger man. The brasses on his belt gleamed.

There was no outward sign on him that they had passed the night together, but her heart fluttered.

She gripped the door handle tightly, hanging on to it as her eyes drank every detail in. It was as if she had not seen him for days rather than for a few hours. She wondered if she would ever tire of looking at him. She had not betrayed the temple with him. Their connection went beyond that. It was a relationship between a man and a woman.

'Tullio, what a pleasant surprise.'

The lines around his mouth became harder and there was a crease between his eyebrows. There was a determination in his movements. His eyes were serious and the twinkle of this morning had disappeared.

Her smile faded under his gaze. The tingles were replaced with a nervousness.

'What has happened?'

'I wanted to make sure you were safely back from your interview with your uncle.'

'Uncle Lichas is better than Captain Androceles led me to believe. He has had many years of dealing with the temple. He respects my aunt and her prophecies. The latest one had caused no little consternation.'

She rubbed the back of her neck and took a few steps away from Tullio. Whatever could be wrong? Then she chided herself for imagining things. She was always imagining. One of her worst faults, according to Aunt Flavia. She had to stop searching for hidden meanings.

'I left him over an hour ago in the tender care of his wife. After that, I have had time to complete an inspection of the temple. Nothing too major to fix—not for your men.'

She took a half-step towards him.

He nodded, but made no attempt to embrace her. It bothered Helena that she wanted to feel his arms about her. She returned to the dressing table and made a show of straightening her mirror and combs. Still he was silent. Something had happened. She could feel it in her bones.

'Is there a problem, Tullio? Has one of your men fallen ill? Or become injured in the storm? You don't have to ask, simply take him to the hospital wing.'

'Do I need a reason to want to see you?' He gave a crooked smile, one that turned her heart. The twinkle in his eyes was back. 'As I said, I wanted to see you, to make sure you were safe.'

'Why wouldn't I be safe in the temple?' She gave a laugh, but felt pleased that he should care enough to be concerned.

'Androceles seems more eager than ever to station guards in the temple.'

'It was Androceles's suggestion, not mine. I swear that man twists and turns more than a tangled piece of wool.'

'But it was your trick with the mirrors that convinced his men you had enough guards to handle any problems.'

A shiver ran down Helena's back. Something had happened, something bad. The temple was about to be blamed for something. There was more than simple concern in his voice. She gulped a breath of air. She had to keep her head. She could not give into panic. Everything could be coincidence.

'You gave me your word that you would obey the dictates of hospitality.' She searched his face for any sign. But it was impassive, his feelings as hidden as if he were a statue. She glanced down and saw the white knuckles of his right hand. Maybe her uncle's visit had unsettled him. 'The temple is not without its defences. There is no reason I should worry.'

The furrows on his brow increased. 'Something might happen that would give the pirates an excuse.'

'My uncle is frightened of his sister, always has been. And it turns out that my prophecy about the black mist was correct. The harbour was surrounded in a black mist when he docked. He broke his leg when the mast fell.' Helena toyed with a pot. She couldn't understand Tullio's mood. If there was some problem, why didn't he just tell her? Or was he seeking reassurance?

'I was wrong to worry. Perhaps I do have some sort of gift after all.'

'Perhaps, but it is nothing I would like you to test very often.' He reached out and pulled her into his arms. The faint scent of olive oil from his bath tickled her nose.

She rested against his chest, feeling as if she were a ship that had come to its harbour. He bent his head and touched her mouth with his. This kiss was different from the others, Helena thought as the kiss deepened. There was some sort of desperation about it, something had changed. There was more to his concern than he let on.

What had happened? A shiver ran through her. What did he know that she didn't? What was he trying to hide from her? She did not need his protection. She had not asked for it.

She broke free, and stood facing him. He reached out and smoothed a tendril of hair from her forehead. His eyes had a sorrowful look that made her stomach twist.

'We need to speak, Helena.'

This was it. This was where he asked for the temple's allegiance. Something she had no power to give. And the affair ended. She knew it had to be, but she wasn't ready yet.

Before she could open her mouth to reply, the sound of metalled sandals echoed from the hallway. Marching. Hurrying. Helena's stomach dropped to the tops of her sandals. She ran to the door and flung it open. The temple guards were standing at the door to the sibyl's apartments.

'What can I do for you?'

'Kimon, the son of Androceles, craves an immediate audience with the sibyl.'

'The sibyl is not to be disturbed. I told you that. I will meet with him. But he should wait until the normal audience time.'

'It must be now. The integrity of the temple has been compromised.' The guard paused. 'Those were his exact words, Helena. The integrity of the temple has been compromised and he demands satisfaction.'

Chapter Fourteen

Helena forced her footsteps to be measured and even. She refused to run. She must not appeared flustered when she met Kimon.

The seafarers were increasing the pressure on her aunt. She would have only a few more days until her condition became known. And then what? She paused just before the entrance, drew a deep breath and adjusted the folds of her gown so that the folds fell in even pleats and her belt was snug about her hips. She had to appear the picture of calm and control.

'Ah, Helena, you appear. I had expected to see your aunt.' The tall pirate captain was in shadow, standing next to the libation bowl. Helena's eye widened. He retained his sword. The gleam of the hilt. 'I had requested to see the sibyl.'

'Weapons are not permitted in the temple grounds. It is sacrilege. You will not pollute this place.'

'These are dangerous times. There are dangerous men about.'

And you, one of the most dangerous. Helena held back the words.

With an arrogant swagger, he walked over to the altar,

lifted the lid of a jar and peered in. He dipped a finger and tasted it.

'Olive oil. One of my father's gifts?'

Helena felt clammy sweat break out on the back of her neck. She hated the way Kimon's eyes roamed over her as if she were a tasty morsel.

'State your business. There had better be a good reason why you are in this temple armed.'

'It does surprise me that you leave such valuable things unguarded. Kybele's statue with its gold sword and this little trinket.' Kimon picked the Neptune's horn up and balanced it in his hand, examining the engravings. 'Could such a thing really save this island?'

'Only if blown in a time of direst need,' Helena retorted. She went over and re-adjusted how the horn lay.

'Are you sure the temple is up to its appointed tasks of safeguarding the treasures? After all, there are Roman soldiers on the island.'

'The Romans are guests within this complex. We have had no trouble from them.' She glanced over her shoulder to the shrouded mirror. Did she dare use that again so soon after the last time? 'They respect the temple and its traditions and know that it is adequately defended.'

He gave a cruel laugh, which echoed throughout the hall. 'I have heard of the temple's defences. I have little time for legends.'

'Why ever not? Your father does.'

'My father is a superstitious old fool. He believes in portents and prophecy.'

'Your father respects the sanctity of the temple.' Helena crossed her arms. She refused to panic, refused to allow this man to intimidate her. She hated the way he was talking to her as if she were a child. 'You should give me a good reason why you do not. Why you come here armed, when the sibyl has expressly forbidden it. You should be grateful that she does not issue an edict against you.'

He smirked then, came over and patted her shoulder. Her skin crawled at the familiarity.

'I have come to return something that you misplaced,' he said.

'I can't think you have anything of mine.' Her mind raced. Had she left something at the palace? No. Kimon was enjoying toying with her much as the temple cat toyed with the mice in the warehouse.

What did he have? She glanced about the temple, seeing nothing amiss. What could she have misplaced?

'Oh, but I have. Guess.'

Helena's scalp prickled. What had he taken? What had his men stolen as a test? Her eyes searched the altar. Everything appeared to be in place. Libation bowls, statues and artifacts, including Neptune's horn. Everything.

'I have no time for guessing games, Kimon.' Helena tapped her sandal on the mosaic-tiled floor. 'Return it this instant and we will forget about this unpleasant episode. Perhaps there will be no need for the sibyl to curse you.'

'She won't curse me.'

'I am waiting, Kimon, son of Androceles. Return the object.'

She crossed her arms to prevent her hands from trembling. No doubt after he returned this object, he'd demand his sailors were stationed here. She had to think of a reason why they shouldn't be.

'Very well, if you insist. You always did enjoy spoiling my

fun, Helena, even as a little girl. You continuously ran off to tell on me.'

He snapped his fingers and Helena watched with horror as three bloody bundles were dragged forth. The cloaks flopped open, revealing the belts hung with brass.

'My men had a bit of sport with them.'

He prodded the first bundle with the toe of his sandal. A long moan came from it.

Bile rose in her throat as she realised that these were men, Roman soldiers. Their faces bloodied and bruised. The marks of whips and worse stood out clearly.

Where had he found them? How dare he beat them for sport!

'You had no right to beat those men.'

'I had every right.'

Helena struggled to control her temper. Kimon's actions were a direct challenge to the temple's authority, but she could also see that he wanted her to lose her temper, that he enjoyed making her angry. Helena curled her fingers around her amulet and took a deep breath before continuing.

'These men are under the protection of the temple, under Kybele's protection. How dare you invade and inflict punishment!' Helena fought to control her voice, and not to give way to her anger. 'Your father and the other heads of the seafaring houses will be informed. You go too far this time, Kimon. You will be cursed and set adrift.'

'I had every right,' Kimon repeated, curling back his lip to reveal yellowing teeth. 'My men found them, hiding under a pile of canvas by my ship during the storm. I thought they should enjoy your hospitality a little while longer. Next time, you should not be careless with your charges. Allowing them to roam free! Whatever could the sibyl be thinking?'

Helena put her hand in front of her mouth and stifled a scream. She knew these men. The grizzled one was the Roman who had helped fix the warehouse door. He was the one Galla was sweet on. He had given her a fig bread recipe.

Maybe there was another reason. Maybe Galla had sent them in search of her. What if they had been caught and beaten because she tarried with Tullio? She should have tried to cross that stream.

'I am sure there is a perfectly reasonable explanation.'

'I am not concerned about explanations. You are too lenient with the Romans. That is quite clear. My father and Zenobia agree with me. Measures must be taken.'

'And what did you do?'

Kimon's eyes gleamed. 'I made them fight and when they could fight no more, I beat them. It is what you should have done.'

'These men can barely stand up.' Helena gestured to the three would-be escapees. 'If they are beaten further, they will die.'

'Let them.'

'They are human beings.'

'These are Roman scum.' Kimon dusted a speck from his cloak. 'You undertook to keep them safe for my father. Next time, do not make me do your job for you.'

Kimon turned on his heel and left the room.

The groan from one of the bundles brought Helena to her senses. She called for the guards to take the injured men to the hospital. Her whole body felt numb.

How had this happened?

It gave Androceles the perfect excuse to insist on stationing his own guards. How could she refuse now, when the temple guards had proved to be so inept? And once that happened, it would be only a matter of time before her deception was uncovered and the true state of the sibyl was revealed.

What had seemed such a beautiful morning had turned blacker than night within a few breaths.

What had been Tullio's role in everything? She had trusted him. Had he just used her?

Helena bit down on her fist, willing the cries not to come.

After checking that the escapees' wounds were being treated, Helena made sure she was occupied with tasks that took her as far away from the Romans as possible. She did not want the slightest excuse to visit them. No doubt she would have to face Tullio at some point, but for now, the sense of betrayal was too new and too raw.

She had to take refuge somewhere and the storeroom stocked high with the seafarer's tributes appeared the ideal place. Above all, it served to remind her why the seafarers were important to this island and why the islanders could not live without them.

Helena paused in counting the jars of olive oil. They would need more than twice that number if they were to make it through the winter season. She wrote down the number and compared it to last month's figure. If they went down to four lamps on the main altar, instead of the usual ten, that would save a considerable amount. The amphorae of liquamen, the fish sauce used in cooking, were down as well, but Androceles had had the amphora of Falerian wine delivered. Absentmindedly, she tapped the stylus against her teeth.

'My lady, a word.'

She turned and Tullio stood in the doorway. He started forward. Helena grabbed the tablets and held them in front of her like a shield. She contemplated skirting around the large amphora of oil and making a somewhat undignified exit.

He shut the door to the storeroom with a quiet click. His face had more planes and hollows than this morning. She remembered the taste of his lips, his skin.

She closed her eyes.

All the time he was kissing her, his men were escaping. It was nothing but a sham. He had used her.

An awful thought struck her.

Had Pius been bribed? Was the whole seduction an excuse to betray her trust? She had thought he wanted her and all he had done was cynically use her. Aunt Flavia was correct. All men, seafarer or Roman, were alike.

He took a step closer and his sandal crunched a piece of pottery. Her eyes flew open to see his hands were outstretched. She stepped to one side, bumping the top of her legs on the rim of an amphora.

'How dare you! I gave strict orders!'

'We need to speak.' He continued his advance. She could feel the warmth of his breath against her cheek. Her treacherous body delighted in it. 'I want to explain. You should hear me out.'

'Explain what? Your men escaped.' She forced a harsh laugh from her lips and turned away, rather than look into his eyes. If she looked there, it would be tempting to look for some reason to forgive him. She refused to forgive him. 'You gave me your word, Tullio.'

'Are you saying that I had something to do with what happened out there in the harbour?'

His hand grabbed her shoulder and attempted to turn her around. She shrugged it off.

'Encouraged them, led them. Those men are soldiers, Tullio, they do not act without orders.' She slammed her fist down on the amphora's cork lid and enjoyed the thump it made. 'I know that much about the Roman army and its ruthless efficiency.'

'Will you listen to me! I knew nothing about the escape attempt. If I had, I would have stopped it.'

'Why should I believe you?'

'Because, unlike the pirates, I don't lie.' Tullio pointed to the amphora of Falerian wine, his eyes narrowing to slits of molten black. 'You asked for proof that the seafarers raided. There it is. That Falerian wine bears the mark of my ex-wife's husband. It was stolen the night of their murder and none has appeared on the market.'

'We're not discussing raids. We're discussing your men.' Helena crossed her arms in front of her. Her stomach turned over. She had no doubt Tullio told the truth about the wine, but that did not excuse his behaviour. She refused to be distracted.

'I'm asking you to believe me.'

'Are you asking me to believe that your being away from the temple had nothing to do with the escape? You kept me in that cave for a purpose. You seduced me for a purpose. Now I know what that purpose was.'

She heard the sharp intake of breath. If she listened, she could hear his heartbeat. Every nerve tensed. She wanted to hear that she meant more to him than a diversion, that he had spent the night with her because he had wanted to.

'What do you take me for?' His hand closed on her

shoulder, refused to be shrugged off and forced her to face him. 'More importantly, what do you take yourself for?'

A terrible coldness filled Helena. Tullio had betrayed her. He had given her his assurance that his men would behave. He had given her his word, but he was a Roman like any other. Her heart shattered into a thousand pieces, and it took all her hard-won training not to collapse into a heap of tears.

'What did you hope to gain with this sort of behaviour?' she asked in a low whisper.

He held out his hands, palms upwards. His face was the picture of injured innocence. Her heart twisted. She had believed him. She wanted to believe him now. That was what hurt. If he could give her an explanation and tell her it was a terrible mistake, she'd run to his arms.

'Jupiter's beard, are you saying I had something to do with this unholy mess?'

'They are your men, and you knew they had escaped.' Helena forced the words from her throat. 'You knew before Kimon came here. You knew when you took me into your arms.'

The room went still and cold. Helena fought to draw another breath. Silently, she urged him to tell her that he had known nothing, that it had been as big a surprise to him as to her, that he would never have sanctioned such a foolhardy mission, that he'd waited to see if they'd return. That she meant something more to him than a conduit to the sibyl.

'You knew,' she repeated.

'Yes, I knew they had escaped.'

The chasm between them opened. She felt alone and cold. She drew her shawl tighter about her. This was the end.

A look of anguish passed over his features. He reached out

towards her and then changed his mind, raking his hand through his hair.

'I swore that I would not lie to you, Helena. Before Kimon arrived with my three men, I did know they had made an escape attempt, but—'

Helena covered her ears with her hands. She knew he was still speaking. That did not matter. What mattered was that he had not sought to warn her. He had come back, taken a bath, come to her room and taken her in his arms, never saying a word about the escape. He had known.

No matter how he tried to portray it, he had betrayed her. She had believed in him, and he betrayed her.

'I warned you what would happen if they tried to escape.' She poked a finger at his chest. 'Do you know what danger these men have put the temple in? Everything my aunt and I have worked for over these past years gone!'

His hands drew her into his arms, held her against his chest, his strong arms like bands of iron. She struggled briefly, then stood still.

'I was trying to tell you what had happened when we were interrupted,' he said into her hair. 'If the guard had not called you away, I would have told you. I wanted to make sure you heard the news from me first.'

Helena shivered. Her body wanted to lean into him. She broke free of his grasp.

'You should have warned me. You gave me your word. You had a duty to obey your promise.'

'My men felt they had a duty to escape.'

'That is no excuse. I trusted you.'

'And now?'

'Why should I?'

He gave a military salute. Gone was the man who held her gently, in whose arms she had woken, and in his place was the perfect soldier, upright, unyielding, single-minded in the pursuit of Rome's glory. 'I will rejoin my men.'

Helena stared at the place where the men had lain. All she could see was Tullio's body, broken like those three. Had he known about the escape plan? Was that why he had attempted to keep her away from the temple? And all she could do was worry that one of those bloodied bundles might have been him.

'You have taken your time, niece. I had expected a report of the damage before now. The wind and rain kept me awake for a long while last night. Tell me what has happened.'

Helena pinched the back of her neck and stared at her aunt, who was seated in a woven chair. Her snow-white hair was gathered at the back of her neck. She wore plain white robes tied with a gold belt at the hips. Other than the slight drooping of her right eye, her aunt looked as healthy as she had the day before Helena had found her. Several scrolls lay by her side. The box containing the sibyl's mask was on the table in front of her.

'There were things I had to attend to.' Helena shifted from sandal to sandal. She did not want to reveal the real reason that she had avoided meeting with her aunt—her aunt's eyes were too sharp, too likely to guess what had passed between her and Tullio.

'I understand you spent the night out on the mountain.'

'I went looking for Niobe. I thought she might have become trapped by the storm. You know how she hates storms.'

'It is commendable you wish to look after the innocents,

but did you ever consider that there are others under your charge? We have had this discussion before. The temple must come first in all things you do. And here you have hopes of becoming the sibyl when my powers desert me.'

Helena traced her toe along the mosaic flooring. Aunt Flavia was right. She always was. Even here, confined to her apartments, she knew more about what was going on in the temple than Helena did. Aunt Flavia already knew about the escape. The way Tullio had duped her. She had given him her heart, her trust and he used her.

He had to have known when he came to her in her room. It was all an illusion. Her mouth twisted. Everything was an illusion.

'At the time, I only thought of Niobe and the danger she was in. After the thunder and lightning started, I knew I had to take shelter. There was a flash flood and I had to wait for it to subside. We…that is, I came back as I quickly as I could.'

Aunt Flavia inclined her head. She placed her scroll on the small table and raised her gaze to meet Helena's.

'At least you showed more sense than your mother.'

'I trust and pray I learnt the lesson of my mother's death.'

'And what was that?'

'The gods are not to be tempted.' Helena looked straight ahead at the frieze. The words took her back years. How many times had her aunt drummed that particular lesson in her head? Too many. 'You should not mock the gods. You must only ask when you can be sure of them answering.'

'Ah, some things I attempted to teach you have made an impact. There have been times that I wondered.'

'Uncle Lichas returned just before the storm hit. His trireme is damaged.'

'Word reached me.'

'Zenobia would like you to perform a re-dedication service.'

Her aunt sat, her brow furrowed with concentration. Helena waited and willed her to succeed. Her aunt lifted her right hand and tried to make a fist. She allowed the hand to fall back on her lap. 'Annoying things.'

'Be patient, Aunt Flavia. You will be able to perform the ceremony.'

'There is much you don't understand, Helena.'

'I'm trying, Aunt. There is much you've hidden from me.'

A lop-sided smile crossed her aunt's face, but her eyes looked distressed. Helena awkwardly patted her aunt's shoulder. Comforting the older woman was something new. Aunt Flavia had never been one for sentiment or comfort. As a child, whenever Helena had banged a knee or bumped an elbow, she had gone to Galla for hugs and cuddles.

'I shall have to tell the seafarers of my infirmity. I understand what you have tried to do, but it is the only way. Too much has happened, Helena.'

'We'll find another solution. You are too important.'

Her aunt's smile widened and became genuine. 'You already have many things to think about. I fear my recent illness has become a burden.'

Helena knelt down and caught her aunt's hand. So small and frail, more like bird's claw than a hand.

'You are not a burden. You are the heart and soul of this temple.'

Her aunt stroked Helena's head and she started at the unaccustomed gesture. She reached up and touched her aunt's withered cheek.

'Aunt, what should I do about the Romans? My uncle and the other chiefs are sure to demand swift punishment, but these men have been beaten and have been returned to the temple's care.'

'Your care.'

'My care?' Helena stared at her aunt. Those men were not her sole responsibility. They were under the temple's protection. She had thought that her aunt would have a sensible idea about how she should behave. 'How can you say that?'

'You were the one responsible for bringing them here. You are now the one responsible for making that decision.'

'But what should I do?' Helena could hear the pleading note in her voice and cringed. Her aunt had taught her to stand on her own feet. And now, facing her first major test, all she could do was beg for guidance and help.

'Your heart will tell you what to do. When in doubt, I always find it useful to listen to my heart. It is where the goddess speaks.'

Her aunt closed her eyes and Helena knew she had been dismissed. She hesitated, and wondered if she should confide in her about Tullio. She pressed her lips together. This was one burden she would not share.

She waited until she heard her aunt's soft breath. Then she walked with quick steps towards the hospital and, she hoped, some sort of resolution.

The stiflingly sweet scent of incense intermingled with acetic acid assaulted her nostrils. The three would-be escapees were there, battered, bruised but alive. One of the acolytes glided over and gave her an account of what they had done for the men.

Helena expelled a breath. All the men should live. The

question was what to do with them. They had already been beaten. It would be weeks before they would walk properly again, she was certain of that.

Chains?

If they couldn't walk, how could they escape? She hated the sight of chains, but probably it was the only option. Something to show her uncle and Captain Androceles when they called in the morning.

It was a blessing they had not called before now, but she had to assume checking the status of *guests* was far down the priority list. But once they had finished assessing the damage, then their attention would turn to the temple. Helena shivered and drew her shawl tighter about her body.

'Helena,' Galla called in a low voice. Helena turned to see Galla sitting on a low stool next to the most badly beaten of the Roman soldiers. 'This is all my fault.'

'How so?'

'I…I told Quintus to go to the harbour…to look for you and to see what the commotion was about. I showed him the secret way the sibyl uses. I was so worried about you.'

'Why wasn't I told this earlier?' Helena stared at her maid in disbelief.

'I was afraid. I…I had gone to look for them when Androceles arrived.' Tears streamed down Galla's face. 'If I had told you earlier, then none of this would have happened. The sea-farers are going to station guards in the temple, aren't they?'

Helena felt sick to her stomach. The men were innocent? They had been searching for her? Oh, Kybele!

'Galla, you should have told me earlier. Something could have been done then.'

'She lies,' the figure on the pallet croaked out.

He struggled to raise his body on his elbows. Galla tried to get him to lie back down. Impatiently he pushed her away. Galla gave a little cry and covered her face with her hands.

'Your maid lies. This was my fault and mine alone.'

Helena moved closer. Her heart started to thump in her ears. She wanted to believe the centurion. She knew she was grasping at slender pieces of wool, but she needed hope.

'What are you saying, centurion?'

'I wanted to escape. I thought I could. Galla knew nothing about it. Tullio forbade it, but I would not listen. I planned it. I slipped out and placed that shawl. Your maid has nothing to do with it. We were going to attempt to escape that night. I had it all planned.'

'Where did you get the shawl?'

'I stole it when that girl came to see Tullio. He has befriended her and was trying to teach her to speak.'

'And Galla had nothing to do with it?'

Quintus shook his head, but he reached out, captured Galla's hand and brought to his lips, then released it.

'In my stubbornness and pride, I thought that I knew best,' Quintus said. 'I was wrong. My eyes were on the grass crown and other honours, not on my duty. If you must punish someone, punish me. Your maid was innocent. I used her. And I cannot let another take responsibility for my actions.'

'Marcus Livius Tullio knew nothing?'

'No, my lady.' He closed his eyes and shook his head slowly. 'In fact, he forbade any attempt at escape. When we return to Rome, no doubt I shall be disciplined. In my arrogance, I broke my military oath. For that I am deeply ashamed.'

Helena pressed her hands to her forehead, seeking to relieve the pain. Her stomach turned over. She'd never have suspected Galla. She had wronged Tullio. She had thrown all sorts of accusations at him, and had not listened to the explanation. She had wanted to believe everything but her own heart.

'You have given me much to think about.'

Quintus reached out a hand. 'My lady, speak to him. Convince him that I have suffered enough. My retirement is coming up in a few months and I was hoping for a good settlement, but my former tribune is dead and I now must hope.'

'He said he would buy me,' Galla said with a trembling voice. 'I don't believe him, of course.'

'Jupiter and Saturn as my witness, I planned to. And if I survive, I plan to.' Quintus's voice rang out through the hall. 'She was prepared to speak for me. For me? Can you believe that? And she makes honey cakes. I want her by my side for the rest of my days. I mean to marry her.'

Helena saw Galla grow bright red. Her heart twisted. Somehow Quintus had conquered Galla's natural mistrust of Romans. She also knew that, if Quintus did offer, her aunt would refuse. Galla was too important to the temple. But looking at Galla's shining face, and tender smile, Helena also knew that such a refusal would be wrong.

'When that day comes, I will be the first to wish you joy and happiness,' Helena said and swept from the room before she gave way to tears.

Chapter Fifteen

Silver clouds skittered across a yellow moon making the world look a strange and different place. Although Helena knew every crevice and foothold on the way to the tower, she had to stop several times and once missed a turning. In near pitch-black darkness she had to grope her way back.

The night-time scent of the jasmine that twisted and clung to the tower walls was cloying and oppressive. So heavy that, with every breath she took, the scent seemed to fill her lungs, pressing down on her, making this part of the passage more difficult than usual.

A scream welled up within her as her fingers touched a gecko, who scuttled away. Its claws dug into her hand before scraping the stone. She had never liked the little lizards who inhabited the crevices and cracks of the temple walls. She liked them even less when they ran over her toes and hands.

She had decided to go to the tower when sleep evaded her. Back in her bedroom, she'd closed her eyes and all she'd seen was Tullio's face. She'd gone over and over the words she had hurled at him and she knew there was no way to retract them.

He had tried to explain and she had refused to listen, preferring to believe the word of a man she knew was a cheat and liar.

The top of the turret was her place of refuge, the place where she always went. Up there, surrounded by the air and sea, she could think out her problems and decide what to do next. Her head always cleared there. For as long as she could remember it was her special thinking spot.

If she could, she would replace the sands of time. Then she'd listen, not only to his words but to how he said them. Before she had listened with her ears and not with her heart. Somehow, she would have to find a way to apologise. Then she would get on with her life and stop wishing for things that could never be.

She had strong feelings for the Roman tribune. Feelings that grew by the day, by the hour. She knew that. It was impossible to deny. She admired his clear thinking. Niobe trusted him. She appreciated the way he helped the temple, asking for nothing in return. He had come looking for her when no one else had dared.

Twice.

But could she trust him? Truly trust him? He must have known his men had escaped, and he had not warned her.

After today, she knew that, despite his feelings for her—and she had to believe he had feelings for her—he would side with Rome.

That hurt.

It pained her to her very core. Her heart had shattered. She could not get away from the fact that she had trusted him, and he used that trust to betray her.

Except he hadn't. He had been manipulated in the same way as she was.

Now, instead of being the injured one, it looked as if she had betrayed him. She had taken the first opportunity to denounce him. She'd denied him a chance to explain. Her prejudice blinded her. She'd ruined everything.

Although things could never be the same between them, she had to find a way of letting him know how sorry she was.

She turned the last corner and stared at the battlements before her. She blinked twice in case it was a trick of the moonlight.

Standing with his back to her, his face turned firmly towards the sea, was Tullio. His crimson cloak was black in the moonlight, making a contrast with the pale skin of his just visible forearms.

Helena stopped and stood, unable to do more than stare.

It was one thing to think about Tullio and to plan her apology. It was quite another to actually have the courage to make it.

Why was he here? Had he sought her out? But he could not have known where she'd be.

She turned to go as silently as she came. However, an invisible thread seemed to connect them. As she turned, so did he.

'Helena.'

A single whispered word, no more. A question. A plea and so much more was contained in that one word.

It was enough.

Helena stopped and went into the silvered moonlight. 'I wasn't expecting to find anyone here,' she said around the sudden lump in her throat.

'I couldn't sleep,' he said.

His face looked remote, stern and unyielding. The lines were more pronounced than ever, his eyes black stone.

Helena's heart contracted. She thought of all the accusations she had heaped on his head. Never once had she paused and asked what she might do in a similar situation. All the warmth seemed to have vanished from him as if it had never been.

'I'm worried about my men.' His hand pushed a lock of hair off his forehead. 'The pirates ill treated them.'

'It is right to worry.' She bit her lip and wished she could unsay those words. They sounded so unfeeling, almost threatening. She was no better than Kimon. 'They will survive. I have been assured of that. Galla is taking a personal interest. And she has snatched patients from the very jaws of Cerberus.'

He raised an eyebrow. Helena waited and mentally prepared a light remark. Something that would lead into her apology. He shifted slightly. She thought she detected a relaxation of his crossed arms.

'That is good to hear.'

'Galla seems quite taken with Quintus,' Helena tried again.

'That is no concern of mine. Quintus knew what he was doing.'

He wasn't going to make this easy for her. One small gesture and she'd run to his arms. Helena knew that. She adjusted her shawl more tightly around her shoulders and let the silence grow.

'Why you are up here? Your men are in the hospital. There is no reason for you to be here.'

'I could ask you the same question.' His face was back in shadow. His voice was soft, lazy, yet she could tell from the way he held himself that he was watching her with a deep intentness.

'I come here to think. I found it difficult to sleep.'

She forced her feet to move sedately over to her favourite spot. The black shapes of the boats bobbed up and down on a silver sea. The quiet lapping of the waves hitting the boats was clearly audible even in the turret.

There had been less damage than she'd first thought, but enough to keep everyone busy for the next few weeks. A precious few weeks to get her aunt well enough to stand and perform the blessing. Within a few weeks, everything would have returned to normal.

Within a few weeks, days, he would be gone and she'd be left here to face the future alone.

Helena shivered.

How could she begin to explain any of this to Tullio? With each lap of the water, she felt the time of her destiny was coming closer.

'When sleep is difficult, this place calls to me. Only here can I find peace.'

'My commiserations.' Tullio gave a slight bow. 'We all have problems.'

Helena pressed her palms together. She refused to get angry. Anger would not serve her purpose. She had to think and to plan. She had to approach her problem with a level head. She turned from the harbour and faced him.

'I hadn't expected to find anyone here.'

'Sleep is impossible, so I came here. I remembered the way from the last time. Perhaps I seek some sort of peace as well. A lasting peace.' He made a sardonic bow. 'I came to watch for the tribute ship. It should be here any day. I watch the water and hope.'

Helena hesitated. She did not voice her fears—fears about what would happen when it did arrive or what might happen if the ship perished in the storm. She walked over to the battlements and gripped the stone with both her hands. She listened to the sound of the waves lapping and the softer one of Tullio's breath.

'No doubt the ship will arrive soon. And then what will you do?'

'I will be free to go and will have no obligations here. I will pursue my vow.'

'Of destroying the seafarers?'

'Yes. I told you that it is the one thing I live for.'

'I know you took no part in the escape.' Helena said the words to the silvered sea. He had moved nearer. She could sense that without looking up to confirm it. Her whole body tingled with anticipation. 'Quintus confessed.'

His hand reached out and touched her shoulder. Warm fingers against the coolness of her skin. She forced her body to stay still.

'What has happened to change your mind? You were positive before. You threw it in my face.'

'I interviewed the men in hospital. Galla tried to say it was her fault, but Quintus refused to let her. He explained what he had done and how he had tricked us all.' She tightened her grip on the stones until the white of her knuckles showed.

'The seafarers will wish to see them punished,' she said. 'They abused the temple's hospitality.'

'And being beaten is not enough? Being forced to fight and make sport is not enough?' His voice held a note of incredulity. 'What more do you propose to do?'

'I said that it was not my decision. I do not speak for the sibyl. You seem to think that I control everything that happens in this temple. It is simply an illusion. I have little power.'

'Just as I have little control over the determined actions of my men. And yet twice you have held me to account for them.'

Helena stared at him. The moonlight made the planes of his face shadowed and his hair appear blue black. Her hands itched to touch his curls again and to feel them spring back against the pads of her fingers. She wanted to go back to that easier time when there were no shadows between them.

'What would you have me do?' she whispered.

Tullio tore his gaze from Helena's face and the way the moonlight highlighted the curve of her bosom. The light breeze moulded her thin robe to her body. He remembered how each and every curve had felt under his fingers. He remembered how her skin had trembled underneath his.

He had come up here to think and to get away from the memory of her lips and the way her body fitted against him. He wanted to make sense of what had happened and how he was going to reconcile the feelings he had for Helena with his duty towards Rome.

What Quintus's escape attempt had shown him was that he had put his own desires ahead of his duty. It was the first time such a thing had happened. If he had stayed, those men would not now be fighting for their lives. Quintus did it because Tullio had vacated his post and gone in search of Helena.

'It is not up to me to decide their punishment. For this, I thank the gods.'

There was a troubled expression in Helena's eyes. Tullio hated making things worse for her, but she had to make a decision. She had to decide where she stood—with the pirates or with the rule of law.

'You had no idea what Quintus and the other two were intending to do.'

'I was busy attending to other things.'

He lift a hand towards her and smoothed the one ringlet back from her face. Her skin trembled slightly under the touch of his fingers. It felt warm against his cooled hands. Cold? Or something more? Tullio hesitated. He could feel the stirrings of a response to her nearness deep within his body.

'What sort of things?' There was a teasing quality to her voice.

'Just things.'

He used one finger to tilt her chin. He gazed at her face. There were words he wanted to say to her but he was neither a poet nor a smooth-talking senator. He was legionary, a man who lived his life by the sword.

He had never felt like this about anyone before and it frightened him. This woman meant far more to him than his military oath. He had nearly betrayed his men for her. He had gone to the brink, but now he was back. He had regained command of his emotions.

Her eyes were wide, her mouth inviting.

He bent his head and captured her lips, allowing the touch of his mouth to speak for him. If she rejected him again, he would know that this was the end.

Her lips parted at his first touch. Her mouth opened, warm and enticing. Tullio hesitated, applying the lightest of touches. Her hands reached up, grasped the back of his neck and drew his head closer, deepening the kiss, demanding more.

His arms came around and grasped her, fitting her curves to him. Within a heartbeat, his body hardened, responding to her softness.

She quivered in his arms.

He lifted his mouth from hers and stared into her moonlit eyes. His hands buried themselves in her tangled mass of hair.

'I'm sorry,' she whispered, touching his mouth with her fingers, tracing its outline.

'Sorry for what?'

'I should have believed you.'

'It is in the past.'

Tullio ran a finger down the side of her face. He knew what that admission had cost her. He knew he should press forward, demand that she declare for Rome, but this was beyond that, this was between him and her.

Nothing else mattered except the taste of her mouth, the feel of her body against his.

'Do you mean that?'

'Hush, Helena,' he said, recapturing her mouth.

He heard the moan in her throat.

Her tongue touched his, retreated and returned for a long caress. He pulled her closer, running a hand down her back to the narrow indentation of her waist, crushing her beasts against his chest. Through the thin material, her erect nipples teased him.

He ran his palm down her side, rubbed a nipple with the back of his thumb, and watched her face change in the starlight. Her body writhed against him. Slowly, carefully, his fingers circled her breast, now brushing, now rubbing more firmly. The thrusts of her hips became more frantic, circling. His body grew tighter. He held on to his self-control with the thinnest of threads.

He wanted to give her pleasure, and bind her to him.

Her fingers plucked at his tunic, slipped between the cloth

and his skin, ran along his collarbone. A slender hand slipped down and caressed his chest, making the points of his nipples as erect as hers.

With difficulty, he kept the fire beginning to rage within him in check. He had to allow her the chance to explore. She withdrew her hands and then ran them down the side of his body. He drew in his breath.

Her hands hovered at his belt. His manhood tightened to an ache. It took every ounce of self-control he had not to lower her to the ground, part her legs and plough himself into her.

He wanted to be sure. She was too important to him simply to be bedded.

'Helena, this is not an ideal place,' he croaked, his voice barely recognisable to his ears.

'We have your cloak, and the stars.'

Helena tilted her head and peeped at him from under her lashes. She knew what he was offering, but she also knew that she wanted this man once more. She wanted to feel as she had felt in the cave. She wanted to feel like a woman, not a priestess.

He took off his cloak, lay it on the ground, then relaxed against it, inviting her. He patted the ground next to him. The invitation was clear.

She knew what she had to do.

Her hands loosened the simple tie about her hips and let it fall to the ground. She watched Tullio for any sign. Her tongue licked her lips. Her fingers were all thumbs. She wanted to please this man. She wanted to make him feel the way she was feeling. The points of her breasts ached and her skin tingled from his touch.

She swallowed hard, wondering what to do next. How to

proceed. How did one disrobe for a lover? Instinct only guided her. She started to shrug the gown off one shoulder, saw the possibility of it becoming stuck and stopped.

She wanted to get it right.

Tullio watched her. He held his body still. He had to let her take her time because he wanted her to come to him. He had no wish to frighten her. He had so very nearly lost her. He waited, feeling the desire within him grow.

With one swift movement, she took off her gown and stood there shimmering. The dusky place between her thighs contrasted with her starlit limbs.

A goddess.

He had to touch her, to worship her.

She held out her hands, beckoning.

Tullio knelt up and encircled her waist with his hands, before running them down her sides. She quivered under his touch, but did not draw back.

He laid his cheek against her abdomen and felt her hand stroke his hair. Skin against skin.

With a slight turn of his head, he touched his lips to her midriff and tasted the sweetness of her flesh. His tongue curved around her belly button, lingered there. Then his lips moved ever downward, sampling, nibbling until he reached her short curls.

He paused and glanced upwards. Her head was thrown back. Her nipples were tight buds poised above him. He lifted a hand, touched them and then returned to the point where her thighs met.

A gasp came from Helena's throat.

Her hands buried themselves in his thick dark hair, drawing him towards her. This was unlike anything she had ever experienced before—the touch of his mouth against her, parting her. He made her feel as if she were a precious vessel made of glass.

She wanted him to continue.

She needed to feel the heat of his mouth.

His tongue delved deeper within her and heat surged over her. The only thing she knew was his tongue making forays into her innermost space. With each new caress, the heat within her built. Her limbs melted.

'Please, Tullio,' she begged, not knowing if she was asking him to continue or to put an end to this feeling inside her.

He loosened his hands and gently lowered her to his cloak. She lay wondering if she should touch him in the same way he was touching her.

His hands opened her thighs, exposing her to the warm air. He placed his mouth on her. She bucked at the sensation, rose to meet him, her body demanding his mouth drive further into her. His tongue swirled and swayed. Her hands sought him, finding first the cloak, then his soft hair, holding him there.

When she thought she must die from the pleasure, she felt him slide himself upwards, and enter her with the tip of his erection. He filled her and her body opened to receive the full length of him.

She moved her hips, and he followed her rhythm. Slow. Fast. Until the whole world was moving. She felt him shudder a breath before she did, watched his face and saw the bliss in his eyes.

This was what she was born for, she thought and then her own climax overtook her.

* * *

Helena's face was pale in the moonlight. Her eyelashes made black smudges against her skin. Her skin touched his with no more than the faintest sheen of sweat between them. Tullio felt his body begin to harden again, but he forced himself to roll away from her and lie on his back, staring up at the sky.

He hated to wake her up, but he had to. He could detect the first faint streaks of rose in the slate grey sky. Soon everyone would stir. They had tarried there too long. He might not have another chance to speak to her again alone. With each passing day, the tribute ship would draw closer. He couldn't leave her. He wanted her by his side.

'Helena, we must speak.'

Her eyes flew open. Deep green pools. Tullio wondered what it would be like to wake every morning to those eyes. Her hand reached up to touch his cheek and her lips curved into a smile. 'I wondered if it had been a dream.'

'It was no dream.'

'Good.'

Tullio captured Helena's hands and held them tight. The simplest of touches and his body responded. He wanted her again, but not here and not now. It was most emphatically not safe.

'Helena, we did not take any precautions.'

'Precautions?' Her eyes looked confused, sleep laden. 'What are you talking about?'

'I am talking about if a child should result from this encounter or the last.'

Her eyes grew wide and the sleep vanished. He felt cruel for reminding her, for destroying the moment, but it had to be said.

'There are ways. My aunt taught them to me. You need not worry. Rue and raspberry leaves.' She pulled her gown back over her head, covering her magnificent body. She wrapped her arms about her knees and fell silent.

A queer stabbing went through Tullio's heart. He should have known. Sibyls and priestesses would have their ways, but it did not lessen the danger.

'And if Androcles and his son should find out? They will brand you traitor.'

'What do you propose?'

'Leave, leave with me when the tribute comes.' He caught her right hand and brought it to his lips. 'You will like Rome. It is as no other city in the world. Its markets are filled any number of goods, and the buildings are made of brick and marble. Let me show it to you.'

'What are you saying, Tullio?' She withdrew her hand.

'Let me look after you. Leave this behind you and come with me. There is little for you here. Put yourself first for once.'

Helena felt the aching in her stomach grow. This was not how she had envisioned a proposal. She knew that everything Tullio said was correct—if her liaison with Tullio was discovered, it would go ill for the temple. But it was not going to be. She forced her mind to think clearly, the cobwebs of the night vanishing as they had never been.

He was more worried about what the consequences might be for Rome than for her. He had to be.

'I can't just leave. The temple depends on me. People depend on me.'

'You are not the sibyl. You don't have the responsibility.'

'You have no idea what you are asking of me. The sibyl needs me.'

He grasped her forearms.

'Think, Helena, what might happen if Androceles discovers what has passed between us. You must come away with me. It is dangerous for you.'

'But Aunt Flavia needs protecting.'

'For how much longer do you think you can continue this charade? It is clear that Androceles and Kimon suspect.'

'I'll think of something,' Helena said with more confidence than she felt.

'Helena, all my life I have waited for you, for what we have. Let me show you Rome. The world is so much bigger than this island.'

Helena looked out at the sea. Soon it would be rose-coloured and the sounds of the harbour would echo. Could she leave all this and go away? If she thought he truly loved her, she might be tempted. She was tempted. He was right— none of this was her responsibility. She thought of her longing to hold her own child in her arms. And of the dried up look of her aunt who had never known pleasure in a man's arms.

'How? Walk on board ship with you? Androceles and the rest might let me, but then they would take their revenge on the temple.'

'You vanish.'

'Vanish?'

'You said that one sibyl did. There is a faint pathway down to that beach, the one where you said that the lover met the sibyl.'

'Only goats wander up and down that path and even they never go to the bottom.'

'But it could be done. My trireme could meet you there. The seafarers would never know.'

'I'll think on it.' Her arms trembled as she wrapped them about her waist. Leave everything, abandon all that she held dear. But what sort of future did she have here? It was only a matter of time before Aunt Flavia discovered what a fraud she was. And when her aunt lost her powers, there would another sibyl, a different one.

'Rome will look after you. You have done a great service to my soldiers. Rome always rewards its friends.' His face became boyish as if he had been given an unexpected present, something he had longed for, but had not expected to receive. 'You will see.'

Helena nodded and wished he had said something that showed they had a future together. She wanted to know they were going to be together. But he hadn't. Her mouth twisted. He was a Roman patrician and she was the daughter of a disgraced sibyl. They lived in different worlds.

She stood up and adjusted her gown, straightening the creases. Her hair she allowed to flow down her back. She'd worry about putting it to rights when she returned to her bedroom. Her shawl should hide its disarrayed state. She held the belt in her hand. Out of habit she neatly tied it around her hips. She hesitated, undid the knot and tied the belt firmly under her breast. She would be an ordinary woman, no longer an acolyte of the temple.

'Do you want me to come with you when you tell the sibyl?'

Helena shook her head. 'There are some things that I have to do alone,' she said.

Chapter Sixteen

'You're dressed in your robes, Aunt Flavia.'

Helena stared. Flavia was standing in the middle of her reception room, dressed in her white robes with the sword of power hanging by her side. Save for the golden mask, she could be just about to embark on a ceremonial visit.

'I thought it was time I reclaimed my authority.'

Her aunt's green eyes bore into Helena's soul. She was convinced that her aunt could detect the imprint of Tullio's touch. Helena bowed her head and concentrated on the mosaic tiles at her aunt's feet.

'Is there something wrong with that?' her aunt asked. 'For far too long I have allowed you and Galla to nurse me. I am not an invalid. I never have been. Now I discover things have been happening in the temple which I have no knowledge of. Important things.'

'No, no, there is nothing wrong with that. I welcome it. Truly I do.'

Helena wondered how she would tell Flavia that she had doubts. That she had decided not to take the final step, but to depart from the life of a priestess. She had to choose her words carefully.

She should be rejoicing that Flavia had regained her strength. It would make leaving easier. Tullio was correct. Her destiny was not here. Her destiny was out there. Somewhere where she would not have to worry about if the incense burners had been filled or the robes washed, or if the correct amount of tribute had been received. She was about to become free.

Her aunt raised the ceremonial sword, and held it aloft over her head. It wavered in the air, then crashed to the ground. Flavia bent down and started to retrieve it and a pang went through Helena. She went forward and took the sword from her aunt's grasp. The elderly woman let it go with a sigh.

'A few days more, Aunt, and you will be strong again,' Helena said quickly.

A few days more and she would be gone. None of this would be her concern. Her hand reached for her amulet, but it had gone. Helena closed her eyes.

'Is this another of your prophecies, Helena, or mere words?'

'Another prophecy?' Helena tucked her hair behind her ear. She opted for a smooth smile, but her stomach churned. 'I would never dream of making a prophecy to you, Aunt. I can just tell from the way you are recovering. You will be well, just as you have been a hundred times before.'

'You are a good supporter, Helena. I appreciate it.'

'You are a good sibyl, Aunt Flavia. You have done more for this island than anyone else I know.'

Helena shifted under her aunt's gaze and drew a breath. She would tell her now. She owed Aunt Flavia that much.

'You flatter me,' her aunt said, but her smile was pleased.

It troubled Helena that Aunt Flavia had not regained the full use of her face, but a half-smile was better than none.

'Not flattery. I tell the truth.'

Her aunt's eyes narrowed at the word—truth. Helena took a step backwards. The table bumped into her legs and she put out a hand to steady herself. She had to work the conversation around to the right words. She had to find an opening. Surely her aunt would notice where she had tied her belt. Surely she would comment on that. She knew where her destiny lay. But how to tell her aunt? How to explain she had changed her mind? It was one thing to be sure up there on the turret in Tullio's arms, and quite another here in her aunt's chamber, faced with the evidence of Aunt Flavia's infirmity.

'Tell me, Helena, how did you get that prophecy? Out of a matter of curiosity.'

Helena paused. Her aunt's voice reminded her of the times when she had made an error of judgement, when she had chosen the wrong sort of incense to burn or had not thrown the correct combination of knucklebones. She busied her hands with returning the sword to its box. The lid snapped with a click, and Helena turned the key.

'Does it matter?' she asked.

'It would appear that Kybele has spoken to you with a great deal of accuracy. Prophecies like that are not found through tossing knucklebones or gazing into libation bowls.'

A chill breeze seemed to blow through the sibyl's apartments. Helena started forward, and knelt at her aunt's feet. The time had come to confess what she had done and how she had entered the prophecy cave without permission.

'I went into Kybele's lair,' she said, holding her head up and looking directly at Flavia. 'I know it was strictly forbidden, but the temple had to remain strong. I could not risk you going down there. You were too weak. It was for the good of the temple. The prophecy came from what I saw there.'

'Surely that was something I should have decided.'

Helena shifted under her aunt's sharp gaze. The explanations she had planned died on her lips. She held out her hands, imploring her aunt to forgive her.

'I could not take the risk. Another spell in the cave so quickly after the last and you would have died.'

'That was for Kybele to decide.' Aunt Flavia inclined her head, but there was an immense sadness in her eyes.

'I know.' Helena stood and ran her sandal along the floor.

'The prophecy came from your efforts and yours alone?' Her mouth twisted as if the words tasted bitter.

Helena's hand plucked at her skirts. How much longer was she going to have to endure this? She knew what was coming—banishment. It was well she had already decided to go.

'Yes, that's right.' She regarded her hands, the floor, anywhere but her aunt's eyes. 'I take full responsibility. No one knew I was going to go down there. I spoke with no one about the prophecy before I wrote it down.'

'You have confirmed what I suspected.'

Helena took a big breath. She had to tell Aunt Flavia what she intended on doing now, before her aunt banished her.

'Aunt, I must tell you—'

'There, Flavia, it was not so difficult after all.' The Lady Zenobia came from Aunt Flavia's bedroom, her green silk gown rustling with every step she took. Her face wore a triumphant smile. 'You played your part admirably, Flavia— but then you were always a good performer on the day.'

Helena glanced between her aunts. Aunt Flavia seemed to shrink and become much hunched while Zenobia positively glowed. Helena took a step backwards, knocking over the table. She heard the sword case crash to the ground, but ignored it.

'What is going on here? Aunt Flavia? Will someone tell me?'

Aunt Flavia shrugged, and looked pointedly at Zenobia. Zenobia's thin lips were stretched into an unpleasant smile. She advanced towards Helena, snapped her fingers and one of her slaves righted the table. A simple but significant act.

Somehow, Zenobia had discovered Aunt Flavia's recent illness. She had taken control of the sibyl's apartments. Helena's eyes widened as Zenobia clapped her hands together and armed guards streamed into the room.

Helena's heart rose to her mouth. A trap. Perfectly executed and she had walked into it. She offered a prayer up to Kybele, to any god who might be listening, that she emerged alive.

'You have been hiding much from the seafarers, Helena. You were naughty, but then you were always disobedient, even as a child clinging to your mother's skirts.'

'It was not their business,' Helena retorted.

'The sibyl's health is everyone's business,' Zenobia spat. 'Everyone suffers when the goddess does not speak to the sibyl. You forced me to learn the truth from my cousin.'

'There is no evidence of Kybele's desertion. The prophecy was accurate. Uncle Lichas arrived back in a black mist.'

'Pah.' Zenobia made a movement with her hand. 'It was not Flavia's prophecy. Surely you must know that the goddess only speaks to one sibyl at a time. Kybele has abandoned Flavia and chosen someone new.'

'No, that is not right.' Helena threw up her hands and backed away. She wanted what she'd agreed with Tullio. She wanted to renounce everything. 'Aunt Flavia is still the sibyl.'

'You said the prophecy was accurate.' Zenobia's smile was pitiless. The same expression Helena had seen her use to order a flogging of a slave. 'You went into Kybele's lair and emerged alive. You are the one. Deny if you dare.'

Helena looked at Aunt Flavia, hoping to see something, reassurance, help. Her aunt had her head bowed on her hands. She had aged years in the last few breaths.

Cold swept over Helena. How could she explain now that Kybele had not spoken to her? That she hadn't done as Aunt Flavia always did—waited for the first mist to lift and then received the proper prophecy? It hadn't lifted and she couldn't. It was a very tangled web of lies she had woven. Galla had been correct that first day. She should never have attempted the deception.

It had all gone wrong, dreadfully wrong.

No, not all wrong, there was Tullio. She refused to think that what they had shared was wrong.

'What do you want me to do?' She glanced at her hand with its shortened finger. A few weeks ago to be proclaimed sibyl would have been her dearest dream, but everything had changed. She wasn't sure what she wanted. 'I am not ready to be the sibyl.'

'The goddess knows when you are ready, Helena.' Zenobia's eye glittered, reminding Helena of snakes. 'She would not have spoken to you otherwise. You survived the cave.'

'Aunt Flavia...I have not made the final ritual.' Helena turned towards her and held out her hands in a gesture of supplication. This was all a mistake. It could be solved. But not here, and not now.

'The final ritual is to confront the goddess and see if she gives any indication of her favour,' Zenobia replied.

'Why can't you let my aunt speak?' Helena turned towards Zenobia.

'If you don't wish to be the sibyl, I am sure arrangements can be made…'

There was no mistaking the note in Zenobia's voice. Helena stumbled her way to a stool and sat down before her legs gave out.

'What happens to Aunt Flavia?'

She saw her aunts exchange glances. For the first time, Helena detected fear in Aunt Flavia's eyes.

'What happens to the old sibyl is a matter for the new sibyl and her alone.' Zenobia straightened her robes. 'However, I do think it is a mistake to have an old sibyl. We had problems with the old sibyl, didn't we, Flavia?'

'Helena, you should leave the room.' Flavia's voice held a note of her old authority. 'I need to speak with Zenobia.'

From force of habit, Helena started towards the door. She trusted Aunt Flavia's judgement.

'She will learn the truth soon enough, if the goddess does speak to her,' Zenobia replied.

'What do you mean…problems?' Helena stopped and turned towards Flavia. She trusted Aunt Flavia to tell her the truth, however unpalatable. She had never flinched from her duty before. 'My mother's death was an accident. You told me that. She chose to go out in that storm. Didn't she?'

'She did not want to accept Kybele as the new chief goddess.' Flavia gave a weary shrug and collapsed into her chair. She motioned for Helena to come and sit next to her. 'When your mother discovered she was pregnant, she refused to go into the goddess's lair. She wanted to do everything in her power to keep you safe. She preferred Aesculapius anyway, but we were attacked and lost several triremes. To make peace, Lichas agreed to marry Zenobia.'

'The sibyl needed a stronger goddess to protect this island,' Zenobia interrupted. 'Flavia accepted my sensible suggestion to change the temple's allegiance to Kybele. Her predictions became accurate and the house of Lichas went from strength to strength.'

'We quarrelled, Helena. That is why your mother went out in the storm, and I have always regretted it. It is the reason I took you in when others would have left you.'

Zenobia's cheeks coloured. 'We have discussed this enough. I accepted your decision. The goddess spoke through you.'

'Jupiter spared you, Helena. The goddess Kybele protected you that day. She has chosen you for my successor.' Flavia's cool green gaze met hers and seemed to bore into her soul. 'Such a responsibility is not tossed away lightly.'

Helena bowed her head. She could not desert her aunt now. There had to be another way. She had to follow the path she was born for. Too many people depended on her. She shuddered to think what would happen if Zenobia chose another woman. There had to be a way of defeating her and the seafarers.

'If you say that I am the next sibyl, then so be it.'

'We must speak, Marcus Livius Tullio.'
At the sound of Helena's voice, Tullio turned from the

window. His heart leapt. She looked as lovely as she had earlier. But rather than rushing into his arms, she stood beyond his reach and retreated as he stepped forward.

He searched her face and saw a new dignity there. Instead of her usual robes, Helena wore the white robes of the sibyl. Her hair flowed down her back and a gold belt was looped about her hips. But even with such authority, she seemed uncertain.

'What has happened?'

'My aunt's illness was discovered.' She inclined her head but her big eyes looked luminous. 'I have agreed to become the sibyl.'

A wealth of meaning was in that simple statement. Tullio's heart contracted. She could not leave the people of this island. Silently he cursed. He should have known that on the turret. It hurt that she had chosen glory. He wanted her, not the symbol. He knew what this could mean for Rome, but selfishly he looked for any sign that she regretted giving up her earlier promise.

'Does the old sibyl live?'

'She lives. Aunt Zenobia has insisted on looking after her in her illness.'

Again, Helena spoke in an almost toneless voice, but Tullio knew what such an occurrence must mean to her. For one wild instant, Tullio completed storming the palace, then he rejected it as being suicidal. He needed men and arms. There had to be something he could do. Some way he could help.

He reached out to touch her face, her shoulder, but she moved neatly away as if she were frightened. Tullio's hand hung in mid-air for a heartbeat and then he returned it his side. Helena's action told him far more than he wanted to know.

'Do you need protection?' he asked in a low undertone. 'Tell me what you want my men to do. Rome can help.'

'Rome, it is always Rome. Whenever is it anything else?'

'My duty lies with Rome.'

'And my duty lies with my people. It always has done. To think any other way was misguided. I'm sorry. It should never have happened.'

Tullio peered deep into her eyes, trying to understand what she was saying.

'The offer is there. I want to help you, Helena. Let me protect you.'

'I have all the protection I need. Androceles has helpfully stationed some of his seafarers here to aid in the transition process.' She shook her head and indicated the shadowy figures standing behind her.

Seafarers. Pirates.

Tullio's guts twisted. She'd made her choice. She'd avoided them for so long and now this. She had been content to go with him when she had thought there was no hope of advancement. But she had embraced the seafarer's offer very quickly.

He had trusted her, and she had betrayed him. He refused to give her the satisfaction of seeing how much he was hurt. All he knew was that she had spurned his offer and him.

'I wish you all the joys of your new post. You are well suited for it.'

'It is something I trained for years for. I hope to be a credit to my people.'

'I am sure you will be.'

He wanted to crush her to him, and ask if last night's promise meant nothing. His hands clenched as he hung on to his temper with the narrowest of threads. He had lost her. He had never really had her. There was a great gaping hole in his middle. He wanted to think he could survive this, but he knew his life would never be the same again.

'My formal investiture will be in forty days on the Calends,' she said with quiet certainty.

'Why so long?'

'It will give me time to prepare, to ensure that I am properly ready to meet the goddess.'

Helena watched for signs that Tullio understood what she was saying. But he stood, forearms crossed, the very picture of the immovable soldier. She wanted him to take her in his arms. She wanted to go back to the closeness they had shared, but it was impossible to speak freely.

She had to trust that he could understand her coded words and that he would help her, but his face looked remote.

She wanted to tell him how she needed him. How much she wanted to leave with him and turn her back on this island but, in the end, how she couldn't. She had to try to save her aunt and everyone else's life. She had to try to prevent the seafarers from attacking the Italian coast and harming women and children.

The very walls of the temple had become spies for Androceles and Kimon. Helena knew if she made one mistake, she would be killed before her reign could even begin.

There was no choice. To keep Aunt Flavia alive, she had to become the sibyl. Then to save both their lives, she had to hope that Tullio understood what she was trying to say to him, that he could look beyond her rejection of him to the wider stage and see what had to be done and why.

Glancing over her shoulder, she saw the seafarers with their crossed arms and curved swords hanging from their belts. She had very little time. He had to understand what she was telling him.

'I wish you good fortune for that day.'

'Thank you. I appreciate that. Please think of me then.'

'If that is what you want…' He bowed stiffly. His voice was colder than the snows on Mount Olympus itself.

Helena's heart plummeted. He had not understood. He thought she wanted this.

'I refuse to abandon my people in their hour of need.'

Don't abandon me, Tullio, her heart whispered. Find a way to rescue me.

'Easy words.'

Helena stamped her foot slightly. He was deliberately choosing to misunderstand her. She might not have another chance to speak to him in private. He had to understand what she was asking.

'I wanted to thank you for all your help.' She emphasised the word help and did not dare look into his increasingly cold eyes. 'The chiefs of the seafaring houses will be impressed when they arrive for the investiture.'

No response from him. Helena bit her lip. There was no point in making a stand now, but surely he could see what she wanted him to do.

A long low blast on a cornu filled the temple and he tilted his head.

'Another of the seafarers arriving? With goods that don't come from pirate raids?'

Helena winced. She longed to tell him that she believed him now. She was certain of everything, but there was no time for explanations. The Fates had run out of wool on this particular spindle.

'The tribute ship has arrived. I hope that all the money will be there.'

'Down to every last *as*. My men and I hope to spend no more time than is absolutely necessary on this rock.' He bowed again. 'You will give me leave to depart. I must tell them the good news.'

Helena watched him go. She had to hope that when he got beyond the pain, he would see what she had asked.

'I hope we will meet again. Some time in the future,' she said, making one last attempt.

'That, my lady, I sincerely doubt.'

Tullio thanked Jupiter for the familiar weight of his mail coat and helmet. Things to remind him who he was and why he was here. His men were all assembled on the quayside. Not much remained to do and then they'd set sail for the nearest Roman port.

He stared at Androceles with intense dislike. The pirate's mood had lightened considerably since he saw the strongboxes being unloaded off the trireme.

Helena, with the gold mask firmly in place, stood next to the pirate captain. The wind ruffled her gown, moulding it to her legs. She showed no sign of nervousness or regret.

Tullio regarded her. Why he had thought she'd be different, he didn't know. She had made her choice. It was quite clear where her sympathies lay.

'You are free to leave, Tribune,' Androceles said, testing a final *denarius* with his teeth and throwing it on the pile with the rest of the tribute.

Tullio raised his hand and started to give the order for his men to embark.

'Halt! We have a traitor in our midst.' Helena's voice cut through the quayside sounds and made every nerve in Tullio's body tense.

Had she changed her mind? What was her game now? She had played him expertly, but what did she want?

Tullio motioned for his men to keep quiet.

'You wish to say something, Sibyl?' There was a contemptuous curl to Androceles's lip. The respect of a few weeks ago was gone. Tullio could almost bring himself to feel pity for Helena, but she had chosen this life.

'Yes, I have something to say. Here is the traitor.'

She snapped her fingers and two guards dragged her maid out. Galla's wrists were chained together and her face bore the bright red mark of a slap. She gave a terrified shriek as the guard made her kneel before Helena and Androceles.

'I have discovered this woman has betrayed us. She fed the Romans special food, gave them medicine. She has gone beyond what was required by Kybele.'

'And what do you propose to do about this?' Androceles asked.

'I will allow no treachery on this island. No one who fraternises with Romans shall remain here while the purification ceremony takes place.'

Tullio lifted his head and met Helena's eyes. There was more to this. She was up to something. Why was she getting rid of her most staunch ally? Then he had it. The terrible noble thing she was doing. His insides twisted. She was not trying to punish Galla. She was trying to save her. He grabbed Quintus's elbow and held him there, preventing Quintus from moving and alerting Androceles.

Galla fell to her knees. 'No, I beg you, my lady. I repent of my mistake. I swear it. I will never betray you again.'

'Get up.' One of the seafarers prodded her. 'You should have thought of that earlier.'

'There are other ways of punishing the maid.' Androceles licked his lips.

'She goes with the Romans. I will not have her on this soil…not when there is an investiture to plan for.'

Tullio reached out and touched Galla's arm, raising her to her feet. Her icy hand clutched his.

He glanced at Helena and saw her eyes held a satisfied look before she turned her head.

Utter despair washed over him. He had wronged her. Helena was sacrificing herself to save Galla, to save her aunt. He should have seen this before. What had she tried to tell him before? He winced. She had tried and he had not wanted to listen. He had been so wrapped up in his pride and hurt that he had not paid attention to the hidden meanings.

'We will take the woman and gladly. Rome does not forget its friends.' Tullio plucked a handful of gold coins from his arm pouch, and tossed them at Helena's feet. 'That should pay for her with interest. Does that satisfy you, Captain?'

'I'm impressed, Sibyl, at your negotiating skill.' The pirate captain picked up the coins and ran them through his fingers. 'Profit before revenge. We will get on well.'

I will return, Tullio vowed silently. I've wronged you, Helena. There was much I should have said when I had the chance.

Tullio jammed on his helmet, saluted Helena and marched on to the ship. He did not trust himself to look back.

* * *

Helena reached the top of the turret in time to see the last of the trireme disappear over the horizon. She raised an arm and waved.

He was gone. Truly gone.

Her insides were hollow, a great black hole in her middle.

On the quayside she had been tempted to give in to her desires and run to him, cling to him and beg him to take her with him. But she had held back. A coward. She should have declared herself the traitor, and departed.

Tullio looked so different and remote in his armour. If only she had had more time.

Helena swallowed hard. The scene swam before her. She blinked once. Twice. Three times. She refused to cry.

The shouts and sounds from the quayside floated up. Somewhere a goat bleated and a goose honked. Normal sounds. Helena choked back a sob growing in her throat. Nothing would be normal again.

She had never felt so alone, not even when she faced the goddess. Then, there had been hope, expectation. Now there was nothing.

She closed her eyes and thought of Tullio's last blazing look. Did it mean something?

She made a line on the stone. Day one.

Forty days until her investiture and her next trip into the black cave. Her mind shied away from the black mist. This time, the pirates would surely guess. Fortunata would fail her.

There would be no Tullio to rescue her.

Did he understand the message she had tried to send him?

She had to trust him and to trust Galla. She hated how she had treated Galla, but, if she had known, the maid might have objected. She had had to get Galla out of danger. The Roman centurion would look after her. He had said that he wanted to buy her. Galla was better in Roman hands when the seafarers discovered how much Helena had duped them, when it became apparent that the goddess did not speak to her.

She drew a shaky breath.

Forty days. It wasn't much time. Helena tried to think how long it would take to get to the nearest Roman settlement and to get the men Tullio would need. If he understood the message. If he would come back to her.

It wasn't enough time.

It had to be enough.

Helena went down on her knees and prayed for a miracle. On the floor next to her hand a silver disc lay. Helena picked up and turned it over. It was a medal stamped with a laurel crown. Tullio's? She tucked it into her pouch. This was her new talisman.

She had to believe help would come.

Chapter Seventeen

'You want to do what? Marcus Livius Tullio, you have lost your mind!' the tribune shouted.

Tullio tightened his jaw and stared straight ahead, ignoring the receding-chinned tribune. It was just his luck that the prefect for the garrison was away and he was left with this imbecile. He had explained the situation three times already.

There had to be something more. Something he had forgotten. He had to find a way to save Helena and her aunt. He had gone over and over the clues that Helena had given him. He should have listened. He should have asked questions then.

'The pirates are massing for the investiture of the new sibyl.'

'Are you sure of your information?' the tribune asked with an arched brow. 'It hardly seems credible.'

'I know it for a fact. We can strike a blow at the heart of the pirates' enterprise.' He waited for a breath. 'It is for the good of Rome.'

For the good of Rome. Tullio hated that he had to lie. This

was no longer about the good of Rome. It was about rescuing Helena, pure and simple. It was about asking her to take another chance with him. His pride had got in the way. He wanted to rectify his mistake.

There were things he had to tell her. If he had said that he loved her, he was certain it would have made a difference.

'Tell me the true reason, Marcus Livius. Why do you want to commit the men and the ships? It is not in Rome's best interest at the moment. There is unrest on the Spanish peninsula, we have problems with Mithridates in the near East. Why should Rome care about the riff-raff?'

Tullio spotted an amphora standing in the corner. From where he stood, he could see a distinctive blue patterning on the top.

He nodded, understanding. The mark of Androceles's house.

'Rome does not take kindly to those who traffic with known pirates.'

'I…that is to say…' the tribune's ears grew red '…by Hercules, Marcus Livius, everyone does it.'

'Not everyone, and not everyone trades with a senator's murderer.'

'He murdered a senator.' The tribune's Adam's apple bobbed up and down. He bore a distinct impression to a fish gasping for water.

'I need men and ships.'

The tribune was silent. He made a notation on his papyrus scroll. Tullio forced his body to stay rigidly to attention.

'I will think about it.'

'You will do more than think.' Tullio grabbed the stylus out of the startled tribune's hand, and forced him against a wall. 'For six days, you have been telling me that you will think, consider and I need to come tomorrow. But tomorrow never arrives. Guess what? Tomorrow has arrived!'

'You can't do that.'

'I just have.' Tullio leant forward. 'Now, are you going to get me the ships I need or am I going to tell the legate just where you have been obtaining all that fine Falerian wine?'

Thirty-nine. Helena made one more mark. Forty. Forty lines on a stone wall. So many lines, so quickly.

She rose from her knees and stared out towards the still harbour. The triremes bobbed in the gentle breeze. More ships than she had ever seen before. But not one of them Roman. The hunting eyes on the prows of the ships no longer a comfort. Helena knew exactly what these ships did and what Androceles intended to do. She had been blind before.

Her hands tightened on the battlements. She had never expected it to take this long. The first few days and nights had past in a blur of activity and ritual. She could not expect him back. It would take time to get men.

Then on the tenth day she had begun to hope. She found every excuse to look at the horizon. Each new sail caused a tightening in her belly, hope springing in her heart. She'd raise her hand to shield her eyes against the sun's glare, imagining Tullio standing on the prow, chain mail gleaming, and sword held aloft. But it remained a dream.

By the thirtieth day, she had stopped running to the battlements. She forced her hands to continue to their work. Each day brought a new purification ceremony. Aunt Flavia insisted the robes be made from the finest wool, and be sewn only by the sibyl. A time-consuming process, but one that kept her busy.

Each new sunrise brought greater loneliness. Particularly when her time of the month arrived and she discovered that she would not be carrying Tullio's son or daughter. She knew she should feel relief, but a small part of her wished for a baby, something to bind her to him. It made her realise that a child was not a disgrace. A child was a blessing from the gods.

Helena took one last look at the harbour. He was not coming. He had promised she would not have to face the cave alone and he had not returned. Only now she realised how much she relied on his promise, how it had carried her through those meetings with Androceles, Kimon and Uncle Lichas.

'I wondered if I would find you up here.'

Helena turned towards the steps at the sound of Aunt Flavia's voice.

'I thought to have some time to myself.' Helena moved in front of her tally of days.

'You are up here watching for Roman ships.'

'How…how did you know?'

'Instinct.' Aunt Flavia dropped a hand on Helena's shoulder. 'Don't be concerned. No one will have guessed. Remember, the goddess moves in mysterious ways. She has her own time. Marcus Livius Tullio is a good man.'

'The goddess does not speak to me, Aunt.' Helena stared directly into Flavia's eyes and watched them widen. 'I nearly died in the cave. I would have died if Tullio had not rescued me. When I put on the mask, I feel nothing.'

Aunt Flavia's face grew grave. Helena shifted on her sandals. She had to make a clean breast of everything.

'I was coming to tell you the day I was made sibyl. I was coming to tell you that I was leaving. I was going to go to Rome and start a new life. I have no desire to be a sibyl.'

'Niece, everything happens for a purpose. If the goddess did not intend you to be sibyl, she would not have made you one.' Aunt Flavia's clawlike hands caught Helena's. 'You need to trust her and to trust your heart. You have a good heart, Helena. You will do what is right. That is what your mother said to me on the night she made me sibyl and I have lived by it.'

Helena's mouth dropped open and she hurriedly closed it. Aunt Flavia had experienced the same doubts and fears as her. She always thought Aunt Flavia a tower of strength. The goddess spoke to Aunt Flavia. She was positive of that. The enormity of what she was about to do made Helena's knees weak.

'I can never be you. I can't wield power in the way you did. Day by day I see the seafarers, in particular the ones from Cicilia like Androceles, gaining power. Kimon swaggers around the temple, bragging what he will do, the raids he plans on the mainland. He is careful to couch it in bland terms, but I know.'

'How do you know?'

'The Falerian wine they gave the temple. It came from an earlier raid. The rings they wear came from the same raid. Tullio told me, but at first I did not want to believe.'

'Are you sure of this, niece? You need to be positive. A cursing is not a matter taken lightly.'

'I know it is true.' Helena squared her shoulders. 'At first I didn't want to believe, but now I do. I see Zenobia becoming closer than ever to her distant kinsmen. She will pervert and use this temple for her own ends.'

'What do you think they are planning?'

'They intend launching a major raid on Rome. Women and children will die, Aunt, and I have to find some way of stopping it.'

'Lichas should never have married into that clan.' Flavia's mouth held a bitter twist. 'It was an evil day when we made an alliance with that family.'

'Is there anything we can do? Is there no way you can continue as sibyl and issue an edict against them?'

'Do you think they'd listen?' A green spark showed in her aunt's eyes, making her look younger. 'Do you think they'd pay attention to me? A woman who is a mere shadow of her former self?'

'The other chiefs would. They respect you still, Aunt Flavia, despite what Zenobia says.'

The hope that had sprung in her aunt's eyes died. Her hands fell to her sides.

'The last bout in Kybele's cave took my breath away. My hands are useless claws. It is time for me to pass on my robes, mask and sword. If not to you, then who?'

Helena put an arm about her aunt's shoulders. She felt as fragile as one of the doves. Helena did not trust herself to speak. Another dream gone. She had had a faint hope that Aunt Flavia would simply agree to stay on as the sibyl, that she understand what a horrible mistake had happened.

'What is left for me to do?'

'The only thing left to us, you and me, is to be as strong as possible. I will guide you as much as I can, but you must listen to your heart. It may be that the goddess is speaking, but you are not listening.'

'I pray you are correct.'

Aunt Flavia withdrew a sundial from her pouch and held it up.

'It is time to begin the purification, Helena. We cannot delay any longer.'

* * *

The brown and green coast appeared as a line on the horizon. Tullio's shoulders relaxed ever so slightly. They were here. On the appointed day. In time, he hoped.

A smaller battle group than he would have liked, but he prayed that it would be sufficient. This time, it would be the pirate chiefs who were caught off guard.

'You'll lead the attack, Quintus, once the *corvus* has been lowered.' Tullio nodded towards the plank with a long spike on the end. Its main purpose was for boarding ships and allowing the infantry to cross easily carrying their shields. 'Once you are on shore, have some men torch the triremes, but take the bulk to the temple.'

'And what will you be doing, sir?'

'I'm going a different way to provide a counter-attack.'

'But Galla told me the only way on or off the island is through the harbour. Come with us. We will go the back way, the way the sibyls use.'

'There is another way. It is how I planned to get Helena off the island. Now, I will use it to get me on.'

Quintus grasped Tullio's forearms, preventing him from moving. 'Seven men. You are only taking seven men with you. Are you sure that is enough?'

'It will have to be. The shore is not very wide there. I don't want to risk anything more than a small boat. You will wait until you hear a loud horn blast. This will be the signal for your part of the attack to begin. If the pirates start to swarm out of the harbour before then, block them.'

'What horn?'

'The horn of Neptune. I intend to deliver a lesson to the pirates that they will never forget.'

'But how can you be sure?'

Tullio stared out over the sea. Small waves danced in the sunshine. All peace and tranquillity.

'I am more sure about this than I have ever been about anything.'

'Should I not make it, you will ensure that Galla gets my veteran's settlement.' Quintus touched his hand to his chest. 'I promised her I'd marry her and become a farmer after the remaining five years of my service is up.'

'You'll make it, Quintus.' Tullio clapped his centurion on the shoulder. 'We'll all make it.'

'It was a noble thing that Helena did—getting Galla out like that. I hadn't expected it. Galla is the sort of woman I could spend my last days with. I feel I owe Helena an apology.'

'Helena acts in the most unexpected ways.' Tullio kept his eyes on the island drawing steadily closer. He did not trust himself to look at his centurion.

'Don't you worry, sir, Helena will be fine. Galla told me that she has been training for this all her life. It is what she wants.'

'Yes, I know that, centurion.'

'Sir, I wanted you to know—it has been an honour and privilege serving with you.'

Tullio's jaw tightened as he stared at the island's shore. Helena had been training to be sibyl all her life and he was about to launch an attack that could potentially destroy her life. But if he did nothing, she'd die. He felt that in his bones. He woke up in cold sweats. He knew he should never have left without telling her how he felt about her, without pleading his cause. He had to tell her that his life was nothing without her.

With each passing wave, each breath of wind, the ships sailed closer.

* * *

'It is time, Helena. The drums have started. The heads of the seafarers are all in place.'

Helena rose slowly from her chair. She allowed Aunt Flavia to fasten the gold belt about her hips, to slip the bronze hands over her fingers and to fit the mask on to her face.

Tullio was not going to come. He had failed her. The heads of the seafaring houses would dispose of her once they knew the truth, but she had this little piece of time to try to do some good. She would accuse Androceles and Kimon of their crimes and bring them to some sort of justice.

Tullio had said that they killed his ex-wife in a raid. She had not wanted to believe then. She could believe now. She had peeped out through a curtain and had seen Androceles, resplendent in purple with a multitude of rings on his fingers. And the Falerian wine with the markings. Tullio was correct about that as well.

She would do this for Tullio and he would never know. He was right. Someone had to stop Androceles. She had to hope the goddess would help her—somehow.

She felt the weight of the mask bear down on her face, and struggled to breathe. Then she came through it and felt a kind of peace. She could do this.

'Sound the drums to begin the ceremony.'

Tullio stood ankle deep in seawater, pulling the boat on to the rocky beach when he heard the boom of drums. A solemn sound. His hands stilled.

'By Hercules's club,' Rufus exclaimed. 'The sound sends shivers down my spine.'

'I will be happier when I hear the sound of the *gladii*

hitting the shields as our men advance, but for now the drums will do.' Tullio cocked his head and listened again to the slow steady rhythm of the drum. 'They are calling people to worship, not to war. We have landed undetected.'

'Having landed here, what do we do now?'

'We climb.'

Tullio spat on his hands and slung his shield over his shoulder. His *gladius*, a short sword made in the Spanish fashion, was at his side. Unlike the one he had lost to the pirates, its hilt was only smooth wood and its blade had never been tested in battle, but Tullio prayed it would serve him well.

This time, Jupiter and Hercules were with him. He had arrived before the investiture started, and therefore he had a chance of saving Helena.

His fingers dug into the soft red dirt, failed to get a good grip and he slid back a few feet.

'Do you really think we are going to be able to climb that?' Rufus asked, giving a low whistle.

'I don't think. I know.' Tullio pulled his body over the narrow ledge. The muscles in his shoulders protested as he started reaching for the next hand grip. He came face to face with a lizard and watched it scuttle away. Then he saw the track he had seen that day on the turret, faint but there. Enough for one man.

He turned back and saw the last rays of the sun hitting the sea.

Helena advanced slowly to the sound of the drum. One step for every beat, just as she had practised countless times before.

The temple was full to overflowing. At the front were the different heads of the seafaring houses. Twenty in all. Behind each ranged their captains, pilots and seamen. Further back still were the ordinary villagers. Helena saw Niobe's wide eyes as she clutched Pius's hand. Helena's step faltered. She wanted to stop and explain, but the drumbeat urged her on.

She reached the altar where Flavia and Zenobia stood and mounted the short flight of steps. The drum fell silent. In a high-pitched nasal whine, Zenobia intoned a long piece about why they needed to change sibyls and how Flavia had brought Kybele's wrath on the entire population of the island.

Helena listened in growing disbelief. She saw Aunt Flavia stand rigidly to attention.

Zenobia ended her piece, allowing her hands to drop to her sides.

The drum boomed again three more times.

Helena's hand brushed Tullio's medal. Her back straightened. She would do this. It was her last chance. She had to trust her heart.

She made the ritual supplication to the goddess and turned to face the sea of upturned faces. She removed the bronze hands, and took the gold mask from her face. The crowd gasped.

'My friends, we are gathered here today to make me the new sibyl. People have spoken about Kybele's desertion.'

A swell of murmuring started to gather, a ripple, but gathering pace. Helena held up her hands, motioning for quiet.

'Kybele is not angry with the old sibyl but with what has been happening. What we have allowed to happen. The sibyl forbade raiding, but there are some who have not listened.'

'She lies!' Kimon jumped to his feet. 'She consorts with Romans and lies!'

'Here before you is one such man.' Helena forced her voice to remain steady. 'He and his father murdered in cold blood and gave the temple tainted goods.'

'Strong words, Helena.' Androceles rose to stand with his son. She heard the whisper of his sword being taken out of its sheath. 'I hope you are able to prove them.'

She tried to speak, but the lump in her throat was too big.

'We're waiting, Helena. Prove to us that it was not the sibyl's fault. Show us that Kybele guides you.'

The doors of the temple clanged open. Zenobia screamed. A figure with a drawn sword stood in the doorway.

'I have returned. I kept my promise.'

Helena's knees sagged with relief as she heard Tullio's voice boom out.

He had come. Tullio had arrived.

'You dare much, Roman.' Androceles sneered. 'Is it for the tribute you come?'

'No.' Tullio's black gaze met hers. 'I come for another reason. Something infinitely more precious than gold or silver.'

'Let the Roman speak.' A small voice echoed through the chamber.

Everyone fell silent. Then Pius yelled. 'My sister, my sister speaks.'

Helena recovered first. 'Kybele has performed a miracle. We should heed her words. She has shown us a sign. Ill will come to any who do not obey her.'

The mass of people parted and allowed Tullio to walk to the altar. He kept his eyes straight ahead. What he was about to say was bigger than Rome. Rome's interests were secondary to his. He hoped Helena understood that.

When he reached the foot of the altar, he stopped and turned.

'My friends, Rome does not have a quarrel with the vast majority of you. Only those who rape and plunder. To any man who lays down his arms, I promise to resettle you on my lands in North Africa as I would settle any of my veterans. A colony with land to farm, and no need to rob or plunder.'

He waited, hearing the collective indrawn breath. Would it all be over simply?

'Pretty words, but is this truly what the gods want us to do?' Androceles stepped forward, curved sword in his hand. 'Neptune has blessed my every venture.'

'Shall we settle this man to man, Androceles?' Tullio asked between gritted teeth. 'Then we shall see whom the gods favour.'

'Let me fight him, Father,' Kimon said. 'I have seen Romans fight. This one will be no match for me.'

'I am not so old that my son must fight for me. I too have seen this Roman fight.' Androceles made a mocking bow. 'Very well. I accept your challenge.'

Helena stuffed her hand in her mouth. She wanted to cry out and stop this madness, but it was impossible. The seafarers were urging the fight on, making a ring. Tullio advanced forward and saluted her.

'May the gods favour the brave,' Helena said.

Androceles crouched, tossing his sword from hand to hand. A maniacal gleam was in his eyes. 'I have waited a long time for this, Roman. When you are dead, know that I will take the temple and use it. The gods will favour me.'

The swords clashed. Metal against metal. Tullio blocked the first blow, felt the jar go up his arm. He prayed his sword would hold. Androceles's sneer deepened.

'You will have to do better than that, Roman.'

'I intend to.'

Tullio pressed forward, stabbing rather than slashing.

They circled each other. Tullio watched Androceles's movements and waited. He saw an opening and took it. This time Androceles brought down the hilt of his sword on Tullio's wrist, nearly knocking the sword from his hand.

Tullio retreated, the old injury to his shoulder aching. He glanced upwards and saw Helena's white face.

He would do this. He had to do this. For Helena.

Helena watched, unable to look away as the two combatants circled each other. Surely the gods could not be so cruel to allow him to die before her eyes. Around and around they circled. First Tullio had the advantage and then Androceles. Then Tullio again.

Androceles pressed forward. Tullio stumbled and half-fell to his knees.

'Blow the horn, Helena. Call for aid!'

Helena looked at him, not understanding. Tullio knew that it was just a relic, a superstition. She started to move towards it.

'Now, Helena, blow it now!'

She did not believe Neptune would send aid, but perhaps the sound would distract Androceles for that slightest of breaths and allow Tullio to escape. She filled her lungs with air. A long low sound filled the temple, echoing and reverberating off the walls. Everything went still.

Then nothing. No parting of the seas. No destruction of the temple. Nothing. It was simply a device. She had failed.

'You see who the gods favour, Roman.' Androceles stood poised over him, sword gleaming.

Tullio waited, then thrust upwards with his legs, throwing Androceles backwards. The pirate flew through the air and landed at the base of the statue of Kybele. The statue rocked and then crashed down on top of Androceles and he lay still.

Everyone froze.

'Kybele has spoken,' Flavia's commanding voice said. 'Let no man doubt that.'

'My father is dead? I will avenge my father's death.' Kimon advanced with his sword drawn. He motioned to his men. 'We will take this temple by force.'

Tullio crouched low. If he took Kimon, he could at least prevent Helena's death, hold off the pirates until reinforcements came. If they came. He wiped a hand across his mouth.

The doors of the temple were flung open. Quintus stood at the entrance with his soldiers ranged behind him.

'You called, Tullio?'

'You might say that.' Tullio brought his fist back and connected with the open-mouthed jaw of Kimon, who crumpled to the ground. 'Neptune sends his regards, but is a bit busy. He sent the Roman legion instead.'

The soldiers streamed in, swords drawn and beating against their oblong shields. Tullio held the sword over his head.

'You see how the gods favour me and punish those who would commit sacrilege in this temple.'

At that, the pirates laid down their arms. Tullio turned towards the centurion.

'For once, Quintus, your timing is impeccable.'

'I do but try, Livius Tullio.' Quintus's face wore a broad smile as he gave a smart salute.

'Shall we round these miscreants up and return the temple to the sibyl?'

'You're the tribune.'

Lichas stood up and motioned for quiet. The entire hall fell silent.

'Once again, sister, I appear to have underestimated you,' Lichas said. 'We will abide by the goddess's decision and take the Roman's offer of lands.'

'But, but—' Zenobia protested.

'Be silent, woman!' Lichas roared. 'If I hadn't listened to you in the first place, the gods would not have turned against us. I will not fight the will of Neptune and Kybele. The gods' will be done.'

A general cheering broke out.

Tears pricked Helena's eyes and she turned her head. Aunt Flavia stood at the edge of the altar, hands held high in the traditional gesture of a blessing. Tullio and the rest of the Roman legion knelt down. Without hesitation, Helena handed the gold mask to Aunt Flavia.

'Your time as sibyl is not finished, Aunt.'

'Do you know what you are doing, niece?' Flavia's fingers closed around the mask.

'I do. I renounce my claim as sibyl. My destiny lies along another path. All I want is to spend the rest of my life with Tullio.' Helena went and knelt by Tullio. 'If he will have me.'

'With the utmost pleasure.' Tullio's fingers curled around hers. 'I came back for you. I love you, Helena and I mean to have you for my own.'

'And I love you,' she whispered. 'But how did you get the soldiers to arrive like that? How did Quintus know?'

'There are some things that should not be left to the gods.' Tullio placed a finger on her lips to silence any more questions.

'The senate and people of Rome will be proud of what you

accomplished today, Livius Tullio,' Quintus said, coming up to him and laying the pirates' swords at Tullio's feet. 'The gods were with you.'

Tullio look down on the pile and over at the prone figure of Androceles. Both Kimon and Zenobia were in custody. The legate would decide what to do with them, how best to make an example. It was a good day's work. But his life meant more than battle honours.

'Rome can go to Hades as long as Helena is safe. She is the only thing in my life who matters.'

In the warm circle of Tullio's arms, Helena watched Aunt Flavia go to Niobe and speak to her. She knew that she was no longer alone. She had found her home.

Epilogue

Eighteen months later—Near Cyrene in North Africa

Helena stood on the terrace of the villa she shared with Tullio and looked down at the farms dotted about the countryside. The remaining seafarers and villagers had taken to farming with great vigour. Where there was once untilled land, vines and olive trees grew.

Aunt Flavia had even engineered a move of the temple away from the island and now presided over the thriving community with Niobe at her side. After her outburst at the temple, Niobe had regained her power of speech. It was Helena's belief that in due course Niobe would become the next sibyl.

'You are looking very pensive, Helena.' Tullio mounted the steps to join her. 'Is something wrong with one of the children?'

'Both are doing fine. Asleep.' Helena nodded towards the twin cradles where their three-month-old daughters slept.

'They are beautiful like their mother.'

'You are an idle flatterer. I am sure you did not break off from your work just to tell me that.'

'I have had a message from Quintus. He is enjoying being the first centurion of the legion. Galla is very happy as well. Pirates have started raiding again. He believes Kimon is among them. It was an evil day when that tribune allowed him to escape.'

'Rome will catch him.'

'In good time. Quintus assures me that he will not need help from Neptune this time.'

'And when he is captured, what will Rome do?'

'Execute him, I hope, but Quintus favours making him a gladiator—to pay him back.'

'Yes, a gladiator would be better.' Helena looked out over the peaceful land. 'There has been enough bloodshed. Let the gods decide if he lives. I hold no feelings of revenge towards him or any of the seafarers. That is a matter for Rome to sort out. The past is done with and there is a bright future to look forward to.'

'Whatever my sibyl desires,' Tullio whispered in her ear, his hand going about her waist.

'A sibyl no longer, but your wife.' She glanced over at the cradles. 'I do believe our girls will be asleep for a while longer.'

'My very beloved wife who offers wise counsel.'

Helena laughed, and gave herself up to his kiss.

* * * * *

Author's Note

The kidnapping of Julius Caesar in 73 BC and the destruction of Delos and the Sanctuary of Apollo in 88 BC inspired this book. After Carthage fell in 140 BC, in the absence of a Roman navy, piracy grew. Once the Ptolemy dynasty effectively turned over the eastern shipping lanes to the Cicilian pirates in 96 BC, the pirate problem spiralled out of control, menacing shipping and capturing Roman citizens for ransom or, in some cases, slavery.

Delos, a major trading port, was raided and destroyed by Archelaus, an ally of Mithridates. A small group of Italian militia organised resistance, but ultimately the increased threat led to the abandonment of a thriving port.

As a young man on his way back from North Africa in approximately 73 BC, pirates captured Julius Caesar's trireme and Caesar endured several weeks of captivity. Once ransomed for a large sum, Caesar returned with a massive force and killed the pirates who had captured him. However, despite the success of this and other minor battles against the pirates, piracy continued and it was left to Pompey to solve the problem in 67 BC.

After assembling one of the largest fleets in ancient times, winning a battle or two, Pompey promised the remaining pirates land and resettlement. The pirates accepted the offer. The largely intractable problem that had plagued Rome since 139 BC was solved in forty-five days.

For anyone wishing to read more about the period, I found the following books useful. Tom Holland's book is perhaps the most readable, but I did enjoy making some of the recipes from Grant's book on Roman cookery and can wholeheartedly recommend the pyramid cakes!

Bibliography

Goldsworthy, Adrian *In the Name of Rome: The Men who won the Roman Empire* (Weidenfeld & Nicholson 2003) London

Grant, Mark *Roman Cookery: Ancient Recipes for Modern Kitchens* (Serif 1998) London

Holland, Tom *Rubicon: The Triumph and Tragedy of the Roman Republic* (Little, Brown 2003) London

Matyszak, Philip *The Enemies of Rome: from Hannibal to Attila the Hun* (Thames and Hudson 2004) London

Rauh, Nicholas K. *Merchants, Sailors & Pirates in the Roman World* (Tempus 2003) Stroud, Gloucestershire

Woolf, Greg, ed. *Cambridge Illustrated History: Roman World* (Cambridge University Press 2003) Cambridge

THE STEEPWOOD

Scandals

Regency drama, intrigue, mischief...
and marriage

VOLUME FOUR

An Unreasonable Match by Sylvia Andrew

Hester has learnt the hard way that men look for pretty
faces, not stirring debate. Accepting of her life as a
spinster, the last thing Hester wants is to accompany her
family to London for another Season.

An Unconventional Duenna by Paula Marshall

Athene Filmer seizes the opportunity to act as a
companion to her decidedly timid friend when she
enters the *ton*. Could this be Athene's chance to
make a rich marriage?

On sale 2nd February 2007

Available at WHSmith, Tesco, ASDA,
and all good bookshops

A young woman disappears.
A husband is suspected of murder.
Stirring times for all the neighbourhood in

THE STEEPWOOD
Scandals

Volume 1 – November 2006
Lord Ravensden's Marriage by Anne Herries
An Innocent Miss by Elizabeth Bailey

Volume 2 – December 2006
The Reluctant Bride by Meg Alexander
A Companion of Quality by Nicola Cornick

Volume 3 – January 2007
A Most Improper Proposal by Gail Whitiker
A Noble Man by Anne Ashley

Volume 4 – February 2007
An Unreasonable Match by Sylvia Andrew
An Unconventional Duenna by Paula Marshall

2 FREE

BOOKS AND A SURPRISE GIFT!

We would like to take this opportunity to thank you for reading this Mills & Boon® book by offering you the chance to take TWO more specially selected titles from the Historical Romance™ series absolutely FREE! We're also making this offer to introduce you to the benefits of the Mills & Boon ® Reader Service™—

- ★ **FREE home delivery**
- ★ **FREE gifts and competitions**
- ★ **FREE monthly Newsletter**
- ★ **Exclusive Reader Service offers**
- ★ **Books available before they're in the shops**

Accepting these FREE books and gift places you under no obligation to buy, you may cancel at any time, even after receiving your free shipment. Simply complete your details below and return the entire page to the address below. You don't even need a stamp!

YES! Please send me 2 free Historical Romance books and a surprise gift. I understand that unless you hear from me, I will receive 4 superb new titles every month for just £3.69 each, postage and packing free. I am under no obligation to purchase any books and may cancel my subscription at any time. The free books and gift will be mine to keep in any case.

H7ZED

Ms/Mrs/Miss/Mr ....Initials ....
BLOCK CAPITALS PLEASE

Surname ....

Address ....

....

....Postcode..................................

Send this whole page to:
UK: FREEPOST CN81, Croydon, CR9 3WZ